1

Charlotte

Pride & Prejudice Continues
Book One

Karen Aminadra

Published in 2012 by Karen Aminadra

Copyright © 2012 Karen Aminadra.

Second Edition

A CIP catalogue record for this title is available from the British Library.

Cover art by Carriage Publishing featuring iStockphoto/©2011 Igor Demchenkov

I dedicate this book to my fabulous husband, who has been my encouragement and support throughout this whole process. *Charlotte* would never have been written without him.

Special Thanks to:

My husband, for his patience when I asked him for silence to concentrate, for keeping me laughing and wanting me to read it all aloud to him.

Mary Lydon Simonsen, who helped to guide my steps and gave me invaluable advice.

Lana, for being a precious encourager and motivator.

Joan, for being my daily word-count cheerleader.

Brenda Rogers-Fiscus – you are fabulous, thank you.

Last but not least, Jesus, without whom I would never have had the strength to follow my heart.

Contents

11

Chapter One

I ask only a comfortable home. How many times had Charlotte's words to her friend Lizzy come back to haunt her recently, reverberating round her head, tormenting her? What price was she paying for her comfort?

She shuddered as she looked around her sitting room, which Lady Catherine, their patroness, had decorated and fitted out and was not to her own taste at all. The wallpaper, although expensive and elegant, was heavy and oppressive. She sat and thought about the changes that she would have liked to make to the room. After a while, she began to feel more at ease again.

Her sanguine attitude, of which she so confidently assured Lizzy, her oldest friend, had left her long ago. She often felt dread at the thought of intimacy with Mr Collins and avoided it as much as she could do. The act often repulsed her, but she knew she had to steel herself for this very night because, as he left the breakfast room that morning, he had given her one of his strange flirtatious waves, a sure indicator that he felt amorous.

Charlotte knew little of the state of marriage when she had married Mr Collins. Her mother's advice to her was to *bear it as well as she could do,* but this meant nothing to her until her wedding night. She remembered thinking at the time that if someone only warned young girls of the marriage beds, then they would not marry in the first place. Perhaps then, it was better that they usually knew nothing and were innocent of such things, or there would be no more marriages and certainly no more children. Her stomach knotted at the thought of her own experiences. The thought of their fumbled encounters in bed made her feel uncomfortable, and she hurriedly turned to her new book '*Langue des fleurs*'. She stroked the cover page, and more of her own words came back to haunt her: *I am not romantic, Lizzy.* And yet here she was, holding and enjoying reading a book on such a romantic subject. Charlotte was beginning to realise that she did not know herself at all.

* * *

Mr Collins had interrupted Charlotte's walk through the woods that morning by rushing to her to declare the arrival of Colonel Fitzwilliam at Rosings Park, their patroness's home. Why this caused her husband to be in such a flutter, she did not fully understand. He was waving his hat and bidding her make haste. She sighed and asked herself if the inhabitants and guests of Rosings Park were to be always her highest priority. She did not return to the parsonage with the called-upon haste, but instead took her time picking some late wild flowers to study in her book.

Upon her arrival, she found the house and servants in pandemonium, for all his shouting and flapping, Mr Collins had not produced the haste, which he so desired, but had made all about him unable to discern whether they were coming or going.

She rolled her eyes. "My dear, calm yourself, and explain to me what has happened."

"My dear Charlotte, I cannot emphasise enough how valuable the patronage of Lady Catherine de Bourgh is to us and the sovereign importance of performing the duty owed to her. She has written to us and requires us to be present at dinner tonight! We must prepare ourselves!" He bellowed breathlessly, staring about him as if his wife and their servants all should have understood this perfectly.

The clock bell chimed in the sitting room, and Charlotte patiently counted each chime taking the time to calm her nerves and temper before she spoke. "There, as we have heard, Mr Collins, it is only eleven o'clock in the morning. There is indeed no need of haste and we are in no danger of being late at all. We may proceed with tranquillity."

This, however, would not suit her husband, who flapped his way into the sitting room to examine the clock - because it must have been faulty. He remained standing there for some minutes, examining in turn the clock and his pocket watch, which both, Charlotte was sure, declared the same time.

She left him to his activity and retired to her room to rest. She sat at the table and looked out of the window. She knew when she met him that he was not a sensible man, and the deficiency of nature had been little assisted by education or society. When she

14

tried to rescue her friend Lizzy from him by inviting him to Lucas Lodge, she knew he had come to Longbourn on a wife hunt and knew him to be awkward and foolish and, subsequently, his feelings for her to be entirely of his own imagining. He declared such passionate feelings for her as she knew he could not possibly truly feel on such a short acquaintance, but here an opportunity had presented itself. Charlotte had long felt herself to be getting past her bloom. She smiled at the thought. She had never had a bloom. And she was plain-looking, especially next to her dear friends, the Bennet sisters, although she had the blessings of good sense and intelligence. She had heartily feared that she would never have a proposal of marriage and that she would end her days a spinster and a burden to her family. Yet there he had been, standing in front of her, professing an ardent love for her, and in so doing, also unwittingly declaring he was a silly man indeed.

She had not needed long to deliberate on whether to accept his hand or not. At twenty-seven years old, and close to being declared a spinster, the decision was easy for her to make. She had always thought that happiness in marriage was entirely a matter of chance. That to be ignorant of the defects of one's future spouse was best. Mr Collins' had been her only proposal of marriage, and she was sensible of it and doubted whether she would ever receive another. With that in mind, and knowing that Mr Collins was an excellent match for her, and feeling a sense of duty and obligation to her family, she accepted. She consoled herself with thoughts of bringing happiness to her family. It pleased her to become mistress of her own house, and the thought of having children to occupy her time gave her pleasure. That is exactly what she did now, regardless of her heavy heart.

* * *

Mr William Collins sat down in his study and looked out of the window too. He liked that room, his study and book room, as it afforded the best possible view of the road in case Lady Catherine's carriage pass by. He was acutely sensible of his considerable fortune in his patroness the Right Honourable Lady Catherine de Bourgh. Her beneficence and his known connection to her had been invaluable to him. He felt it keenly. He could not have hoped for a more propitious living and a better patroness. He hardly could understand why his wife did not feel it as keenly as he did. *Perhaps she does not have the capacity to feel as deeply as I do,* he mused.

He thought back over the events leading to his marriage to his *Dear Charlotte* and blushed at the memory of the unfeeling and impolite way in which his cousin Elizabeth had refused the offer of his hand; he could not have borne to stay in that house any longer. To his vast relief, his dear Charlotte had come along, invited him to Lucas Lodge, and saved him from further humiliation. Although he had promised never to reproach Elizabeth on the subject again, he could not but feel saddened that none of the Bennet girls would continue at Longbourn and take their mother's place as mistress of the house upon their father's demise, when subsequently he took possession of his inheritance. However, he did congratulate himself on having been saved from an unfortunate match, as he must now view the hoped-for alliance between himself and his cousin Elizabeth since the infamous elopement and subsequent marriage of her youngest sister, Lydia, to the notorious cad and blackguard Mr George Wickham. Mr Collins was heartily relieved that he had escaped the misfortune of having to call such a man brother-in-law.

Turning his attention to the pile of letters on his writing desk, his eyes fell once again upon the wedding invitation from Longbourn. A double wedding. As exciting and fair a prospect it was for all those concerned in Hertfordshire, he could not but feel deeply the pain and disgrace that Lady Catherine now felt upon the announcement of her nephew's marriage. To be married to a woman whose position in society was so far beneath their own upset Her Ladyship so much, she could not even bring herself to utter Elizabeth's name without shaking and starting to weep.

"Yes," he nodded to himself, "as Lady Catherine says, Pemberley is to be thus polluted."

He had, of course, driven to Longbourn and sought an audience with both Mr Bennet and Elizabeth, being sensible of the high standing, which he believed he had in that family, but neither of them seemed to take his kindly meant advice with any seriousness and, in fact, seemed to deem his visit with levity. He could not understand it. Surely, they would not wish to be the cause of injuring such illustrious families as the de Bourghs, the Fitzwilliams, and the Darcys? Yet the wedding was to take place, the evidence of which was on his desk before him. He felt honour-bound, as Mr Bennet's heir, to attend, but equally duty-bound to Lady Catherine to refuse. He contemplated his predicament for some time and then, taking his Bible in his hands, drew out his hassock from under the desk, turned, and knelt down, leaning his elbows on his chair to pray.

Chapter Two

C harlotte never did speak much when at Rosings Park. In fact, Lady Catherine rarely needed anyone to respond to her or to converse with - she just spoke *at* her visitors and required them merely to agree with her every word. This visit was no exception. Charlotte sat demurely, smiling, nodding, frowning, and shaking her head in turns when Lady Catherine's speech demanded such responses. Mr Collins simpered and tried to soothe their hostess, but he failed every time to form even one whole sentence, as Lady Catherine gave him no pause to interject.

One person, Colonel Fitzwilliam, enlarged their party that evening, and the remainder of them sat in their usual places. Anne de Bourgh, Anne's companion, Mrs Jenkinson, and the Collinses all sat facing the inimitable Lady Catherine. Charlotte noticed Colonel Fitzwilliam's countenance. She had seated herself at such an angle to him to see his mouth, which he had deliberately hidden behind his hand as he rested his face against it and his elbow on the arm of the sofa. Was it the candlelight, or was he smirking? She could understand how Lady Catherine's ranting could be seen as ridiculous and how the scene in which they were a part was, indeed, comical. However, it astonished her to see the Colonel seeming to enjoy his aunt's display of ire as she fervently condemned the match her nephew Darcy was about to make.

"Mrs Jenkinson, will you play the pianoforte?" Lady Catherine barked as she rose to ring the bell for coffee. It was not so much a request as an order, and Mrs Jenkinson hurried off to oblige her.

Colonel Fitzwilliam leant towards Charlotte a little as the music started, "I, for one, think your friend Elizabeth an amiable lady and wish them both the best in their marriage, Mrs Collins."

He returned immediately to his former position on the sofa as Lady Catherine re-joined them. Charlotte could hardly contain her smile and could not wait to write and tell Lizzy all about it, knowing that she would be highly diverted. The coffee things arrived, and Lady Catherine continued her speech as though there had been no interruption at all.

"What vexes me most is how that woman and my nephew have trifled with me. Her arts and allurements have, I am sure, made him forget what he owes to himself and to all his family. She has quite drawn him in, such a fortune hunter is that girl!" She turned to Colonel Fitzwilliam and smiled kindly at him. "But at least I have one nephew whose constancy and sense of duty I can rely upon."

The Colonel reached out and kissed his aunt's hand as she proffered it to him. Charlotte noticed that he did not make a reply. How she wished Lizzy could have been there to listen in. What fun they would have had going over every part of the conversation afterwards at the rectory. *Perhaps that would not be fair on Lizzy,* she thought, *this is about her personally, her own future and happiness.* This reflection saddened her, and she felt sorry that the aunt of her friend's future husband could abuse her to her friends and family thus.

Lady Catherine saw this change in her countenance, smiled and nodded. "Yes, Mrs Collins, I see, feels as I do. She is right to be ashamed of her friend. Yes..." She nodded with satisfaction.

Charlotte had learnt almost from the beginning of their acquaintance that there was no use in contradicting anything that Lady Catherine said, and this made her feel more upset, that she could not even defend her dearest friend in the world.

Mr Collins took the silence to mean he could interject. "I undertook to do my best to warn them. Indeed I did. I wrote to Mr Bennet to dissuade them from making the match."

"Yes, yes, Mr Collins," Lady Catherine had found her voice again and cut across him, "but it was to no avail was it? The match will take place, and we must all suffer from this debasement."

* * *

Charlotte always liked the drive home from Rosings. She felt it was pleasant to breathe the fresh air after the stifling atmosphere surrounding Lady Catherine. Mr Collins was often silent; he just sat making little noises to himself as he replayed the evening in his own head while a contented smile suffused his face.

It gave her time to reflect and, invariably, to calm her nerves, but tonight she wanted to talk, "My dear, may I presume to interrupt your reverie?"

Mr Collins looked surprised at the interruption but smiled sweetly at her. "Of course, my dearest Charlotte, pray speak, and I will give you my undivided attention."

She took a deep breath. "I think we should go to Hertfordshire and attend Lizzy's wedding."

Mr Collins looked shocked but turned to face her. "But, my dear, I have determined that it would be the utmost insult to Her Ladyship if we were to attend. One must pay every kindness to one's patroness, to whom we owe everything. We heard this evening how upset she is over it all!"

Charlotte turned to face him, and chose her words carefully. "Could it possibly be, William, that you might be in error?" She did not give him time to respond. "One day you will inherit Longbourn, and you will be an independent gentleman. Therefore, do you not owe just as much to the Bennet family?" His face crumpled, and he was about to retort and contradict her when she continued, "For the sake of the comfort of your wife and your future children at least."

This gave him pause for thought, and he had to agree that she was correct. Although he was not in the habit of admitting to making mistakes, he knew he was wrong. "My dear Charlotte, you have given me something upon which to think. You may indeed be correct, and I am sure that when we fully explain ourselves and beg her forgiveness, Lady Catherine could not continue to be displeased with us for long."

"Indeed I should hope not. You will be thinking of your family honour. Do remember, William, that we know how valuable you are to the Bennets," she applied to his ego and then appealed to his piety directly, "And did not our dear Lord say, 'Blessed are the peacemakers'? William, only you could stand as peacemaker between Mr Darcy, Elizabeth, and Lady Catherine."

Mr Collins' eyes lit up. He raised them heavenwards and puffed out his chest. "I do believe my position as a clergyman makes me perfectly suited for this task. I thank you, my dear

21

Charlotte, for presenting to me such a vital mission as this is." He smiled, reached out, and took hold of her hand, which he held for the rest of the way home. "Yes, indeed, I think that is exactly why we should go to the wedding."

* * *

Charlotte spent the next morning writing to her friends and family. She wrote her longest letter to Lizzy, an acceptance letter to the Bennets, and informed her family that they would be staying at Lucas Lodge in Meryton for one week. She could hardly contain her excitement as she handed the letters to the maid to take to the post into Hunsford Village.

Mr Collins had gone early to Rosings to explain their decision to Lady Catherine. He also intended to ask for her forgiveness for wishing to attend the wedding. Charlotte had bit her tongue over that. It saddened her that he felt it necessary to plead Lady Catherine's forgiveness. It was a surprise, however, to Charlotte to see Mr Collins arrive home, running and much later than expected, well after luncheon.

"Mr Collins, is all well?" she asked as she greeted him at the front door.

"Oh, my dear Mrs Collins," he gasped, "Lady Catherine…"

Charlotte allowed him a moment to catch his breath, and then led the way into the sitting room.

He flopped down onto the sofa and continued, "My dear, Lady Catherine was in such a rage of temper when I informed her of our decision." He withdrew his kerchief from his pocket and wiped his forehead with it. "Of course, such an unsurpassed, amiable, Christian person as she is, she could not but understand our predicament." He gasped, "I pointed out to her that although we are duty-bound to her – indeed, we are eternally grateful to her - we ought to attend my cousin's wedding, as I am the heir to the Longbourn estate. 'Mr Collins', she said, 'I am most disappointed by your decision and feel it acutely as a slight against my person.' My…" he paused to wipe the perspiration from his top lip. "My dear, you cannot imagine my agitation at her consternation. I beseeched her not to think too severely of us and to contemplate how affected we are, too, by the marriage." He paused to catch his breath, "You have the right, my dear Charlotte, of being proud

22

of your husband as I lead her to understand by stages, and by the compliments that I know a woman of her standing to deserve, to enable her to see that we ought to attend. She was most charitable indeed. I wish you could have seen how graciously she bore it." He dreamily looked out of the window, and Charlotte could not restrain a smile. "Such condescension, such affability." He collected himself and came back to the subject. "Oh, my dear Charlotte, her generosity of spirit will astound you, I have no doubt, as much as it does me. She has also deigned to offer us use of her carriage as far as London. What do you say to that, Mrs Collins?"

Charlotte was, of course, speechless. Mr Collins thought her to be awestruck by the beneficence of Lady Catherine. However, it disappointed her that her husband had felt the need to implore Lady Catherine to permit them to go to a family wedding and not to be angry with them in wishing to do so.

Sometimes the intimacy that they enjoyed and relied upon with Rosings tried her patience. Today was one of those times, and she went for a walk before dinner to clear her head.

Mr Collins, having received his instructions for the following day's sermon from Lady Catherine, retired to his book room to work.

23

Chapter Three

Colonel Fitzwilliam visited Mr and Mrs Collins at the parsonage after church on Sunday to take his leave of them. He conveyed how glad he was that they were to attend the wedding of his cousin and that they had not felt compelled and obliged to stay at home in Hunsford. He had never had time before to become truly acquainted with Mr and Mrs Collins but now, studying them in their sitting room, he expressed a desire to do so. He knew that Mr Collins was an odd, sycophantic man, and wondered what his wife was like. He had been tremendously surprised to discover her to be a woman of sense and bright conversation. He was on leave and not required to be back on the Continent immediately and hoped to winter at his aunt's house. He was glad to find that Mrs Collins would be pleasant enough company and sincerely hoped that Mr Collins would improve upon further acquaintance.

* * *

Colonel Fitzwilliam's visit had, however, highlighted to Charlotte that they had a decidedly limited acquaintance in Hunsford and that Lady Catherine had disapproved of her even visiting with some families within the Parish. She did, however, see Lord and Lady Metcalf's governess, Miss Pope, occasionally in the village. She was a bright young woman whom Charlotte liked exceedingly, and she wished they could meet more frequently. Her Ladyship's interference had confined their society and secured it for her pleasure alone. Charlotte looked forward to the return of Colonel Fitzwilliam over the winter months.

She intended to form more friendships without the knowledge of Her Ladyship, since she felt that the presence of the minister's wife was in much need within their parish. There were two spinsters, the Misses Thomas, who lived close by, and their neighbour, the widow Mrs Brown, with whom she met frequently to do needle and crochet work for the poor. She enjoyed Tuesday mornings with those ladies and felt a deep desire to become closer friends with them. She was also of the opinion that, because of his devotion to Rosings, her husband was neglecting his pastoral duties, and she resolved to endeavour to do something about that upon their return. She knew that he would be mortified to discover that he was not perhaps the personification of what a clergyman ought to be, and knew she could successfully persuade him in that area.

In the beginning of their marriage, Charlotte was eager to encourage Mr Collins to visit Rosings. She also encouraged him to be out of the house as often as possible. This was perhaps to blame for the fact that he visited there more frequently than he did with his parishioners, where he could be of use. His parochial duties were not irksome, nor were they many. *However, a man in his position who was fortunate enough to enjoy the condescension and patronage of the Right Honourable Lady Catherine de Bourgh ought not to be remiss of his duties in other quarters.* Charlotte smiled at the thought. She was beginning to know how exactly to appeal to her husband's sensibilities. *If only I could be such a mistress of my own feelings as I used to be,* she thought.

* * *

The drive into London was peaceful and uneventful, having had the luxury of Lady Catherine's carriage, but from thence onward, things took a different turn. They had stayed only long enough to take refreshment and change to the post coach at Bromley. They were approximately three miles past Cheshunt when the post coach they were travelling in hit a rock in the road and one of the rear wheels broke. It was only because of the skill of the coachman and the fact that they were not carrying too many passengers that they did not overturn completely. A young woman and her son had joined them at Cheshunt, making the number of passengers four, and seemed shaken by the event.

Despite the Coachman's deft handling, Charlotte was mortified when Mr Collins began to berate the poor coachman for his actions, as though it was entirely his fault. "I say, do you have any idea of the importunity and distress which you have caused? I cannot stress enough the importance of my lady wife and myself arriving on time at our destination, and in once piece, I might add. I am most displeased at this turn of events. What on earth possessed you to do such a thing?"

"What?" the astounded coachman replied.

Charlotte hurried to help the young woman and her child alight, ashamed by her husband's words.

"Indeed I am sure you could have avoided this if you had just taken care. Exactly what do you propose to do now? Hmm…?"

Mr Collins did not at all realise his folly or the possible danger of speaking so to such a seasoned coachman as the one standing before him then. The man had dealt with drunkards and highwaymen, and here was Mr Collins, a mere clergyman, attempting to scold him. The coachman and the mail guard did, indeed, think about teaching Mr Collins a lesson. The thought passed between them as they looked at each other in disbelief; but instead, they both shook their heads and just laughed at him. The coachman unhitched one of the horses and set off riding bareback in the direction of Cheshunt to fetch a blacksmith, and the mail guard began to unload the trunks and bags.

This gave Mr Collins time to recover his composure and, to Charlotte's dismay, he continued speaking in much the same vein as before. "I am not accustomed to such behaviour as this, indeed not. Such a man as I, who is so fortunate as to enjoy the patronage and condescension of the Right Honourable Lady Catherine de Bourgh of Rosings Park…" he proudly boasted.

The mail guard simply turned to face him from his position atop the coach and interrupted. "I couldn't care less if you enjoy the patronage and condescension of the King of England! You'll keep your trap shut if you want to continue your journey onwards and know what's good for you!" He returned to the task in hand, whilst pointedly moving his livery coat to show his pistols and, patting his flintlock he added, "*Sir.*"

Mr Collins' consternation one can imagine. He was perspiring more than usual, but Charlotte's humiliation was evident. Her face was so red that it reached her ears, and tears welled in her eyes.

She implored her husband, "My dear, perhaps you ought to help to place the luggage by the side of the road?"

Mr Collins considered objecting but thought better of it and did as his wife had suggested, much to his own chagrin.

27

They did not have long to wait before they saw, on the road heading towards them, the blacksmith's cart and the coachman. Charlotte knew that most of London's blacksmiths kept a spare Post Coach wheel, understanding that the fines the guards and coachmen were likely to incur if they were late in delivering the mail and the blacksmiths' desire not to lose Post Office business made certain of such things.

The wheel was changed in a relatively short period, much to Charlotte's relief, and they were soon able to continue their journey once more. She was eager to get her husband back into the coach before he caused yet another scene embarrassing to more than himself, but he seemed strangely quieter than it was customary for him to be. They gave their thanks to the blacksmith and boarded, continuing their journey further into Hertfordshire and towards Meryton at a much greater pace than previously to make up time and, consequently, in much greater discomfort.

* * *

Finally, they rounded the last bend in the road that led to Longbourn Village and then on to the market town of Meryton. Charlotte lowered the window to see if she could spy anyone of her acquaintance as the carriage passed by the residence of her friends but could not see anyone. They came, after another mile, to Meryton, where the guard blew his horn, and they knew they had arrived. The joy with which Charlotte alighted from the carriage showed on her face as clearly as daylight. It certainly felt agreeable to her to be back at her former home.

"Charlotte!"

She turned to see her sister Maria waving and heading in their direction. "Maria, I am heartily glad to see you."

The sight of her sister brought her to the brink of tears. She felt such felicity in her embrace, and then felt the arms of her mother enfold her; and from that, she drew the strength to steel herself against such an outpouring of emotion.

Lucas Lodge was then a further mile to travel out the opposite side of Meryton, and Lady Lucas had brought her carriage to convey her daughter and son-in-law thence. While Mr Collins and Lady Lucas chatted away, Charlotte paid them little attention; she was watching her former home-town as it passed by, familiarising herself with every house, window, door, tree, and bush anew. She held Maria's hands tightly while the latter rested her head against her sister's shoulder. She, too, had acutely felt their separation.

They alighted at Lucas Lodge at the right time to coincide with Sir William's arrival home.

"My dear daughter, home again – I am glad you have come!" He kissed her lightly on the forehead and bowed to Mr Collins.

"My dear sir, it gives me immense joy to be welcomed into your home once again. Great joy! Indeed, I cannot express how irksome our journey here was," declared Mr Collins.

"Aye," interjected Lady Lucas, "the Post Coach lost a wheel! What do you say to that? Our dear Charlotte and our son-in-law could have been killed."

"Mama, it was not as grave as that. The coachman behaved remarkably well. The situation could have been much more serious if it had not been for his skill," she stated pointedly, avoiding her husband's eyes.

Mr Collins laughed indulgently at his wife. "My dear, I see what you are doing. You are endeavouring, I believe, to prevent your beloved parents from suffering too much from the thought of our mishap. Your sensitivity to their feelings does you credit." He turned back to Sir William as they went into the house, "But indeed I shall certainly be writing a strong letter of censure to the Post Office about this. Indeed I shall!"

* * *

The double wedding of Mr Charles Bingley to Miss Jane Bennet, and Mr Fitzwilliam Darcy to Miss Elizabeth Bennet was to take place the day following their arrival at Lucas Lodge. The morning dawned bright but bitterly cold. There was a hard frost on the ground, which gave an elegant beauty to the surrounding countryside. The little village church at Longbourn was overflowing, and the guests felt the love, pleasure, and felicity of the couples exceedingly. The whole party walked the short distance in jubilation from the church to Longbourn house, the home of the Bennets, which allowed the villagers to see the brides as the couples departed for Netherfield Hall, there to celebrate the wedding breakfast.

Charlotte was unable to spend more than a few minutes that day in the company of her dearest friend Lizzy. She was, however, extremely glad to see Lizzy looking so happily in love. Their embrace in the reception line was of true friendship and filled with deep emotion, but as the day wore on, these emotions once again threatened to overpower Charlotte. She danced as little as possible with Mr Collins, preferring instead to save her own feet from so much pain, as he repeatedly stepped on them, and sat alternatively with her mother and watched the dancers, especially Elizabeth. Charlotte grew concerned at how little she could control her emotions. When she saw Elizabeth and Mr Darcy in intimate conversation, she felt a new emotion, unfelt by her ever before, that of jealousy. *What nonsense*, she rebuked herself, *I am not jealous of Lizzy and Mr Darcy*! Nevertheless, the realisation then dawned upon her that she was, in truth, jealous of their intimacy and love.

Colonel Fitzwilliam broke her reverie by asking her to dance. She was glad of the distraction and the chance to talk; and, as she overheard, her husband was proud that the nephew of his patroness had singled out his wife with whom to dance.

* * *

The week in Hertfordshire passed more quickly than Charlotte would have liked. They attended a party given by the Phillipses in Meryton and dined at Longbourn. Maria and Charlotte had resumed their long walks, and she saw how much more grown up her little sister seemed, and it pleased her. They had visited all their friends, and she took much pleasure in shopping at the local merchants with her mother. It was, as Lady Lucas had said, "just like old times."

Therefore, it was with a heavy heart, indeed, that she supervised the loading of their luggage into the carriage for their return journey home. Sir William persuaded Mr Collins to take the slower and, he assumed, safer stagecoach on their return, so the journey home to Kent took much longer.

The drive was uneventful, and Charlotte slept all the way into London while Mr Collins read; then, after changing at Bromley, she slept the remainder of the journey home. Her husband awoke her as they drew near to Hunsford Village.

Chapter Four

Mr and Mrs Collins certainly felt that it was pleasant to be home. They were both tired from the long journey, so ate a quiet collation and then retired early.

Despite sleeping the majority of the way home from Hertfordshire, Charlotte surprisingly slept the entire night through and awoke as the maid opened the curtains to light the fire in their room.

Mr Collins rose first, went to his book room to pray, and left Charlotte to wash and dress in peace and solitude. She would walk into Hunsford village before breakfast today and knew that they would be required to take tea at Rosings that afternoon.

It was such a beautiful, crisp, frosty morning, that Charlotte felt her spirits lift as she walked into Hunsford. She called at the inn and enquired of the keeper if the post had been, but there were no letters to take back home with her, and she arrived home to find breakfast laid in the dining room.

The day passed with the usual occupations of having returned from a journey, and soon the bell rang, and the maid gave Mr Collins the expected invitation from Rosings in his book room. With the arrival of the invitation, Charlotte's spirits sank, and she found she could not abide the thought of taking tea at Rosings that day.

"My dear Charlotte," Mr Collins declared happily as he entered the drawing room, "Lady Catherine always gives little attentions to those of her acquaintance that are deserving. We are exceedingly honoured. Indeed we are. As I expected, it has arrived not too soon and not a minute too late. You see," he waved the letter at her; "an invitation has arrived from Rosings asking us to take tea with Her Ladyship. What say you to that?"

Charlotte had no desire to go to Rosings to deliver a minute account of the entire proceedings of the wedding of her dear friend. She stated as much to her husband.

"My dear, surely you are unwell. Indeed you must be, for I cannot believe you would be so unkind or unjust to our cherished patroness!"

The term *cherished* irritated her, and she gave her tongue free rein. "Indeed I am not unwell. Why did she not attend the wedding if she is so interested in it? I do not like gossip, I do not like gossips, and I will not ruin the memory of such a delightful event and week as we have just enjoyed by giving into such activities. Please, William, you must see it is not becoming."

"My dear Charlotte, I cannot see that any fault or injury should arise from informing Lady Catherine of the happenings of a wedding! There is nothing of gossip there!"

Charlotte was not to be placated. She sat down heavily on the sofa, and he, seeing her distress, joined her. "Charlotte, I have not convinced you. Indeed, you are discomfited." He was uncomfortable too now; Charlotte did not usually counter him, and it disconcerted him exceedingly.

"William, I believe that *our* behaviour could be seen as wanting."

Mr Collins was taken aback. "Our behaviour? Whatever could you mean? Honestly, Charlotte!"

"A family of our close acquaintance suffered a tragedy: a daughter eloped; Mr Darcy found her; and fortunately, then she married."

"Yes, it was a terrible situation. Lydia is a stupid, thoughtless girl!"

His statement piqued her even more. "I would have said the same thing about the conduct of the clergyman who related the entire situation to someone wholly unconnected with the family. Someone, I might add, who had no rights whatsoever to know such information. Had the information been withheld, then after the resolution there would have been little or no damage to the family in question. However, the said clergyman, having told the greatest gossip in all England the exact facts of the matter, did more damage than he could have imagined to that family's reputation."

He sat agog listening to his wife.

She did not want to say these things. She knew they would hurt his pride, but she did not have the willpower now to prevent

34

herself. "Do you not realise that the blessed events, which we witnessed at Longbourn this past week, might not have taken place because of gossip and the damage arising from that gossip, Mr Collins?" A tear escaped down her cheek, much to her embarrassment, which she quickly wiped away.

"I see what you are endeavouring to do. You mean to put me on my guard." He blushed, profoundly humiliated by his wife's scolding but refusing to take her words seriously, and, making light of the situation, continued, "But my dear, it is done, and no harm has come of it. Truly, no harm, I am sure, can ever come from relating any events or circumstances whatsoever to Lady Catherine."

Charlotte looked at the man she had married and watched in disbelief as he continued to ignore her remonstrance and persisted in praising Lady Catherine.

"Indeed there is no greater woman in all of England with such a kind, generous heart. She would never act out of selfishness or malice. Dearest Charlotte, you must not make yourself uneasy on behalf of the Bennets. Indeed, you must not. I insist upon it. Come, let us make ourselves ready to go to Rosings." With that, he rose from the sofa and quitted the room, leaving his wife to weep desperately.

She knew that crying in such a way would give her a headache, but was glad of it. She was a little ashamed of the way she had spoken to her husband, even though she had told him only the truths she thought he needed to hear; she knew she could have done so in a more sensitive manner. The headache, when it came, she was glad of. It gave her an excuse not to be part of the conversation that evening at tea.

* * *

She need not have been anxious. Colonel Fitzwilliam had also returned into Kent and was not in any mood to relate the details of the wedding either. He sat close to Charlotte and asked her about her family while Lady Catherine spoke loudly so all present could benefit from her wisdom and conversation.

"My nephew Colonel Fitzwilliam has not provided me with any of the particulars of the wedding, Mr Collins. A man like my nephew is seldom wont to remember or to convey the details of flowers, lace, etc. However, you, I am sure, Mr Collins, will be able to furnish me with all the information I desire." She paused to allow her meaning to be understood. "It could not, however, have been an elaborate affair. Of course not. I am sure the Bennets have not the income for such extravagance."

Colonel Fitzwilliam saw Charlotte stiffen and purse her lips together to prevent herself from speaking out. He poured her another cup of tea to calm her nerves. "Here, Mrs Collins, drink this. It will make you feel better."

* * *

The next morning, Charlotte awoke late to the sound of Mr Collins entering the bedroom. He placed a small posy of flowers on the counterpane. She picked them up and smiled.

"You have been out of sorts of late, my dear, and these Christmas roses are flowering early this year. I thought they would make you smile." He made to leave, but before closing the door, he popped his head back into the room. "Will you join me for breakfast?"

"Yes, and thank you." She stared down at the flowers her mind reeling. To how many of her words had he truly listened and paid attention? He had never considered her feelings before, let alone presented her with flowers because he deemed her out of sorts. *What could he mean by this? Could he have listened to what I said? Has he taken my words seriously?* She asked herself.

* * *

Christmas was one week away, and Charlotte had finished embroidering the Psalter cover and was making a bookmark with a nativity scene as a present for her husband to commemorate their first Christmas together. She knew they would be finished in time and so decided to enjoy the break in the weather and take a walk. She took her usual route through the avenue of trees at Rosings and then intended to take the way back through the lanes from Hunsford when she came across Colonel Fitzwilliam approaching in the opposite direction.

"Mrs Collins, Good afternoon!" He bowed.

"Good afternoon, Colonel." She curtseyed.

"I see you had the same excellent idea that I had, of enjoying the break in the weather to get out of doors."

"Yes, there is only so long a person can be trapped within doors."

"Oh, indeed, especially when one has my aunt and her hearty conversation for company." His eyes twinkled with amusement, and she smiled at him. She knew him little; however, she had at least discerned his dissatisfaction with his aunt on more than one occasion. "I hope you have recovered from your headache?"

"Yes. Thank you for asking, Colonel."

"Shall we walk together? Which way were you headed?"

"I was about to walk back towards the parsonage through the lanes."

"Splendid! I shall join you, if you do not mind?"

"Not at all." She smiled, thinking he was returning the way he had come simply to join her, and they set off down the lanes together.

Chapter Five

C harlotte had no idea at all what the arrangements were at Rosings for Christmas. She did not wish to ask her husband about their own arrangements, for she was sure to ask in such a way that would send him off immediately to Rosings to ask permission to celebrate the blessed day at his own home, and then end up returning with an invitation to dine there instead. She wanted only to have their Christmas dinner in the evening after church together, quietly and alone.

She chose her words carefully when informing her husband that she was off out on errands. "My dear, I am to visit the butcher this morning to order the goose, and then to go and buy the ingredients for our plum pudding. I confess myself to be quite excited at the prospect of celebrating our first Christmas alone in our home, my dear." She stressed the word *alone* and hoped he caught it. "And then I will visit the Misses Thomas and begin the decoration of the church." She kissed him lightly on the head and left before he could utter a word.

* * *

Charlotte always enjoyed visiting with the Misses Thomas and Mrs Brown, but today was unusual as they were cutting holly sprigs from the hedgerows to decorate the church. Week by week, their friendships were growing, and Charlotte was exceedingly glad to find new friends in Hunsford, as she missed Meryton and Longbourn deeply.

Mr Collins, who had opened the church up especially for them, met them at the church door. "Good morning, ladies." He nodded his head to them.

"Good morning to you, Reverend. How are you today?"

"Why, thank you for asking, Mrs Brown. I am well, as you see. And I am glad to see you are well also, judging by how many

39

sprigs the neighbourhood holly trees have obligingly bestowed upon you all!" He led them to the front of the church and to the altar where they were to decorate.

The church was a typical one of Norman design, and the de Bourghs had added wooden pews, which were heavily polished, leaving a heady scent in the air. The church was cold; their breath lingered, in the air in front of them as they worked. Mr Collins flitted amongst the ladies, offering little pieces of unwanted advice on flower arranging. He had no knowledge whatsoever on the topic and was beginning to get underfoot and be more of a hindrance than a help.

"My dear," said Charlotte, turning to Mr Collins, "I expect we will be some minutes in arranging, so I wondered if you would be so kind as to head back home and instruct Mrs Higgs to prepare a warm luncheon for us all? And I am sure that upon your return, we will have finished and be ready for you to escort us."

He acquiesced, and as soon as he had left the church, the ladies all visibly heaved a sigh of relief. They smiled at each other and left their thoughts on Mr Collins and his behaviour unspoken. He meant well; he simply had no real knowledge and no true discernment of the feelings of others to prevent him from either upsetting someone or insulting them.

Charlotte broke the silence and expressed such thoughts. "My husband's advice is often like his dancing... he is liable to tread on many toes in so doing."

The ladies looked at Charlotte wide-eyed, but relieved to see the glint in her eyes and the corners of her mouth twitching to restrain a smile. They all laughed, and the tension was abated. Therefore, they were glad to continue their task together without hindrance and fell into silence as each of them busied themselves, and after some minutes thus the youngest Miss Thomas began to sing "Come thou long expected Jesus".

Mrs Brown smiled as she listened. "Oh, I do love Charles Wesley's hymns." She then joined her voice to that of her friend's, and soon all four of them lifted up their voices in worship as they decorated the church in readiness for Christmas Day.

* * *

The next morning dawned bright and fair, although dark clouds on the horizon threatened to ruin the day; therefore, Charlotte set off for her walk before breakfast. It seemed also that Colonel Fitzwilliam had the same idea as well, and they met once again in the avenue of trees that ran along the edge of the Park.

He laughed when he saw her. "Good morning, Mrs Collins. I see that great minds have once again thought alike!"

"Indeed they have, Colonel. I hope you are well?"

"Tolerably so. And you?"

"Yes, I am remarkably well indeed; I love this time of year. However, you said *tolerably*. What mean you by that? Are you unwell?"

"Not at all, I assure you, Mrs Collins."

"Good. I am heartily glad of it. It would be a shame to be ill during the Christmas period, especially when we are in need of male voices when we go carolling and wassailing."

His eyes grew wide at the thought. "Oh, am I required to join in the singing? I had thought, being a member of the Rosings family, that I could just stay at home and be visited by the singers."

"Oh, for shame!" she teased. "And miss out on all the fun? Indeed, I am sure you would not!"

He laughed. Yes, she was pleasant enough company, and witty too, and he was thankful for it. "May I be impertinent and say that I am pleased to find you pleasant company?"

It was Charlotte's turn to stare wide-eyed.

"Forgive me if I insult you. I meant it as a compliment. I seldom come into Kent with the hope of finding tolerable company, let alone finding someone with whom I can converse. I am most pleased to find in you, Mrs Collins, an amiable woman with wit and vivacity."

The corners of Charlotte's mouth twitched and her eyes sparkled as she retorted, "I suppose you had known my husband before our marriage and, from what he is lacking, concluded that the new Mrs Collins must also be wanting? Am I right Colonel?" She laughed at his red face and embarrassment.

"Now I see I should have kept my comment to myself!"

"Indeed, no! I am glad to find that you are pleased with my company, and for my part, it is also refreshing to have someone to converse with who does not have an obsession with Lady Catherine." A fit of giggles forced them to stop walking until they could compose themselves once again. It felt refreshing to Charlotte to laugh like that again. That was one thing she missed most about Lizzy, how heartily they would laugh together. She rarely laughed these days.

"It feels good to be frank and honest for once, without the risk of injuring anyone."

"I agree, Colonel, it does!" They continued for some time in silence. "So, are you going to explain the *tolerably*?"

"Oh, yes, that." He paused to collect his thoughts, and his face grew serious. "Well, I received an unpleasant express this morning. I will not bore you with the details, but I am afraid that I may have to cut my leave short and depart on Boxing Day for London."

"Nothing too grave, I hope?"

He looked sad, and she saw a dark shadow pass across his eyes. "I am afraid it could well be."

* * *

The day before Christmas Eve arrived with all the usual excitement, and the delivery of a parcel heightened the excitement within the parsonage. It turned out to be a package from Charlotte's parents with instructions to open the attached letter first. Charlotte was so happy to receive something from her parents, especially as it was her first Christmas away from them and she was beginning to miss them tremendously. The letter informed her that all were well, that they were not to open the package until Christmas morning, and wished them a joyous celebration of the season and many blessings for the coming New Year. She was overjoyed and knew if she put pen to paper immediately that her epistle would reach her parents at Lucas Lodge that same afternoon. She had left them gifts when she and Mr Collins had visited Lucas Lodge, in the care of Maria, and smiled to think of her mother's delight on Christmas morn upon seeing the lovely lace she had worked for her. Charlotte was determined that this was going to be an enjoyable Christmas and Lady Catherine was not going to spoil it.

It was with some irritation to Charlotte that, in the afternoon, a message came from Rosings Park requesting the pleasure of Mr and Mrs Collins for Christmas dinner at the great house. *This is the consideration we are to be given. Only one single day's notice! This is typical of Her Ladyship! So inconsiderate!*

Charlotte marched into the sitting room, opened her writing desk and immediately began to inform Lady Catherine that her invitation had arrived too late to be accepted and that they had other plans. She also gently reminded Lady Catherine that the three days of the Christmas festival were exceptionally busy for a clergyman, and his duties were comparable to the many he needed to perform at Easter. She signed the note with considerable cordiality and then asked the maid to have it delivered to Rosings. There, she had done it. She had committed a deliberate act of defiance, but also a deliberate act of independence. She breathed an unsteady sigh. She was heartily glad her husband was not at home, or her own plans for their Christmas dinner would be ruined and money wasted upon his certain acceptance of such an invitation.

That evening, however, Mr Collins received a note from Lady Catherine; but, unfortunately, this time he was home to receive it. Charlotte's stomach knotted with fear that all her plans would be over and she would be spending Christmas at Rosings.

"My dear Charlotte," Mr Collins turned to his wife and looked most perplexed, "did we receive an invitation from Rosings this morning?"

She had to think quickly. "Why, yes, William, we did, and I replied to it."

"It seems you declined the invitation to dine at Rosings on Christmas Day."

"Well, of course, I did, my dear!"

"My dear Charlotte, I cannot think what would have induced you to do such a thing!"

"Mr Collins, can you not?" He stood perplexed at this answer. Again, he had played into her hands, and she knew she could now manoeuvre the situation. "My dear, I was thinking of us. It is our first Christmas together, and who knows how many years it will be before we have that opportunity again? It has been

43

almost one year since we married and perhaps we can expect our family to grow within this next year." She carefully watched his reaction. His face certainly changed with the thought of children. He blushed, and a smile played at the corner of his mouth.

"Well, my dear Charlotte, yes, perhaps you are right."

"And, my dear, I was thinking of you especially. You work so very hard, and Christmas is the busiest time for you, except for Easter, and I thought you would like the tranquillity of home on such a tiring and sacred day." She spoke carefully watching his reactions. "So it was with you in mind that I have prepared roast goose and plum pudding, and for that reason also, I declined the invitation." She paused and waited for his response.

Mr Collins thought about what his wife had said and was immensely proud of her and her thinking about him in such a way. "You are indeed a devoted wife, and I am prodigiously proud of you. Yes, I believe once I write to Lady Catherine, beg her forgiveness and leave, it will all be well. You have acted as is best, I believe."

Charlotte was in shock at the ease of which she achieved her objective and rang the bell for tea to hide her jubilant grin.

Chapter Six

C hristmas Eve arrived, cold, frosty, but with glorious sunshine that flooded through the windows. *Perfect!* Charlotte thought as she climbed out of bed. Nothing could blight her day, not even the complaining of Lady Catherine, which she was sure to endure that evening at church.

After breakfast, she helped the cook to prepare the potage for the evening guests, as she expected most of the carollers to begin the evening at the rectory for potage and hot chocolate. From thence, they were to go sing around the village and at Rosings, and then on to church for the eleven o'clock service, then hurry home to warm beds.

Charlotte loved Christmas. It seemed to be filled with a magical beauty all of its own. Even Mr Collins was in high spirits, and he could be heard singing "Hark! The Herald Angels Sing" and humming the many words he could not remember. She laughed at the scene in her house, and it was not long before she was cajoling Mrs Higgs, Mrs Jones the cook, and Jenny the maid into joining in with Mr Collins' carol.

He heard the ladies singing in the kitchen and joined that scene of festive domesticity, waving his hands as a conductor, much to the amusement of the womenfolk. For the first time in months, Charlotte looked at her husband and saw a man she could at least learn to like and no longer felt so negative towards him. Was it the Christmas spirit? Alternatively, was it the hot chocolate warming her belly? She did not know, but she was indeed glad that it was so. She wanted to be happy in her marriage, and so for now, she enjoyed the feeling. It was with this sensation of contentment that she began to sing another carol, "Good Christian Men Rejoice!" Once again, they all joined in the song. *If only it was always this happy*, she thought as she sang.

* * *

It had started to snow as the carollers made their way to the rectory to begin the evening's festivities. Hot chocolate was served; potage was eaten, some spilt; and there was a vast deal of laughter, especially from Mr Collins, who appeared only to become nervous when potage or chocolate was spilt on his carpet. Charlotte handed out the candles, and old Jim Harvey tuned his fiddle in readiness. Charlotte had been carolling in Meryton many times over the years, but Meryton was much larger than Hunsford. She felt a delightful sense of acceptance as the group of villagers welcomed here into their numbers, and they readied themselves for the cold night air.

The snow was falling steadily and was beginning to settle as they made their way from the rectory to their first port of call, the house at Rosings. There were many mutterings that they might have to end early if the snow got any heavier, but in general, they were all in high spirits. Jim Harvey started the strains of "The Twelve Days of Christmas" which they estimated would take them within earshot of Rosings when they could begin "Here We Come A-Wassailing" and then sing "The First Noel" for Her Ladyship.

Lady Catherine and her daughter, Anne, stood at a first-floor window and watched their progress across the park towards them. They met the carollers at the entrance just as they finished singing "Here We Come A-Wassailing" and greeted her with the beautiful strains of "The First Noel". Anne smiled with delight, which disappeared as Mrs Jenkinson appeared at her side and placed yet another large, heavy shawl about her shoulders. Lady Catherine, however, was surprised by the sound of a man's tenor voice coming from behind her. They turned to see Colonel Fitzwilliam appear, wrapped up against the cold as though he intended to join the singers. He bowed to the ladies and passed out into the cold night air, taking his place next to Mr Collins. Lady Catherine, not wishing to cause a scene by berating her nephew in front of the villagers, merely stood opening and closing her mouth at his audacity. She obligingly, but somewhat visibly irritated, handed out her wassail Christmas punch to all the carollers, who drank deeply and then wished her a Merry Christmas.

They then hurried on their way, laughing, jostling, and singing, towards Hunsford again with the wassail warming their bellies. By the time they had sung around the village, various members of their group had gone home to warm up or had been lured by the enticing glow of The Bell Inn, and their numbers were dwindling. Charlotte invited the remainder back to the parsonage to warm through before going to church for services.

The fire was already lit, and hot chocolate was once again awaiting them as they entered the sitting room. Charlotte could hardly feel her toes, and Mr Collins said he thought he had lost the use of his hands forever. They were a merry group as they chatted until it was time to leave once again, and Mr Collins left first in order to ring the bell to call all to worship. The atmosphere in the church by candlelight was so serene; it was the perfect way to herald the coming of Christmas Day and to celebrate the birth of the Saviour.

Two uncommonly cold, happy, and muscle-sore Collinses climbed into bed past one o'clock in the morning and were asleep as soon as their heads touched their pillows.

* * *

"Christmas Day, the most wonderful day of the year!" Mr Collins declared as he opened the curtains forestalling the maid who had duly arrived to attend to such a task. "Ah, good morning, Jenny, and Merry Christmas!"

"Merry Christmas, sir, ma'am." She curtseyed to them both. "I shall stoke the fire, and I have hot water for your shave, sir, and I shall bring yours directly, ma'am."

"Thank you Jenny." Charlotte yawned and felt her body ache from walking in the cold the previous night. She was so sleepy that she dozed as she watched her husband shave and then dress. He smiled at her, looking so peaceful on her pillow, before slipping out of the room and heading to his book room to collect himself in readiness for the morning's sermon.

Her hot water arrived, and she dressed slowly, choosing a lovely dress of deep blue, which she had saved especially for such a day as this. She thought of her family and of what they were then doing. *Much the same, I suppose,* she pondered, and then she imagined Lizzy getting ready to attend Pemberley Church. *How much grander life must be for you now, Lizzy.* She smiled at the thought of her friend's happiness and then looked at her own reflection in the mirror as Mrs Higgs dressed her hair. She was still plain-looking, but there was a rosiness to her cheeks she had

47

never seen before, which she liked. She chose earrings and then was ready to meet her husband in the hallway to walk together to church for their first Christmas service as Reverend and Mrs Collins.

Mr Collins' message was on the birth and deity of the baby, much as any sermon was in all of England on any given Christmas morn.

As they gathered in the churchyard after the service, the younger Miss Thomas approached Charlotte and invited her and Mr Collins to dinner on the eve of the New Year.

"We would be delighted to attend, would we not, Mr Collins?" She turned to her husband, but he was following and fawning over Lady Catherine as she made her way to her carriage. Charlotte watched them board and smiled sadly to herself as she thought, *Even on Christmas Day they continue to look miserable!*

Miss Thomas must have been thinking the same thing for, as she linked arms with Charlotte, she said, "I would not change places with them for the entire world. All that money, the wonderful house, land, and title, and not a smile between them."

Chapter Seven

U pon their return to the parsonage, they changed into their morning clothes and then took tea in the sitting room together while waiting for breakfast to be prepared and laid out.

It was then that an excited Mr Collins declared he could not wait to present his dear wife with his Christmas gift to her, "My dearest, beloved Charlotte, mere words cannot express to you how happy you have made me in becoming my wife." She blushed at his outpouring. "Since our union, I have been the happiest, most contented of men. You have made for us a delightful home, which is full of joy and peace. A more relaxed home I doubt there ever has been in all of England." Her blush deepened, but she managed to look at him and smile. "As I am so intimately acquainted with your little likes and dislikes, my dear, I deemed it best to choose for you a gift that would befit a woman in your position. Therefore, I hope – no, I am sure you will be most pleased by my choice, dearest Charlotte." He handed her a package.

She thanked him, began to open it, and could hardly contain herself. In her hands sat, within a gilded frame, a miniature portrait of Mr Collins himself.

"Yes, I can see you are as pleased with it as I am. Indeed, yes," he nodded. "I instructed them to fashion a loop on the back of the frame where you can thread a ribbon and thereby fasten it around your neck and carry my likeness next to your heart and with you always." He smiled with complete satisfaction.

She could not stop her eyes from betraying her feelings as they welled up and the tears spilled down her cheeks, but he mistook them for tears of joy. She stood up, kissed him on the cheek, and said thank you once again. He held his arm out to her and walked her to breakfast, a triumphant look diffusing his entire being.

They had a quiet breakfast, and Mr Collins chatted away, mostly to himself, about what a blessed year they had just had. It was not until after breakfast that Charlotte had composed herself enough to offer her gifts to her husband.

They moved back to the sitting room as the maid came to clear away the breakfast things, and they sat on the sofa together. She handed him the gifts she had handmade and then wrapped in tissue paper and tied with red ribbon.

She looked up into his face and saw something sad there, some emotion that threatened to choke him. "My dear, are you well?"

He cleared his throat and recovered himself somewhat. "Quite well indeed, my dear. I am touched by your generosity."

She smiled and teased a little, "You have not yet opened it. How do you know I have been generous?"

"I am not in the habit of receiving presents, my dear." He shifted uncomfortably and pulled at his shirt collar.

"Surely you received them from your parents as a boy?"

The look of sadness returned to his face, and his eyes darkened. "Sadly, no. Ours was not a happy home." He coughed and collected himself once more. "Not at all like ours, my dear."

He gave her a smile, and she could not but feel moved with compassion for him as she smiled back and reached out for his hand. He maintained her gaze for a few seconds before looking away uncomfortably and then tugged at the ribbon, untying his first Christmas present from his wife.

His eyes fell on the exquisite needlework of the bookmark first, as she had laid it out that way, and beheld the little image of the nativity and the scripture, all neatly embroidered: "Isaiah 9:6 for unto us a child is born, unto us a son is given". Charlotte watched him as his eyes filled with tears, passed him her handkerchief, and waited for him to dab his eyes.

"What exquisite work, Charlotte. I am speechless." Charlotte smiled at the thought of that, but he was not speechless at all and continued, "Indeed, I knew you were a talented woman, but this is beyond even my expectations." She was pleased. "I am sure even Lady Catherine de Bourgh herself would agree with me and, indeed, I believe she would approve greatly of your choice of gift to me."

The smile slipped from Charlotte's face. "Indeed, I thought only of you my dear, not of Lady Catherine at all."

He then placed the bookmark on the arm of the sofa and turned his attention to the Psalter cover. "Now, I believe this to be the finest needlework in all of England, my dear. Look at the way you have so lovingly embroidered my name upon it. I shall cover my Psalter with pride. Yes, I am indeed the most fortunate of all men in England, my dear Charlotte." To her utter surprise, he leaned towards her and kissed her firmly on the mouth. "Now, my dearest, how would you like to accompany your husband on a small walk to the village, around the church, and back?"

She said that would please her enormously and ran to fetch her bonnet and pelisse, while he put on his heavy coat and hat and placed the Psalter in its new cover. Together they walked out of the house, with Mr Collins' Psalter held firmly under his arm.

Charlotte knew what he was about and as soon as they came across another person out for a walk; he seized the chance to show off his new Christmas present whilst she stood silently by watching and blushing.

* * *

As they approached the parsonage on their way back, Charlotte knew by the slowing of her husband's pace that, he was looking towards Rosings, while she was deliberately staring in the opposite direction.

"My dear, I wonder if it would be polite for us to visit Her Ladyship."

"Uninvited, William?" She looked shocked but knew he would disregard such improper behaviour.

"Your sense of propriety does you credit, but I do believe that a visit from a clergyman and friend would be most welcome on this most sacred of days. Shall we walk that way?" It was not such a suggestion as an intention, and she had to steel herself not to give in to him.

She did not relish the idea of seeing Her Ladyship twice in one day, and certainly not twice on Christmas Day. "You go on ahead if you feel you must. As for myself, I have much to attend to in preparation for our first family Christmas meal together."

She did not think she would get away so easily, but the pull towards Rosings was getting stronger; her husband was already turning away from her, his feet moving in that direction.

"Mr Collins," she called after him, "do not be late for dinner. I would not wish to serve you burnt goose!"

Despite her admonition, she knew he would be late and told the cook to start dinner one hour later than they had planned.

She then took the opportunity to return to her room, lie on the bed, and read a novel Miss Thomas had lent her, but her eyes became heavy quickly and she slept, having read only the first page.

* * *

Charlotte awoke when Mrs Higgs came to inform her it was time to begin cooking, as she had asked if she could help the cook with this special meal. They had looked dubiously at her at first, but she told them that she had not always been the daughter of a knight of the realm and that she had some experience. They allowed her to help whilst they giggled at the thought, although they did not trust her with anything more than preparing soup and vegetables.

It was as they were laying the table with the meal hot from the kitchen and Charlotte was anxiously looking at what she was doing, towards the clock, and out of the window by turns that Mr Collins arrived, once again running and in a high state of agitation.

He ran breathlessly into the dining room. "Oh, my dear!" He looked around him and took in the spread on the table. "Oh, I am heartily pleased I am not too tardy. I declare that if it were not impossible, because Her Ladyship is the most pleasant and charitable of all women, I would suspect that she was endeavouring to detain me!" He leant on the back of a chair while he caught his breath.

Charlotte smiled at him and shook her head. "What on earth would give you that impression William?"

Mrs Higgs and Jenny endeavoured to suppress their giggles at their mistress's manner. She shot them a look, and they hurried back to their work.

Mr Collins sat down in his chair at the head of the table. "Well, every time I expressed a desire to depart, she presented me with more tea. I believe I have had enough tea for a lifetime!" He laughed nervously and finally took in the table before him. "I must say, my dear, this is a magnificent meal before me. You have done yourself proud, Mrs Collins!"

She smiled at him indulgently. "Would you wish to freshen up after your somewhat hasty return home?"

"Yes, yes, indeed I would, Mrs Collins. Your patience is infinite. I will be just one moment," as he hurried off to make himself presentable.

Charlotte looked at Mrs Higgs, who shook her head knowingly. "One day, ma'am, one day he will realise he owes more to you than her!" She gathered up her trays and left muttering under her breath, "Ooh, she's a conniving one, she is."

Charlotte sat in silence awaiting Mr Collins' return and wondered what Mrs Higgs had meant. She knew that Lady Catherine was overbearing and would control and manage every single part of the lives around her if she could, indeed, do so. Was there more to what Mrs Higgs had said? Had Lady Catherine overstepped her authority too often somehow? She determined to find out as much as possible once the festivities were past.

While washing and changing his clothes, Mr Collins' thoughts were on a similar train. Had Lady Catherine meant to detain him? What could have been her reasoning? Was she lonely? No, that could not possibly be; she had Colonel Fitzwilliam, her daughter Anne, and Anne's companion for company. Was she still angry and put out that they had determined to spend their first Christmas meal together and not with her? Another thought occurred to him. Surely she could not be jealous because she did not have her own way – No. He frowned at the idea and pushed it aside. He quickly brushed his hair and hurried back to join his wife for Christmas dinner.

Chapter Eight

O n the following morning, Charlotte sat alone in the sitting room putting the final touches to the Boxing Day boxes for the servants while Mr Collins was at the church preparing the boxes for the poor when the bell rang and Colonel Fitzwilliam was announced. She tied the last cord around the final box as he entered.

"Good day, Mrs Collins. I am not disturbing you, I trust?"

"Good day, Colonel. You are not disturbing me at all, I assure you. In fact, I have just this minute finished my task." She indicated that he should be seated. "I am afraid that Mr Collins is not here at present."

"Ah. Well, I had come purposely to take my leave, but I am sure that you would pass on my goodbyes to your husband."

"I would be glad to, Colonel. Would you care to join me for tea?"

The Colonel was glad of the invitation. He had missed the walks they had begun to share and had endured a few days' drought of lively conversation at Rosings.

"I confess I would like that, Mrs Collins. I am in serious need of conversation this morning." He smirked at her, and she knew his meaning immediately. "It is permitted, Mrs Collins, for you to share your sentiments on the subject with me, as I know you feel as I do that conversation should indeed flow in two directions, back and forth."

She stood up the ring the bell to staunch the burst of laughter that threatened to break free from her. "I trust you had a pleasant Christmas Day, Colonel?"

"Thank you Mrs Collins, I did. And may I convey my apologies to both you and Mr Collins for my aunt yesterday?" She looked at him quizzically. "I am afraid she is not one to be gainsaid, and the thought of you desiring to spend your Christmas meal alone irked her terribly. She devised to keep Mr Collins as long as possible so that your meal would spoil." Charlotte could not contain the gasp that escaped her lips. "I see I have shocked you. I am heartily sorry for that."

"I confess I am shocked, Colonel, that Lady Catherine would stoop to such behaviour."

"Oh, I assure you, she will have her own way. Nevertheless, I am glad Mr Collins managed to wriggle his way out of Rosings and back here. Was the meal terribly spoilt?"

She smiled up at him and her eyes twinkled. "No. In fact, I had assumed Mr Collins would be behind time. We began dinner an hour later than planned, so when he did arrive home, we were laying it upon the table at the same moment."

The colonel could not restrain his laughter at her cunning. "Touché, Mrs Collins! Well played indeed!"

The tea things arrived and Charlotte busied herself with the task of making it, all the while conscious of Colonel Fitzwilliam watching her intently. Once she had given him his tea, she poured her own and was glad to be seated again. The intensity of his gaze had made her feel self-conscious and, she was embarrassed to admit, made her legs feel weak.

"Will you be in town long, Colonel?" She was relieved to find her voice steady and calm.

"That is something I do not know the answer to, I'm afraid. It is a sad, messy business."

"You mentioned before that it was grave. May I enquire as to the nature of your business?"

"You may indeed enquire, Mrs Collins, but I can furnish you with as little information as possible. I am to attend a court-martial hearing."

She looked shocked. "It is not your own, I trust!"

He smiled at her, a smile that made her feel uncomfortable and nervous. "No, not my own, but of a young lad who ran away from the war in the Peninsula and was recently apprehended. I am to stand as a character witness for him. Unfortunately, I fear it will not go well for him. The Army does not look kindly upon deserters." He looked sadly down at the floor, a frown creasing his forehead.

"I am sorry to hear it, Colonel." She knew that the boy would be shot. "I am sorry for the boy and his family." He looked into her eyes, and she could see how deeply he felt about the boy. "I think he has been important to you."

"Undeniably, he has been. I took him under my wing. You cannot imagine the horrors of war, Mrs Collins, and the poor boy suffered tremendously from his fears. He experienced recurrent nightmares. I was not surprised when he ran away from the front. Even the hardiest war veterans suffer from nightmares. God knows I do." He reached up and rubbed at his neck, and she remained silent, sensing his need to unburden himself emotionally. "War is a ghastly business." He seemed to collect himself. "I am sorry, Mrs Collins, to speak so freely."

"Do not apologise, Colonel. I think if you did not talk about it, it would be harder upon you."

He looked up into her eyes again. "Yes, you understand. You are a remarkable woman."

Charlotte blushed. *Why am I blushing?* she thought, suddenly uncomfortable with herself.

"I shall return after, in about six weeks, I estimate. I do sincerely hope we can continue our walks and discussions."

"I hope that too. They have been most enjoyable." He held her gaze for longer than was necessary, and her pulse began to race. His eyes traced her face and then fell upon the miniature Mr Collins had given her for Christmas, hanging from a ribbon tied about her neck. "Mrs Collins, may I enquire as to what that pendant you are wearing might be?"

He leant forward to take a closer look at the miniature. Seeing the look of shock interlaced with astonishment and revulsion on his face, Charlotte did then give way to laughter. "I know!" she exclaimed. "It was a gift," she sighed, a wry expression on her face, which said more than her words.

The colonel was relieved to see that she felt the same way he did, as he feared giving her offence, and he smiled conspiratorially back at her, relaxing into their new friendship.

* * *

Once the Colonel took his leave and departed, Charlotte decided to walk into Hunsford to visit the Misses Thomas.

She found only the younger Miss Thomas at home and glad of a visitor. "Mrs Collins, I am so glad you are here. Do sit down."

"Thank you, Miss Thomas."

"Oh, I think it is about time that we dispensed with formalities. We are becoming firm friends. Please, I would prefer it if you were to call me Louisa."

Charlotte was surprised but exceedingly pleased to be able to do so. It was turning out to be a day of improving friendships. She implored Miss Thomas to return the compliment and now call her Charlotte.

They smiled at each other a little nervously at their new intimacy and then giggled like schoolgirls. "I am sad to have missed your sister today, Louisa," Charlotte began, trying out this new familiarity.

"Mrs Thomas is running errands today and has probably been waylaid by Mrs Brown," Louisa smiled.

"Mrs Thomas? I thought she was your sister, another Miss Thomas."

Louisa looked surprised at Charlotte's misunderstanding. "Not at all! Oh, my dear," she moved to sit next to Charlotte on the sofa and laid her hand upon hers, "I am so sorry that you had misunderstood."

She appeared to think for a few seconds and chewed her lip in a way that made her look younger, and Charlotte realised she did not know her friend's age at all, but surmised she could not be above five and thirty.

"I suppose I should tell you the whole history then."

Charlotte turned towards her friend. "I would appreciate that, and I apologise for the misunderstanding."

"Not at all. I suppose when we are usually spoken of as the Misses Thomas, then that assumption is quite natural. Anne is my sister-in-law. She was Anne Fields and married my brother Henry." Charlotte's eyebrows raised in surprise. "Oh, you did not know about Henry either. Oh, my dear, this is going to be a long story. I should call for the tea now."

Louisa giggled in the childish way she was wont to do and rang for tea. Charlotte liked her immensely. She was a kind and genteel woman with no pretensions who found the humorous side in most situations.

58

"Now, Henry was my older brother." She sat back down, and Charlotte took note that she had said *was*. "There were just the two of us, and he married Anne. We all lived here together, and Anne had two children, Charles and Henrietta, in quick succession." She choked on the words, drew out a handkerchief, and covered her mouth. Her eyes screwed up with pain at the memories.

"You need not continue, Louisa, if it is too much." Charlotte felt her pain.

"Oh, thank you. I must correct the misunderstanding. The memories are still so painful." She cleared her throat and collected herself to continue. "I worked sometimes for Lady Catherine in those days. I am rather adept at needlework, and instead of sending to London for small repairs and alterations, she would ask for me. I would also then help Anne with the children, and I was glad of the occupation after my disappointment." She paused once again at another painful memory. Charlotte decided that she could wait to hear that story another day.

"I was at Rosings when Jim Harvey came with a message for me that the whole household was taken ill with the grip that was sweeping through the village. I thought that Lady Catherine was being gracious when she invited me to stay in one of the guest rooms meanwhile. I had never seen such a glorious room, and I confess the bed was far too soft for me to get a decent night's sleep, even if I could have slept in my distress. I spent the days caring for my family, and I returned to Rosings at night. You can imagine how it hurt me one day to overhear Lady Catherine telling Lady Metcalf that she had not asked me to stay out of compassion, but because she did not want to lose her seamstress to the grip, as it would incommode her terribly."

She looked into Charlotte's eyes, her own brimming with tears, and Charlotte once again felt irritation at Lady Catherine.

"I determined to leave immediately, and I wrote a note informing Lady Catherine that I felt obliged to return to my family." Again, she paused to wipe her eyes. "Charlotte I blame myself for not being here so diligently. I blame Lady Catherine for her interference." Here, she had to blow her nose. "Forgive me."

"Not at all." The tea things arrived, and Charlotte took charge of making it while her friend composed herself again.

What had Lady Catherine done to Louisa? This was an indication of Lady Catherine's selfish desire to dominate those all around her, but certainly no reason to be bitter against her. Louisa was obviously implying more than she was saying, and although her curiosity was up, Charlotte did not intend to push the point at that moment.

Charlotte handed some tea to her friend, who drank deeply and then continued with her narration.

"I thought the fever had broken and they were on the mend, but young Charles was the first to be taken. Henrietta soon followed her brother heavenward. I could not bring myself to tell Anne nor Henry. They were languishing in their infirmity; such terrible news could wait." She drank more tea, her face wet with tears. "Henry died two days after his children, and it was on the same day that Anne finally regained herself and came back to us." Her voice was breaking, and she was crying freely now. "Oh, Charlotte! I was beside myself. You cannot imagine the joy I felt that she had come through the worst and the anguish I also felt knowing that I had to inform her of her worst nightmare."

Charlotte refilled Louisa's cup while she continued. "We held the funerals quietly, and I thought Anne would never speak again, she was so badly grieved. Only prayer seemed to comfort her in her sorrow. That was two years ago this spring." She looked up again at Charlotte, clearly relieved to have completed the tale. "There now, you know our history, and I am glad of it. I am sure she will need your sensitivity when the anniversary comes around."

Charlotte placed her hand on Louisa's. "As will you, my friend."

Louisa's revelation had put their friendship into a new light. The Misses Thomas had suffered significantly from the ravages of illness and, as for Anne, losses which no parent ought to know, Charlotte thought as she walked home much more slowly than usual that day. The thought that Lady Catherine had somehow injured Louisa by interfering once too often also worried her. It did not bode well for herself and Mr Collins if that were the case. She was already tired of Lady Catherine's apparent officiousness, Charlotte mused sadly.

Chapter Nine

Charlotte and Mr Collins dined at Rosings in the week between Christmas and the New Year. Interestingly, Lady Catherine was not concerned by her usual subjects of conversation. She felt no need to neither advise, reprimand, patronise, nor demand anything. Instead, she occupied herself with the thought of her daughter, Anne. Anne was a sickly girl, according to Lady Catherine, but Charlotte had never observed any illness whatsoever in the girl. It was true that she had a pale, sickly pallor, but that was most probably attributable to her rarely being out of doors and never taking exercise. Lady Catherine was regaling them with a fine list of accomplishments, which Anne would have had if only she were well enough to attempt them. Charlotte could barely contain a laugh. Poor Anne! She had never been permitted to do anything that Lady Catherine thought would fatigue her or that could lead to her becoming ill, such as taking exercise out of doors.

Then Lady Catherine moved on to talk about Anne having been jilted by Mr Darcy in favour of *that girl*, as she called Elizabeth. Again, Charlotte was close to laughing aloud. It was apparent that Mr Darcy had never had any intentions nor designs to marry Anne and, by the looks of her, Charlotte could not imagine her mustering the desire to marry anyone either. The understanding that supposedly had existed between Anne and Mr Darcy was entirely of Lady Catherine's invention. Lady Catherine was a woman who usually got her own way and, having had her nose put out of joint once, she was not to be outdone again. She then determined to get an excellent husband for her daughter, and was discussing the idea of having a party of young people – by young people Charlotte assumed she meant *gentlemen* – to visit Rosings in the hope that one of them would propose marriage to Anne.

"What an excellent idea, Your Ladyship. I cannot imagine how any gentleman could resist the charms of your excellent daughter," fawned Mr Collins, who had been making such comments throughout the evening.

"Yes, indeed, who could resist." She said fondly, looking at her daughter. "Of course, only suitors with a fortune and, preferably, a title will suffice. Only such a man would be suitable for *my* daughter." She smiled at Anne. Charlotte noticed that Anne looked away from her mother, discomfited by the idea of being sold off to the man with the highest income. "Colonel Fitzwilliam would be an excellent match. Despite being the youngest son of my brother the Earl, he still has a small fortune of his own that he has earned in the war." She watched Anne and seemed to be mulling over the idea. "Yes, indeed. I think I will broach the subject and inform the Colonel that he has my permission to court Anne."

Poor Colonel Fitzwilliam, thought Charlotte. *I wonder how he, a colonel in His Majesty's Army, will take to being told what to do by his aunt and having his marriage arranged for him.* Charlotte was glad he was not present to be embarrassed in front of them in such a way. She knew that being told such information would be better done when alone with his aunt, where he could express how he felt without hurting his cousin's feelings.

She had often heard Lady Catherine bemoan Elizabeth's connections, but sitting there and watching her, Charlotte was not sure who had the worse connections, Elizabeth or Mr Darcy.

* * *

Charlotte was prevented from visiting Louisa and Mrs Thomas during the following days by the weather. It seemed that the clouds could hold more rain than ever before. Charlotte sat in the sitting room, watching the rain beat upon the windows of the parsonage, and slowly monitored the progress of the road turning from slightly muddy to a quagmire. Not even a carriage could pass in such weather, and Charlotte turned her attention to the needlework she ought to have been doing for the poor. Her mind refused to be engaged and wandered from Lady Catherine to Anne, to Colonel Fitzwilliam, to Louisa, to Mrs Thomas and her unfortunate history, and back again. She put down her needlework and went to Mr Collins' book room to find something to read. He was writing his letters and barely looked up as she entered. She browsed the shelves, but nothing took her fancy. Mr Collins' taste in reading material did not extend to novels. He thought them crass and a non-productive use of one's time; therefore, his collection of books was too serious to tempt Charlotte into reading any of them. She then remembered Mrs Higgs was a novel reader and carefully closed the door behind her and made her way to the kitchen. Mrs Higgs and Jenny were sitting at the table and rose as Charlotte entered.

"Oh, Mrs Collins, I have just made some buns. Would you like some?"

She had not seen Mrs Jones, the cook, immediately but was glad of the welcome and the chance to do something. "Thank you, Mrs Jones. I would like that."

Jenny pulled out and dusted off a chair for Charlotte, and they sat down again.

"Would you like some hot chocolate too?" Mrs Higgs asked as she rose once more and walked to the range.

"Yes, please. It is such a damp, miserable day, I need my spirits lifted."

With hot chocolate and buttered buns warming them from the inside, the ladies began to chat away, and Charlotte's boredom abated. She listened to their gossiping and laughed with them at the tales from the village and some of the servants' tittle-tattle from Rosings. She was amazed at what they knew, and was made uncomfortable recalling her chiding of Mr Collins for gossiping, while here she was involved in such an activity.

She then remembered her reason for coming to the kitchen in the first place. "Mrs Higgs, I remember that you are a reader of novels."

"Yes, ma'am."

"Aye, she loves a good bit o' romance at night!" laughed Mrs Jones.

Charlotte blushed and smiled to hide her embarrassment. "I wonder if you could lend me something to read? Mr Collins is not in the habit of keeping novels."

This made Jenny and Mrs Jones laugh more, and the latter could not help but comment, "Wouldn't do him any harm, though!"

Charlotte caught the insinuation and her blush deepened, and she wondered at the wisdom of being so friendly with her servants.

Mrs Higgs caught the look on Charlotte's face and rose. "If you'll follow me, ma'am. I keep my books in my room."

Charlotte thanked the cook for the buns and quickly followed Mrs Higgs out of the kitchen and up the stairs, glad to be away from their knowing glances, and wondered what tales they were telling about her and Mr Collins.

Once they were in Mrs Higgs' room, the housekeeper spoke. "Ma'am, I am sorry about downstairs. Sometimes they just do not know what is inappropriate to say to the mistress. I hope you do not think me presumptuous, but I would avoid such informal visits to the kitchen in future. I would hate for them to start gossiping about you."

"You are right, Mrs Higgs. Thank you." She blushed again ashamed at her own naiveté and looked down at the floor.

"Which novel would you like to read, then?"

She was glad of the change of subject and directed all of her attention to the small collection of books on the shelf. She saw Ann Radcliffe's *Mysteries of Udolpho*. She smiled and wondered how Mr Collins would react to such a book. She decided to take a chance and read it, but she would hide it in their room all the same. She made another choice with Mrs Higgs' advice: Samuel Richardson's *Clarissa*. She took both books, thanked the housekeeper, proceeded to her room, and began to read.

By tea time, there was no let-up in the rain, but Charlotte's mood was much improved from reading and immersing herself in world of her own imagining. She took Mr Collins his tea, as he remained in his book room. She saw that he was reading from Fordyce and sat in an easy chair by the fire. He smiled up at her as she entered and asked if he would like a piece of cake. He did not, and she left him to his reading, grateful that she could also return to her book. She smiled to herself at the vastly different subject matters.

Pleasantly occupied, her boredom passed away and she no longer minded the rain incessantly beating on the windows. She was far too engrossed in the life, perils, trials, and romance of the heroine of her book even to notice. Her tea remained on the sofa table at her side and became cold. She was so interested in the

64

outcome of the plight of Clarissa in her book that she barely noticed even the passing of the afternoon, and she did not perceive the light fading from the room until she came back to reality with a start when Jenny entered to close the curtains and light the candles.

* * *

No invitation came from Rosings asking for them to join the family in celebrating the New Year, and Charlotte was not displeased. She knew that it was a deliberate slight on Her Ladyship's behalf because of Christmas, yet Charlotte knew her husband would never even notice such a thing, and as she had already accepted an invitation from Louisa and Mrs Thomas to dine with them, it relieved her from making excuses. Owing to the terrible weather that week, the Collinses had to use their own gig rather than walk. Thankfully, the rain had stopped that morning or they would not have been able to attend. Still, Charlotte prayed for a long cessation in the rain as, although the gig would save her shoes and gown, it would not keep her too dry if the heavens opened once again. She decided to ask Mr Collins about the purchase of a larger means of transportation.

They were happy to arrive at their destination and get out of the cold, whereupon Louisa directed Charlotte to a chair near the fire. Happily, Mrs Brown joined them, along with Mr and Mrs Abbot. Mr Abbot was a milliner who had retired and left his son to run the business in Westerham. Charlotte had met them when they went carolling on Christmas Eve and welcomed the opportunity to converse with them more. Mr Collins, though, latched on to Mr Abbot immediately and launched into a great discourse on the dreadfulness of the weather and the appalling state of the roads.

Charlotte noticed the vast difference in dining with true friends and dining at Rosings. Here, she was permitted a greater freedom in that she might express herself without being corrected or berated. She also gave opinions without fear of being wrong or belittled. *Yes,* Charlotte thought, *this is how I would prefer to spend my evenings, with true friends.*

Dinner was an easy affair, and as there was no gentleman in residence, the men joined the ladies, and together they all repaired back to the sitting room. Mrs Brown took the opportunity to open Mrs Thomas' spinet. The poor instrument was in need of a tuning, but all the same, Mrs Brown played beautifully, and Mrs Abbot joined her to sing duets.

Louisa sat next to Charlotte and asked her if she would like to go with her into Westerham the next day to do some shopping. Charlotte accepted Louisa's offer, and remembered that she would like to enquire more into their discussion of the previous week. Charlotte realised with some dismay that, in almost one year of married life, she had never once been to Westerham on a shopping trip. She had, of course, been through Westerham by coach when travelling to Hertfordshire via Bromley. This thought surprised her, and she determined also make a purchase or two.

Mr Abbot overheard the ladies talking about shopping in Westerham and interrupted Mr Collins in his discourse to join in, much to that gentleman's surprise. "My dear ladies, why did you not say that you wished to shop in Westerham?" The ladies looked a little shocked at the idea of informing Mr Abbot at all of such a plan. "I will write a note for you, which I must insist on you handing to my son, Mr Abbot Jr. He will see to it that you are furnished with all that your hearts could desire, and I might persuade him to offer a discount, eh?"

Charlotte smiled and looked down at her hands and left Louisa to speak to him on their behalf. "Thank you, Mr Abbot, but that is not necessary I assure you."

"Nonsense, nonsense, my dear girl! What can an old man like myself do when he has no daughters to spoil, eh?" He laughed heartily, and his belly moved with the action. "I will brook no refusal whatsoever. Miss Thomas, Mrs Collins, I insist! And if you might furnish me with pen and ink, I will scribe a note this instant!"

Louisa reluctantly obliged him and led him to the writing table, where he began to scratch and blot a note to his son. He was such a jolly, kind fellow that Charlotte could not but feel grateful for such attentions, although she noticed that Mr Collins looked red-faced and embarrassed.

Mr Abbot signed his note with a flourish and handed it to Louisa. "There, my dear, 'tis done. You have yourselves a lovely day!"

Louisa joined Charlotte once more, and both smiled and blushed. "Anything we can do to please the ladies, eh, Reverend?" Mr Collins merely simpered in response.

Mr Collins did not seem comfortable with the idea that his wife was accepting a gift from a tradesman rather than the advice of Lady Catherine, who had more than once insisted that Charlotte use her milliner in London. That was something that Charlotte would not do; for one, she had no occasion to wear such finery, and two, she would never be so frivolous with her pin money.

* * *

On their journey home from the Thomas house, as she had expected, Mr Collins did, indeed, begin to chide her over accepting such a gift. "My dear Charlotte, I cannot begin to impress upon you the sovereign importance that we must place upon the advice and condescension of Lady Catherine. She would be in a fury if she were to learn that you had not only taken advice but accepted the offer of a discount from such a man as Mr Abbot, let alone that you intend to shop at his establishment and not the elegant boutiques which Lady Catherine herself patronises. Such importance cannot be overemphasised my dear. We must be acutely sensible at all times of doing all within our power to please Her Ladyship."

Once more, her anger rose inside her at such a speech as this. When would he realise his folly? Charlotte knew that she would have to defend herself or cancel her arrangements with Louisa and partake of all the embarrassment of such an action, and she knew that if she did not go with her, Louisa would feel snubbed and their friendship would suffer. Charlotte would no longer allow Lady Catherine to dictate even the minutest parts of her life.

"William, I feel it only right to respond, to defend and explain my decision."

Mr Collins stared at his wife in disbelief and turned to express his disapproval at her once more. At that moment, the gig hit a hole in the road, and he was forced to return his gaze reluctantly to the matter of guiding their equipage, and she was free to continue to speak her mind.

"May I begin," she continued, "by pointing out to you that you lay far too much importance upon the advice of Lady Catherine?

67

I am a person with my own likes and dislikes, Mr Collins. I believe I may be trusted to make appropriate choices, especially when it comes to choosing the clothing I wish to wear. I am also able to choose the merchants I wish to purchase from and in which town I wish to do so." Mr Collins merely snorted, his brow knitted together. 'You have expressed that Mr Abbot is not a man whose shop I ought to frequent. May I ask why you think this is?"

She deliberately did not pause, however, to give him the opportunity of explain. "I know exactly why, Mr Collins, because of Lady Catherine. Everything is because of Lady Catherine! And the only way in which Lady Catherine would find out that I, indeed, went against her wishes is if someone told her that that was the case, and I would be heartily disappointed to find that you, my own husband, had degraded and injured your wife in such a way, sir!"

She twisted her hands in her lap, endeavouring to master and calm her temper, while Mr Collins remained too shocked to reply.

"I might also remind you that you are merely a clergyman. We only have a clergyman's income, and if I, in all honesty, were to patronise the boutiques in London of which Lady Catherine insists upon, then you and I would be in the debtor's prison before Easter, Mr Collins!" She paused for breath, then continued, "I am not an imprudent woman. I have managed our household well this past year and," she added proudly, "have managed to save a little."

He looked at her, and took his eyes off the road again with an expression that showed he was surprised, but not displeased, by what she had said.

"Therefore, Mr Collins, let me keep within the sphere in which we truly are as Reverend and Mrs Collins. Allow me to keep the friends I am making, who are also of the same rank as we, and do me the honour of not chiding me like a child, but accepting my decisions as those of a prudent and respectable woman."

Despite her initial anger at her husband, she had managed to speak her mind in a logical way but, in her fury, sat back afterwards, staring at the road ahead, silently daring him to retort.

He could not respond, despite deeply feeling what he believed he owed to Lady Catherine. His conscience fought against his profound feeling of obligation to Her Ladyship and his duty to his wife. He, therefore, remained silent the remainder of the way home, where, upon their arrival, Charlotte repaired immediately to their room and to bed while he went to his book room to think.

He settled into his easy chair and replayed her words in his mind, trying to find the slight, the flaw, or the point with which he could countermand her decision. It was approaching dawn when he finally fell asleep in the chair.

Chapter Ten

T he next morning was dry again. Charlotte was unsurprised, although a little disappointed, that Mr Collins had not come to bed last night. She dressed quietly, went into the breakfast room, and poured herself some coffee. Mrs Higgs came in presently to discuss the day with her and informed her that Mr Collins was still asleep in his book room.

"Then, pray, do not disturb him. Make up the fire, but quietly. Then when he awakes, make sure that he has something hearty to eat. I am to Westerham today with Miss Thomas but will return this evening before dinner." She buttered some bread and reached for the jam, pausing with her had outstretched as she saw Mrs Higgs was still standing looking at her. "Yes, Mrs Higgs?"

"I just wondered, is everything all right, Mrs Collins?"

Charlotte had acutely felt the awkwardness of the conversation in the kitchen the day before yesterday. After she and Mr Collins had argued in the gig, she was keenly aware of her rank and station this morning, and knew also that she must conduct herself differently at home.

"Yes, of course it is, Mrs Higgs. Mr Collins had a lot on his mind last night when we arrived home and stayed up to mull things over. He must have fallen asleep in so doing. That is all. But I fear he will catch a cold if Jenny does not light the fire in his book room soon." Her meaning was clear. Mrs Higgs bobbed a curtsey and left Charlotte to her breakfast.

* * *

Upon her arrival at Louisa's house, Charlotte noticed a carriage outside. She tentatively rang the bell, wondering if their trip would be postponed due to an unexpected guest. This suspicion proved to be groundless. After ushering Charlotte into the sitting room, Louisa breathlessly explained the carriage.

It seemed that Mr and Mrs Abbot, upon thinking of and talking about Charlotte and Louisa's trip into Westerham that morning over breakfast, had decided upon lending them the use of their carriage. The Abbot's themselves did not need it for that day, and Mrs Abbot had said that she would not have been comfortable or able to settle at anything the whole day long if she had to worry about Charlotte and Louisa going by coach into Westerham.

Charlotte warmed at the thought of such marked attention made out of genuine affection and concern for their safety. *Truly, these are kind and Christian people,* she thought. If only her husband could also see them the way she did.

The two ladies departed on their shopping spree in comfort and style, and Charlotte wondered what her husband would think if he could see her once more in a carriage that was like her father's.

They visited the cobblers, where Louisa had her sister-in-law's boots mended and purchased a new pair of slippers for herself. Amongst her own purchases, Charlotte bought a new pair of shoes for Mr Collins as a peace offering. The ladies then went to a seamstress who was recommended by Mrs Abbot as being not too expensive, but with an excellent eye for the fashion; and then they went on to Mr Abbot's own establishment.

The shop was far larger than Charlotte had anticipated and made the milliner's in Meryton look like a market stall in comparison. Upon their arrival, Mr Abbot Jr greeted them, and Louisa presented him with his father's note. His face changed, and he smiled from ear to ear resembling his father. He could not have been more obliging to them, and Charlotte was so shocked to see how much of a discount he was willing to give them, that she almost lost herself in her purchases. She bought new muslin for some new walking and day gowns; her present ones could be delegated to morning gowns. She also treated herself to some fine, sheer linen for chemisettes and fichus. To these purchases, Charlotte added gloves, a more elegant and fashionable lace cap, and ribbons for trimming.

Mr Abbot was loathe to have them leave, and they informed him that they must take the muslins and linen to Mrs Owen, the seamstress. Upon hearing their reason for leaving so soon, Mr Abbott exclaimed that he would have them delivered to Mrs Owen at once and called an assistant immediately. Charlotte felt giddy at such preferential treatment and was suddenly sure that she had overspent.

She paled at the thought. Louisa did not miss this change in her friend's countenance. "My dear Charlotte, are you quite well?" she asked as she took Charlotte's hand.

"Yes, I assure you. I am tired all of a sudden." She drew her friend aside away from the hearing of Mr Abbot Jr. "To own the truth, my dear Louisa, I am a little concerned that I may have spent more than I had intended to."

"Oh, Charlotte, do not mind that. Come, there is a tea shop not two minutes' walk from here where you can sit in comfort and do your sums to reassure yourself. I know you have not been frivolous, my dear."

They bid adieu to Mr Abbot Jr, thanking him again, and set off in the direction of the tea shop.

Once suitably ensconced in the corner and furnished with tea and scones, Charlotte began to relax a little when she counted her change in her reticule. She realised that, after the ample and generous discount they were given, and taking into account Mrs Owen's fee, that she had, indeed, not overspent, and breathed an audible sigh of relief. Louisa laughed.

"Oh, what a wonderful thing it is to be away from Hunsford!" Louisa declared.

"Indeed, Louisa, although I think I carry some of our acquaintance with me in my head. I believe I can hear their censure at any rate." It felt good to Charlotte to laugh freely and speak so openly. The two friends remained in the shop for some time.

"Charlotte, perhaps we should walk for a while?"

Charlotte could think of no better end to their day than a walk around Westerham. They walked through the market street and paused to look at the construction of a magnificent house, and Louisa told her about the countess who was reportedly going to live there. They then walked to St. Mary's Church and round the churchyard, where they found a bench on which to rest.

"Ah, what a beautiful day!" exclaimed Louisa stretching out. "I am so glad that we have had this day to ourselves, Charlotte."

"As am I, Louisa. It is not often that I can take a whole day for myself and indulge in such activities. I find I am most contented with our day out."

"I, for one, will be sad to return home."

A shadow of sadness crossed Louisa's face, and Charlotte grew concerned for her friend. "What is it, Louisa?"

Louisa took a moment to take a deep breath and then looked at her companion. "Today is what would have been my fifth wedding anniversary."

Charlotte's faced showed her confusion. "I am afraid I do not have the pleasure of understanding you, Louisa."

Again, Louisa took a deep breath before speaking. "Five and a half years ago, more or less, Mr Simmons of Oak Wood Farm and I courted."

Charlotte's expression changed to one of surprise. "I know of the man! He is a gentleman farmer and is very kindly thought of."

Her friend smiled, "Indeed, he is the best of men, Charlotte."

"I still fail to understand. What happened?" She could see that Louisa was now having difficulty finding the words to express what she had begun to relate. Charlotte took her friend's hand to reassure her.

"Everything was going along well," she swallowed down the lump in her throat, "until Lady Catherine heard of our engagement."

There it was again! Lady Catherine's name popping up in the most unconnected circumstances.

"Pray, Louisa, what can this have to do with Her Ladyship?"

Louisa looked grave. "Oh, you may well ask. Her Ladyship makes the entire neighbourhood her concern. I should have been stronger. I should have stood my ground. But I did not." She burst into tears, and Charlotte pressed her own handkerchief into Louisa's hand.

"You remember I told you that I was Her Ladyship's seamstress for small works? Well, it seems her officiousness was at work even then. When the old minister informed her of his intention to read our banns that Sunday, she flew into a rage. She

74

immediately sought me out. I was at home with Henry, and Mr Simmons was due to call within the hour. She scolded me like a fury, Charlotte! She asked how I could be so heartless and so selfish as to deign to make the decision to marry without her permission." She caught a tear with the handkerchief as it traced its way down her face.

"I do not understand why you would need Her Ladyship's consent."

"Neither did I at the time. I told her that we were in love and we intended to marry in three weeks' time, and she replied angrily that she failed to see what love had to do with marriage and that I was only thinking selfishly of my own comfort and to spite her." Louisa's breathing was becoming ragged as the painful memories threatened to overwhelm her. "Lady Catherine said that as I was in her employ, I was under her jurisdiction and the decision for me to marry was hers to make and hers alone."

Charlotte squeezed Louisa's hand as she sat, mouth agape.

"Henry then stood up and said that I was not in her employ, I worked for her on a needs-only basis, did not receive a retainer, and if I wished to marry, the only consent I needed was his and his alone.

"Oh, Charlotte, you should have seen Lady Catherine's face when Henry spoke to her in such a manner! I thought she would have an apoplectic fit!"

Charlotte, instead of being amused at the thought of Her Ladyship's face at that particular moment, was becoming angrier at the overbearing self-importance.

"It was then that I saw that George - Mr Simmons had arrived and was standing in shock in the doorway."

"Oh, no!" Charlotte exclaimed and then winced at her outburst. She did not wish to interrupt her friend.

Louisa merely nodded and continued her narration. "He looked mortified, Charlotte. He stepped forward and declared that we were to be married whether she liked it or not. Lady Catherine's face became so red, she scared me. She almost screamed at George – Mr Simmons.

"'I do not give my consent, and I have refused to allow the banns to be read. You will not be married and certainly not in my church! If you dare conspire to elope together and marry elsewhere, I will see to it, Mr Simmons and Mr Thomas, that no one within my sphere of influence will ever do business with either of you again! Am I understood? I will not be treated in such an infamous manner. Now let that be an end to it!'

"She turned on her heel and left."

It was then that Louisa gave into her distress and sobbed openly. "Henry kicked over a chair; Mr Simmons stood opening and closing his fists, his face so red that I thought he would strike something; and I stood weeping, knowing that my only chance of happiness in life was slipping away from me. Mr Simmons bowed, took a long, sorrowful look at me – oh, such pain was in his eyes - and he departed. He never returned to visit me again."

Charlotte placed her arm around her friend's shoulder, and Louisa sobbed. It was a while before either of them could speak again.

"But was not Mr Simmons married?" Charlotte asked.

The look of pain in Louisa's eyes made her immediately wish the question unasked.

She nodded, "Yes. He married Nancy Fellows, the daughter of another farmer, the following year. He enlarged his land in so doing, but theirs was not a happy marriage. Nancy died a year later after enduring fifty hours of labour, so they say."

"My goodness!" Charlotte exclaimed. "So much sadness to come to such a man. What about now, Louisa? Is there any hope? You clearly still love him. Does he also return your affection?"

Louisa looked her in the eye and blushed. "I cannot be certain as we never meet socially now, but when we do see each other, he looks at me with such an intensity that I…" She could not finish her sentence. She buried her face in the handkerchief and sobbed once again.

Charlotte could find no words to console her friend. She was outraged at such a situation. Nevertheless, one thought did occur to her. Louisa was no longer in Lady Catherine's employ. That had ended upon the death of her brother and his children. Could it possibly be that the shackles that Her Ladyship had placed upon this poor, unfortunate couple were now, in fact, non-existent? Could she possibly play matchmaker and bring these two broken-hearted lovers together again? Such an enterprise would have to be undertaken extremely delicately indeed, and she resolved to discuss the problem with Colonel Fitzwilliam upon his return to Kent. He would know what to do and how to handle things with his aunt.

After regaining their composure, the two ladies arose and took a slow walk back towards the market square. Charlotte helped Louisa into the carriage and then visited Mrs Owen to enquire as to when their items would be ready for collection. She was pleased to learn that they would be sent on to them on Thursday next, and she climbed into the carriage, informed her friend of how quickly Mrs Owen worked. They then set about journeying home. Charlotte knew that she would not be able to rest without trying to do something. She wanted to help find a solution to the unjust and distressing situation of someone who was fast becoming one of her dearest friends.

Chapter Eleven

Upon her arrival home, Charlotte discovered that Mr Collins was out. Mrs Higgs did not know where he was, and Charlotte had a sinking feeling that she knew precisely the whereabouts of her husband. The mere thought infuriated her. She feared that she would receive a summons to Rosings to be castigated. She would most likely be shunned, bemoaned, and belittled for months to come, until Lady Catherine finally deigned to forgive her.

She straightened her back and resolved to not dwell on the matter nor cause herself undue worry; instead she thought of the lovely day she had spent in Westerham with Louisa, and of the sad matter of which she had spoken. The injustice of the situation made Charlotte feel sick to her stomach.

Charlotte had not married for love. She would have preferred to have done so and live contentedly, and she wished that also for her new friend. She decided to become closer acquainted with Mr Simmons. As she put her purchases away, she considered speaking to him at church on Sunday.

* * *

The shadows lengthened, the light faded, and still Mr Collins did not return to the parsonage. Charlotte gave instructions to Mrs Higgs to begin the dinner preparations, then continued to read in the bedroom, her stomach beginning to knot and a sense of foreboding starting to overtake her.

The dinner hour came and went, and Charlotte sat down to eat alone. She ate a few bites and ended up merely pushing her food around the plate. With her appetite gone, all she could think about was the whereabouts of Mr Collins. She could be certain that he was at Rosings. Moreover, as he was there during mealtime, she could be certain that her absence was obvious and that Mr Collins had, no doubt, disclosed full details of her disobedience and rebelliousness to his patroness. That Mr Collins' absence from his own dining table was deliberate, designed to distress her and convey to her a significant message, was clear.

She rang the bell and had Jenny clear away the table. She retired to her room, so angry with her husband that she did not wish to see him at all that evening, and desired to sleep early.

* * *

Much to her embarrassment and irritation, she awoke when Jenny arrived to part the curtains and stoke the fire. Her irritation returned with full force when she realised that Mr Collins' side of the bed was cold and he had not slept there. She swallowed down the desire to ask Jenny where he had slept. She surprised herself by managing to appear aloof and not to notice that Jenny brought only one jug of water for washing for her alone. *Evidently,* she thought, *he told Lady Catherine. He stayed out late and slept in another room and, to make matters worse, the servants know! I never realised how solitary and unhappy marriage would be!*

Mr Collins had spent an awfully restless night. Having grown accustomed to the warmth of his wife's sleeping body next to him, he had been cold and uncomfortable in the unfamiliar bed in one of the guest rooms. Nevertheless, Lady Catherine had been adamant that these measures had to be taken. Charlotte had to be taught consequences of rebelliousness, and it had to be quashed in its infancy. At this moment, he was not sure which of them was being punished the harder.

He had repaired to Rosings immediately after breakfast the day before and had related the entirety of the previous night's discussion to Her Ladyship. Lady Catherine was shocked and affronted and immediately began to lecture Mr Collins on how to handle a *wayward wife* as she now referred to Charlotte. He sat up in bed and replayed the previous day's events at Rosings over in his mind.

When he arrived at Rosings, he was extremely agitated. He sat in the drawing room, where he had to wait for Her Ladyship to arrive. Lady Catherine was not in the habit of rising early, and when she finally did put in an appearance more than two hours later, she was clearly vexed, and the scowl with which she looked at him could not make her displeasure plainer. He got up from his chair and bowed to Her Ladyship, at the same time, beginning to thank her for being so gracious as to see him.

"Yes, yes, Mr Collins, that will do!" She waved her hand at him dismissing his bow. "I am most vexed at being disturbed. I fail to see what could be so serious as to bring you to Rosings at such an early hour as this."

Mr Collins involuntarily looked at the clock. It had just struck midday. "I do humbly beg Your Ladyship's forgiveness…"

"Stop grovelling, Mr Collins, and tell me why you are here. What do you mean by arriving, uninvited and at such an hour?" She cut across him, but he did not heed her interruption. Suddenly he was unsure of how to proceed, of what to say and how to say it. "Well, speak up!"

The volume with which Her Ladyship shouted at him brought him to his senses. "I have come, Your Ladyship, to ask for your kind and generous advice on a subject of great delicacy."

"Of course, I am often sought out for such advice, and I find people are most grateful for my help. But I still fail to see why you felt it necessary to come so early!"

"I fear my untimely arrival is due to my being at sixes and sevens."

"Sixes and sevens? What can a clergyman have to be at sixes and sevens about, I wonder!"

This piqued her interest, and he knew that as her temper was calming, it was safe to proceed. He acquainted her with the New Year's evening party at the Thomas house. A scowl crossed Lady Catherine's face at the mention of such a party. He informed her of what he deemed to be the inappropriate offer of Mr Abbot, and then went on to describe in detail and the most animated language what Charlotte had said to him on their way home that evening. As he proceeded through his narration of the events of the previous evening, Lady Catherine's demeanour changed from disinterested, through shocked, and to infuriated and all the various in-between stages.

Mr Collins had underestimated the level to which Her Ladyship would be affected by his disclosure, and she barely spoke a word for fully ten minutes, other than declaring that she required her smelling salts, which he brought her immediately. He also poured her a glass of wine. After drinking heavily from the glass, she pushed him and the glass aside, resulting in his falling over her footstool and wearing the remainder of the liquid, and stood towering over the hapless clergyman.

"You… you, Mr Collins! How dare you!" Her eyes bulged so fiercely in their sockets, he was afraid she would have a fit of apoplexy.

He scrambled to stand up, moving away from Lady Catherine's advancing form and replacing the glass on the side table. She forced him back so far back by her advancement that he fell backwards onto the sofa.

"Me, Your Ladyship? It is not I who is at fault!" He simpered and cried, his eyes welling with tears at the thought that he had personally angered Her Ladyship.

"Yes, you, Mr Collins! You have come here, and you tell me this!" She could barely get the words out, she was so angry at him.

Mr Collins was afraid that she was going to strike him and so retreated to the relative safety of crouching behind the sofa.

A footman came into the room, alerted by the ruckus, and drew Her Ladyship's attention away from Mr Collins, which had the fortunate effect of abating her anger somewhat.

The footman cleared his throat. "May I be of assistance, Your Ladyship?"

"Fetch me some strong tea and get someone to clean up the wine Mr Collins has spilt."

"Very good, Your Ladyship." The servant bowed out of the room, and Mr Collins relaxed a little.

Lady Catherine made her way back to her chair where she remained silent once more, staring ahead of her until the wine was cleared up and strong tea was brought to her.

Mr Collins could see that her lips were still trembling as she drank her tea. She finally turned her eyes upon him. "Mr Collins, what are you doing behind that sofa? Do sit down and behave appropriately."

He slipped around the edge of the sofa and sat in the corner furthest away from the angry Lady.

"I am most displeased, Mr Collins." He remained silent for fear of enraging her again. "Do you know who I am? Do you not feel the need to show me proper respect? Do you and Mrs Collins forget what you owe to me?" She paused and breathed heavily in and out through her nose, "I am not in the habit of brooking such behaviour as this. To patronise Mr Abbot's shop and to blatantly and disrespectfully disregard my most advantageous recommendations!"

Mr Collins cowered and sank lower down in his seat with every word that she spat at him.

"Mr Collins, when I instructed you a year ago to marry, I remember distinctly telling you to find a gentlewoman for my sake, one who was not brought up too highly; a sensible, useful woman for your own sake. Am I to believe that you are mistaken in your choice of wife, Mr Collins?"

This offended him. "No, Your Ladyship, not at all, I assure you," he simpered.

"Then why, Mr Collins, is your wife acting in such a manner?" She gave him pause to think this over. She eyed him up and down and then continued, "Or perhaps the fault is yours. You have been remiss in your duties as a husband. You have not led her correctly. You have allowed her too much freedom."

Under no circumstances had this thought ever entered Mr Collins' head, and he reddened at the thought of it.

"Yes, I now see where the fault lies, Mr Collins. You have allowed a faulty degree of independence in your wife. Had you taken her firmly in hand, you would not be seeing her behave with such insolent contempt for her betters." She rose and began to pace the room. "Still, the fault may not indeed lie entirely with you, Mr Collins. Yes, I see it all clearly now. She grew up too wild and free. Her parents, Mr Collins, allowed her to associate with that Bennet girl, I know!" She stopped and looked out of the window. "Yes, *she* also is wont to express herself far too freely for one of such breeding." She resumed her pacing. "Mrs Collins needs a firm hand. I am not advocating beating her, Mr Collins. As with a horse, it seldom does anything but break the creature's spirit. But that is not what is required here. She does need stiff correction, clearly. Mr Collins, you have a proud, wayward wife, and she needs reigning in!"

He nodded in agreement with her, too scared to do anything else. She rang the bell and asked for more tea; this time, some for Mr Collins too.

She informed her servants that he would also stay for dinner, and then she sat in her chair once more, leaning forward in his direction, saying, "Now pay strict attention to me, Mr Collins. This will not work unless you obey my every word."

* * *

If Mr Collins and Lady Catherine thought they were punishing Charlotte by metaphorically sending her to Coventry, they could not have been more wrong. In fact, she felt that she would enjoy being without his company, enjoy sleeping alone. The thought of not being obliged to visit Lady Catherine and of being falsely polite pleased her immensely. In fact, being ostracised by Lady Catherine was, to her, more of a blessed relief.

Mr Collins had penned a note to Charlotte informing her of her punishments, stating the reasons that he and Lady Catherine felt such actions were necessary. At the time, Charlotte had thought that if she had not been so affronted by such a letter, its officiousness would have amused her. The worst part of her punishment was that her pin money was halved, but as she rarely went shopping, she did not feel this too keenly; as she had already stated to her husband, she had saved a little too. Charlotte knew that all she had to do was wait it out and that Mr Collins was likely to break the silence before she did.

Therefore, she contented herself whiling away her time, visiting Louisa and her other friends in Hunsford, and reading her own novels, which she bought to spite her husband.

The only part of the whole affair that did not amuse her was that Lady Catherine had written a stern and insulting letter to Mr Abbot. He had informed her that he had not read it in its entirety but had thrown it onto the fire, but his face was red when he told her, and she knew that he was injured by what little he had read. Charlotte worked hard to heal that hurt by visiting the Abbots regularly and enjoyed taking tea with them. She found this new freedom exhilarating and was thankful that Lady Catherine was not aware of the happiness she was enjoying at being snubbed by Mr Collins and herself.

Chapter Twelve

Now unshackled from the responsibilities of Rosings, Charlotte threw herself with energy into Hunsford society. For the first time since coming into Kent, she was, in truth, enjoying herself, visiting or attending to parish business in the mornings, going to afternoon parties, not being obliged to be present at Rosings of an evening, and not being at Lady Catherine's disposal. Nonetheless, after a few days of her liberty and notwithstanding the pleasure it gave her, she was beginning to feel the strain. People were beginning to talk. She was not oblivious to the comments she heard as they walked past her in the street. She did her best to ignore them, but it was injurious all the same to her feelings. She had also, rather embarrassingly, had to decline one or two dinner invitations, as she could not possibly have attended without her husband, and he was not speaking to her at present.

She met with Louisa and Mrs Thomas while taking tea with Mrs Abbot one morning about a sennight after her castigation began. Charlotte was not oblivious to the fact that the ladies were quieter than usual. Their meaningful glances at each other and their pitying looks in her direction spoke volumes. They remained in this way for some time, their conversation stilted and awkward. Charlotte put her cup and saucer down and let out an exasperated sigh.

"Ladies, please be generous to me and, as my friends, which I sincerely hope you still are, pray, voice that which is unspoken and marring our visit today."

"Oh, Charlotte!" exclaimed Louisa, as she reached for her handkerchief. Mrs Thomas comforted her sister-in-law and, with a meaningful look at Mrs Abbot, gave the responsibility of speaking to Charlotte entirely over to her.

Mrs Abbot repositioned herself to sit next to Charlotte and took hold of her hands. "My dear," she paused, not knowing how to form the words she wanted to say, "it has been noted by some of our acquaintance that all is perhaps not as well as it has been and ought to be within the Collins household."

She looked questioningly at Charlotte and had at least the grace to blush at her own words. Charlotte bit her own tongue, all the angst, irritation, and frustration of recent events welling up inside and fighting to burst from her. She fought for composure but could not stop the tears from forming in her eyes.

Mrs Abbot squeezed her hands in a manner meant kindly and as encouragement, but which had the opposite effect, and tipped Charlotte's emotions over the edge. Mrs Abbot put her arms about her. Charlotte rested her head on Mrs Abbot's shoulder and gave in to her emotions, letting her tears flood out until they were spent.

She finally pulled away from her friend. "I do apologise, ladies. Sometimes things are too hard to bear."

They all smiled pityingly at her, but she did not heed them. Her attention was on her lap where she twisted her handkerchief in her distress. She then took a deep breath and began to tell of what had happened. Once the floodgates were opened, the tide of words would not stop until every detail was out and her closest friends in Hunsford were made aware of the true nature of her situation, any gossip that they had heard dispelled. Charlotte sat exhausted and looking down at the floor, waiting for accusations and rebukes from her friends, but none came. Her three companions sat agog staring at her, their faces displaying quite vividly their thoughts.

"Oh!" Louisa cried in anguish. She got up and stomped about the room. She deeply felt the hurt Charlotte was enduring.

"Louisa, please seat yourself, and I will ring for more tea." Mrs Abbot, glad for something to do while she settled her mind, rang the bell and ordered more tea. Louisa, however, was unable to settle and continued to pace up and down the room.

Once fresh tea arrived, along with new cups and saucers, Mrs Abbot spoke, breaking the silence. "Now, let me see if I perfectly understand the situation. You, Mrs Collins, are being chastised for being prudent, consulting your own mind, and, most criminally of all, going against the express wishes of Lady Catherine de Bourgh."

Charlotte looked up at the older woman. When put in such a way, it seemed ridiculous indeed that she was suffering for imagined impropriety. She could not help herself; the laughter burst out of her and would not stop. Soon all four of them were laughing at the ridiculousness of her present state and shaking their heads in disbelief.

It was a minute or two before they had calmed. Then Mrs Abbot addressed them all once again, "Now, ladies, one thing remains for us to contemplate and discuss." She looked at each one of them in turn most seriously. "What are *we* going to do about it?"

* * *

The visit with Mrs Abbot, Mrs Thomas, and Louisa had lifted Charlotte's spirits. She felt her courage renewed and the ability to withstand her punishment. Despite her new-found strength, the next day brought yet more pain to her heart. A letter arrived from Lady Catherine.

Dear Mrs Collins,

You can, madam, have no doubt whatsoever as to why I am writing to you this morning. I refer, of course, to your obvious and hurtful slight against my person and complete disregard for my well-meaning advice and attention to you.

You have by now endured, most painfully, I am sure, one week's castigation and silence from your husband and me and exile from our society. We deemed this necessary, Mrs Collins, to tame your wayward and opinionated behaviour. Such conduct in a woman is intolerable and unpardonable, and we, Mr Collins and I, wish to cure you of it before you inflict injury upon other persons less forgiving than myself.

For my part, I cannot believe that this is in your true nature, but I am sure is from a faulty lack of discipline as a child and the abominable and detrimental connection you have had with my unfortunate nephew's wife. I am sure her influence has swayed you. I will not say I am oblivious to the part in which your husband is to blame for his indulgence of you. I have made myself clear to Mr Collins, and he understands me entirely. Indeed, we are of one accord in this matter, and we both deem it necessary to correct this faulty step in you, one so inexperienced with the ways of the world, and teach you the proper behaviour of the wife of a clergyman, whose living is wholly within my gift. I would

87

consider it beneath me to renege upon the contract into which I have committed myself with Mr Collins, and the living will remain his for the duration of my life, as agreed upon before your marriage. You may rest assured on that point at least.

Now I must insist on endeavouring to aid you in correcting the faults in your own behaviour, faults which are not only injurious to myself, but to the impeccable character of your husband. I surely I need not impress upon you the imprudence of injuring his character by his having a wayward wife, Mrs Collins. I am sure that by now, you have also begun to see the error of your ways, are remorseful, and, indeed, wish to improve yourself.

Now, Mrs Collins, let me advise you further. Adhere to propriety, listen to the counsel of your betters, and do not force yourself or your opinions where they are not wanted nor needed. Mrs Collins, I beseech you to earn humility of spirit, calmness of character, and grace to accept the generous condescension and help from myself. I am deeply wounded by your disregarding my advice and going expressly against my wishes, but I am, to be sure, such a kind-hearted person, that I will, of course, forgive you after you have suffered sufficiently from your impropriety of behaviour and our excluding you from our society. After a sufficient time has passed, I will write again to inform you that you may visit me to beg my pardon and receive my forgiveness. Mrs Collins, I implore you to endeavour to learn from your mistakes and to put them behind you!

I trust this will not happen ever again, Mrs Collins, and may God open your eyes to your folly.

Yours faithfully,

Lady Catherine de Bourgh

Charlotte sat in stunned silence after reading the letter, her eyes fixed upon the words but unseeing, her mind reeling from them, and her heart bursting with frustration and anger. She wanted to cry, but would not give in to such self-pity. She burned with the injustice of the letter. She wanted Elizabeth and her counsel. She wanted to write to her and tell her what she was being forced to endure, but she knew that would be improper, and she must be strong and stand and fight her own battles. It seemed to her that, in actuality, there were merely two options open to her at present: to give in to Lady Catherine and live a life of subjugation to her will or to rebel against Lady Catherine and make her own decisions about her life. Each had merits in its favour, and each had its disadvantages. She certainly did not wish to be the means of injuring her husband.

"He may be a silly man," she spoke aloud to herself, "but he is not deserving of humiliation and degradation. I must make him see that my actions were not and are not foolishness but are solely from a desire to be the mistress of my own life and to be a minister's wife as I ought."

She began to pace the room as she continued to think aloud. "I am not oblivious to the deference owed to Lady Catherine, but surely he can see that above that, she has no and ought to have no authority on how we manage our daily lives. I must somehow devise a way to demonstrate this to Mr Collins or surrender my will entirely to Lady Catherine for as long as she lives."

This last thought brought the gravity of her current situation crashing down upon her. She sat down heavily on the easy chair and gave in to the grief, which she could withhold no longer. How long she remained thus, she knew not.

Chapter Thirteen

M rs Abbot visited Charlotte the following morning to check up on her and to lend her support. They talked in hushed tones, fully aware that Mr Collins was in his book room and might occasion to overhear a word or two. Mrs Abbot had decided that the best way to deal with Mr Collins, who felt it necessary to exclude his wife from his society, was to bring society to him.

She had, with Charlotte's consent, arranged a card party for that evening. Mr Collins was oblivious to this fact, and this day was chosen for the soiree because Lady Catherine was visiting the Metcalfs at their estate and Mr Collins would, consequently, be at home and unable to ignore his guests and, it was hoped for, his wife. Mrs Higgs had been so kind as to supply the information as to Mr Collins' arrangements for the week, and the ladies were grateful to have her as an ally. Charlotte laughed to think how shocked he would be at having his hand forced, that in order to keep his arrangement with Lady Catherine, he would have to shun his visitors and behave with such impropriety that would make his position as clergyman precarious.

Charlotte called Mrs Higgs in, and she informed her that a collation was required that evening for their guests and that Mr Collins was not to be informed whatsoever of their plans. Mrs Higgs was impressed with Mrs Abbot's daring, swore to secrecy once more, and bobbed a curtsey to Charlotte before leaving and attending to her work.

Mrs Abbot stood up to take her leave. "Now, my dear, do not worry yourself about anything. It is all in hand." She looked knowingly at Charlotte.

As she turned to make for the door, Mrs Abbot suddenly turned back to Charlotte. "A thought has occurred to me, my dear. We will be seven: myself and Mr Abbot, yourself and Mr Collins," she raised her eyebrows conspiratorially, "the Misses Thomas, and Mrs Brown. My dear, we need another person to make up a second table! Do you have any thoughts on who might accept at such short notice? It ought to be a gentleman, as their numbers are sadly lacking."

She looked to Charlotte for inspiration, whose eyes twinkled as the thought of just the right person occurred to her and stepped closer to Mrs Abbot to whisper in her ear.

Mrs Abbot's eyes opened wide, her grin spreading from ear to ear. As she left, she called back, "Genius, my dear, pure genius. I shall set the wheels in motion! Good-bye, dearest Mrs Collins."

* * *

Charlotte dressed with especial care that evening. She knew that she had to feign innocence in front of Mr Collins, but he also had to believe that none of their acquaintance was aware of their current situation and all that she was enduring at his hand.

Even Mrs Higgs was catching the excitement in Charlotte and smiled conspiratorially at her mistress as she began to dress her hair. Charlotte had to tell Mrs Higgs some of the plan in order to carry out her part and to avoid her turning away their guests at the door. She had told Charlotte that Mr Collins said to tell visitors that they were not at home, so Charlotte had met each and every one of her morning callers herself out on the driveway to confound his plan and to prevent Mrs Higgs from having to disobey her master.

"I am glad I told Jenny to do something else. I am sure she would not be able to keep her tongue and would go running off to tell the master."

"Oh, yes, Mrs Higgs, wisely done. If this is to work, Mr Collins needs to be kept in ignorance. And may I say how grateful I am that you informed me that Mr Collins wishes all guests to be turned away at the door."

"Oh, ma'am, it was the right thing to do. They are abusing you cruelly, and I cannot abide it…" She paused deciding whether to go on and then changed her mind.

"Go on, Mrs Higgs. What is it?"

The housekeeper took a deep breath and spoke her mind. "Well, ma'am, if you do not mind my telling you, I went to church this morning to say prayers for you."

This affection and loyalty in her housekeeper touched Charlotte, and she was not sure how to respond to this disclosure. She knew then that whatever befell her, she would have a loyal companion and friend in Mrs Higgs.

"Thank you." She fought to keep the tears from coming to her eyes.

When had she become such an emotional woman? She had never been a missish girl and had always been logical and sensible, but that was before she married; that was before she came into Kent and was away from the love and protection of her family. She thought of them now, as Mrs Higgs brushed her hair, and missed them profoundly during this trial. She had not written to her mother to inform her of her present state; she knew what her reaction would be.

It was then that she made up her mind. "Mrs Higgs," she said with a heavy heart, "if things do not improve, if Mr Collins cannot be made to see the merits of his wife and to realise his manipulation by and the conniving of Lady Catherine, then I feel I will have no other recourse than to return in to Hertfordshire and to my parents' home."

Her speech shocked Mrs Higgs, who stood with the brush in mid-air, staring at her mistress's reflection in the mirror.

"Yes, ma'am. I understand. I would miss you immensely, ma'am."

Now it was Mrs Higgs turn to feel the emotion, and her tears fell freely and unchecked as she endeavoured to continue to brush Charlotte's hair.

Charlotte turned and held Mrs Higgs hands. "Mrs Higgs, if I cannot be his wife, and I am neither wanted nor needed but imprisoned, then what other choice have I?"

Mrs Higgs leant forward and embraced Charlotte.

She pulled away just as suddenly, regaining propriety. "I do apologise, ma'am."

"I completely understand, Mrs Higgs."

* * *

Charlotte slipped downstairs, unseen by Mr Collins, and waited in the sitting room for her guests to arrive, frantically praying that he would not discover her presence before they appeared and, in so doing, foil their plan. She sat quietly in the armchair, trying not to move, fearing that the smallest movement would alert Mr Collins to her presence.

She inwardly chided herself for her silliness and walked to the window to watch for any lanterns on the road outside. She did not have to wait long. She knew they would be exceptionally diligent in their punctuality this night. As soon as she spied the lanterns of the Abbot carriage, it took all her will to stop herself from running immediately towards the door. She instead waited where she was and watched the carriage pull up onto the drive. Mr Abbot descended and helped the ladies alight.

"Oh, what a press it must be in there with five of them," she mumbled.

Mrs Abbot saw her at the window and signalled a little wave of her fan at her. Behind her, Charlotte then heard the bumptious voice of Mr Collins in the hallway; fortunately, she did not have to strain her ears to listen.

"What on earth is happening here? Why is there a carriage in my driveway? Mrs Higgs! Mrs Higgs, come immediately and explain this!"

Charlotte heard Mrs Higgs' footsteps coming from the kitchen, though she could not hear the responses, as her housekeeper spoke far more softly than did her husband. It was then that Charlotte moved towards the door.

"Time to rescue, Mrs Higgs, and time for us to begin," she told herself firmly.

She opened the door into the hall, and Mr Collins merely stared at her in her evening gown, open-mouthed.

Charlotte simply looked at him and said, "My dear, what is all this noise?"

Mrs Higgs then took the opportunity, whilst his attention was taken by his wife, to slip by him and open the door.

Mr Collins could not decide whether he should respond to his wife's enquiry or not, but was saved the trouble as Mrs Abbot swept into the hallway. "Mrs Collins, what a pleasure, as always, to see you, my dear!" The two women embraced, and Mrs Abbot turned her attention to Mr Collins and, looking him up and down, asked, "Mr Collins, you are well I trust?"

"Aye, madam, I am indeed. But may I enquire as to why…"

Mr Abbot, clearly enjoying himself, cut off his reluctant host in mid-question. "Good to see you again, Reverend. And, Mrs Collins," as he pushed Mr Collins gently aside, "as delightful as always." He kissed her hand and winked at her as he did so.

Charlotte could hardly contain herself. It was just like watching a comedy at the theatre in London.

The Misses Thomas then swished their way into the hall, which was now overcrowded, and Charlotte called above all the chattering voices, "Do come through, all of you!"

Once all were in the sitting room, Mrs Higgs busied herself with taking hats, cloaks, bonnets, and pelisses and disappeared as quickly as she was able, before Mr Collins could descend upon her for an explanation. Louisa latched herself on to Charlotte and linked arms with her protectively. Charlotte smiled benignly and watched the theatre unfold in front of her eyes.

"Come on in, Reverend!" Mr Abbot bellowed, beckoning him into the sitting room.

Mr Collins stood stupefied in the hall, opening and closing his mouth in disbelief. *What would Lady Catherine say?* He thought.

Mr Abbot took him by the arm and pulled him into the room. "Now, man, where do you keep your port, eh? Thirsty work this, waiting for the ladies to set up the card tables, eh?"

Mr Collins did not follow his meaning. "Hmm?"

"Port, man, or wine or something to warm us after the journey! Is this how you treat your guests? Do you forget yourself?" He burst into that great laugh of his, and his paunch moving with each guffaw.

Mr Collins, although sufficiently embarrassed, did at least have enough of his wits about him to fetch the port. Mr Abbot turned and winked to his wife conspiratorially, and when Mr Collins returned, Mrs Higgs was pouring wine for the ladies already. Charlotte was busying herself and trying her best not to catch her husband's eye.

The card tables were set up; conversations began. Mr Abbot kept Mr Collins occupied by asking him whether he had ever been hunting in these parts. Mr Collins was in such a state as not to furnish Mr Abbot with a sensible answer and barely spoke above two words at a time. His eyes were firmly fixed on Charlotte as she moved about the room. She did not know how she kept her countenance. She began to be afraid that if the evening did not pass well, then Mr Collins might, indeed, have some sharp words for her once they were again alone. She did not look upon such an outcome with anticipation.

Mrs Higgs came and spoke in her ear, "Ma'am, the cold collation is ready in the dining room, as are more decanters of wine. Might I suggest Mr Collins might be exceedingly thirsty this evening?" She looked meaningfully.

Charlotte took her meaning immediately and nodded to the housekeeper, who turned her attention to the guests.

Louisa was still at Charlotte's side, who looked at her nervously. "Oh Louisa," Charlotte whispered worriedly.

"Everything will turn out well. You will be a great hostess, and I believe Mr Abbot plans to toast you later."

Charlotte looked at her friend in disbelief. "Are you certain? Whatever for?"

"Can you not guess? Mr Abbot means to show your husband how valued you are by your friends."

Charlotte's face softened with the realisation of the depth of their scheme.

"My dear, take courage. We will never desert you."

Mrs Abbot and Mrs Brown fussed about the room, setting places, making sure that all the arrangements were to their liking, and surreptitiously stealing looks at each other and nodding.

About half an hour passed in this light-hearted way until the bell at the door rang and another guest was announced.

Mrs Higgs held the door open for a gentleman, announcing, "Mr Simmons."

Mr Simmons was a kindly looking gentleman, not much past five and thirty, and he was lean from activity. He was handsome. Charlotte immediately looked at Louisa, who had turned deathly pale upon seeing him, then a bright red, but she could not remove her eyes from his.

They both stood fixated in this manner until Charlotte felt she should reluctantly break the spell. "Mr Simmons, you are truly

96

welcome to our little gathering. I assume you know everyone here?"

Charlotte played the hostess well and walked Mr Simmons around the room as he greeted all of their party, but his attention was on no one but Miss Thomas. Louisa fought the desire to run from the room. She was amazed that he, of all people, was invited to the party. Despite her inclination, she lifted her chin and resolved to stand her ground; and when Mr Simmons greeted his former fiancée, Charlotte could see that he, too, was blushing. The gentleman took Louisa's hand and kissed it, his lips lingering on her knuckles and his eyes fixed on hers.

Chapter Fourteen

Two rubbers of whist, one of casino and one of loo later, Charlotte declared that she was hungry and invited her guests to join her in refreshments in the dining room.

Mr Collins was reluctantly drawn into making up a four and was so distressed and flustered that he could not concentrate, and he lost quite piteously. He made for his wife in order to take her aside and speak sternly to her. As he drew near to Charlotte, she was rescued by Mr Abbot, who asked if he might escort her to supper.

Mr Collins' consternation was complete, his distress nigh on panic. He kept opening and closing his mouth, but no sound emanated from him. His thoughts were in turmoil, and he could barely keep his countenance. He was sweating profusely, and his breathing shallow. He felt that he might faint away at any moment.

What would Lady Catherine say of my blatantly disregarding her sage and beneficent advice? He thought. *How could Charlotte do this? Especially when she was being taken firmly in hand and knows that she is doing wrong. Whatever am I to do?* He blindly followed his guests into the dining room, where he was pleasantly surprised to find the table spread with an excellent collation of cold meats, pickled vegetables, fruit, and hot potatoes.

Mr Abbot echoed that thought, "Mr Collins, your wife has done you proud, indeed. What an excellent spread!"

"Oh, yes, Mr Collins. Excellent," agreed Mrs Abbot.

Once seated, Charlotte was glad that she was at the opposite end of the table to her husband and that an elegant display of fruit in the centre obscured his view of her and enabled her to avoid his eyes somewhat.

Now seated, Mr Collins' gaze never left her.

What is she about? he mused. *Surely she knows this will result in even more severe consequences? What am I to do with*

99

her? Indeed, I do not know. He took his wine glass and quenched his abnormally dry throat, all the while keeping his eyes firmly on Charlotte. He placed the glass back on the table and Mrs Higgs immediately refilled it without his notice.

Charlotte, of course, could feel her husband's stare boring its way into her flesh. She had to fight the urge to shout across the table at him to stop it. She grew more and more uncomfortable with every passing moment. This behaviour was seen by their guests, except perhaps Louisa and Mr Simmons, who seemed to be attempting to avoid looking at each other and failing dismally to do so.

Mr Abbot stood and tapped his wineglass with his knife. "Ladies and gentlemen, may I have your attention."

A hush descended, punctuated with giggles from the ladies.

"How formal, Mr Abbot!"

"Indeed, Mrs Brown, indeed. Will you all join me in a toast?" He raised his glass, and everyone joined him. "To Mr Collins." Mr Collins' head snapped round to look at Mr Abbot with wide-eyed astonishment. "And his most delightful and charming wife, Mrs Collins!"

"Mr and Mrs Collins!" the whole room chorused. Charlotte blushed, and she was glad to notice that so did her husband.

Nevertheless, Mr Abbot was not finished. "Mr Collins, you are one of the most fortunate men in all of England, sir!"

Mr Collins blushed and mumbled something no one understood.

"You have had the hand of Providence upon you indeed, when the Almighty led you to meet with Mrs Collins."

Mr Collins looked shocked and angry that his *wayward wife* was being praised and toasted under his own roof and that he was the recipient of such a speech.

Nevertheless, Mr Abbot continued in his praise. "She is a delightful creature. She is intelligent, witty, very caring, and highly prudent. She is a lovely friend, an attentive hostess, and I am sure you must be tremendously proud of her, especially tonight, after honouring you so with this gathering, eh?"

Mr Collins swallowed hard and took another gulp of his wine. *What was the meaning of this?* He was sensible of all eyes being upon him and all nodding in agreement.

"Yes, Mr Collins. Indeed, in Mrs Collins you have found someone you can depend upon always to do what is right, respectable, honourable, and prudent. I applaud you, sir." Again, Mr Abbot bid the room to toast Mr and Mrs Collins.

Charlotte smiled down at her plate, not daring to look up at the reaction of her husband. Mr Abbot was clapping Mr Collins on the back and pouring more praise on his head as he took his seat again and the conversation resumed. But Charlotte focussed her attention on what Mr Abbot was still saying to her husband. He was telling him how glad he must be and relieved to find such a wife. To her amazement, Mr Collins blushed, laughed, but repeatedly muttered "Yes".

Mrs Higgs continued to ply Mr Collins with wine until he became sufficiently merry, relaxed, and his tongue was loosened. As they repaired to the sitting room once more and the cards were being shuffled, Mr Collins opted to sit out, and Mr Abbot obligingly joined him on the sofa.

Mrs Brown, Mrs Thomas, Louisa, and Mr Simmons made up a four and began a rubber of whist, enormously enjoying themselves, as their laughter was proof. Louisa and Mr Simmons sat opposite each other, and it was obvious to all who knew their story that the affection between them had never changed and wanted only a mere push in the right direction for things to begin well again there.

Charlotte was pleased for Louisa and hoped to bring the pair into each other's company as often as propriety allowed. She and Mrs Abbot seated themselves next to the fire, but close enough to Mr Collins and Mr Abbot to hear their conversation. That turned out to be unnecessary since, as the wine had loosened Mr Collins' tongue, so had it also increased the intensity of his voice.

"I must say, Mr Abbot, that tonight's little soiree has taken me completely by surprise," he said, as Mrs Higgs brought port for the gentlemen and tea for the ladies. Mr Abbot, for appearance's sake, merely sipped his port to encourage Mr Collins to drink of his own, talk more freely, and perhaps be willing to be talked to about his mistreatment of Charlotte.

"Indeed, I am sure there must have been some mistake."

"Whatever do you mean, Reverend?"

"Well," Mr Collins leaned in towards Mr Abbot conspiratorially, despite his voice being far from a whisper, "I am not supposed to be talking to my wife, sir!"

Mr Abbot feigned to look confused. "Again, sir, I do not take your meaning."

Mr Collins shifted in his seat and moved even closer to Mr Abbot. Had that gentleman not wished to have a private conversation with Mr Collins, their proximity would have mortified him. As it was, he bore it remarkably well and with admirable grace.

Charlotte and Mrs Abbot, upon observing this, looked at each other and giggled. Charlotte rose and handed tea to those who desired it, her attention all the while on Mr Collins' conversation.

"Do you recollect a week or two past when you made an offer of discount to Charlotte and Miss Thomas?" he continued.

"Indeed, I do. I firmly believe I am blessed to be a blessing to others. I was glad of the opportunity to do so."

"Well, you might think so; indeed you might. But you were wrong, very wrong to be sure, Mr Abbot."

The said gentleman had to use all his control not to be angered by such a blatant insult. He was acutely aware that as the alcohol had loosened Mr Collins' tongue, it had also removed his sense of propriety.

"I was?" he meekly rejoined.

"Oh, undeniably, sir. You cannot begin to imagine the grief, distress, and mischief such an action has caused."

"How so Mr Collins?"

"Well, it is Her Ladyship, is it not?"

"Is it, Mr Collins? How so? How can it affect her?"

"Ah, you see, Mr Abbot, Lady Catherine is my patroness, and I must obey her every word"

"I still do not understand, Mr Collins. Her Ladyship has merely provided you with the living, given you a job, so to speak. How does that make her every whim your command? You are not her servant, are you?"

"Indeed I am not, Mr Abbot! I am a gentleman, the son of a gentleman, and one day I will inherit an estate of my own." Here he endeavoured to bring his voice down to a whisper, "Although we do not speak of that, as it would be indelicate because the present occupant would have to go to meet the maker for me to inherit."

Charlotte looked at Mrs Abbot in shame and embarrassment, but the older lady continued to drink her tea without any indication she had even overheard such a speech.

"So then, Mr Collins," Mr Abbot continued, trying to match Mr Collins' whisper, "why do you feel that you are subservient to Lady Catherine and must obey her every word? And what has this to do with my gift to Mrs Collins?"

"Oh, yes, I forget myself. Lady Catherine has within her power the ability to make my burden heavy or light. You see? When she gives her opinion or advice she will not brook opposition; indeed she will not, as Charlotte is experiencing first hand." When Mr Abbot did not respond, Mr Collins continued, "You see, your offer to Charlotte went expressly against the wishes of Lady Catherine herself. She was most vexed and put out. I assure you, she was."

Mr Collins shuddered at the memory of the scolding her received at Her Ladyship's hand and swigged some more port. Mr Abbot picked up the decanter and refilled their glasses.

Mr Collins continued unabated, "Lady Catherine had advised, or perhaps I ought to say *told* Charlotte to patronise one milliner only in London, one that Her Ladyship herself patronises."

"Indeed?"

"Oh, indeed, Mr Abbot. So you may well understand Her Ladyship's consternation at Charlotte's disobeying her."

Mr Abbot merely replied, "Hmm."

"Charlotte ought not to have insulted Her Ladyship thus, and I feel she will endure her castigation indefinitely unless she recants and sees the error of such a course of action as the one she took."

"Castigation, Mr Collins?" asked Mr Abbot.

"Ay, she is to be punished by our not speaking to her and her not enjoying our company whatsoever."

He laughed at such a scheme, and Mr Abbot pondered whether Mr Collins realised he was in his wife's company at that present time.

He was brought out of his reverie when Mr Collins continued his discourse. "Of course, the punishment was not designed to harm Charlotte, but gently to reprimand her."

"Do you think it is working, Reverend?"

"Well, I confess, I feel it keenly; so indeed, Charlotte must. To be deprived of Lady Catherine's company is something that can hardly be borne."

"Really?"

"Yes, really."

"Do you think this is wise? What I mean to say is, do you think that this punishment is necessary and, dare I say, fits the crime?"

"Mr Abbot, whatever do you mean? We are talking of the Right Honourable Lady Catherine de Bourgh. Her deference by us is most necessary. We must endeavour to do our duty to her at all times."

"Well, I cannot argue with that, Mr Collins." This statement pleased the said gentleman, and he nodded happily to himself. "However," continued Mr Abbot, "I cannot see why Mrs Collins' choosing her own milliner could be called duty or why Mrs Collins ought to be punished for such an act. To be sure, such punishment is petty and childish, would you not say?"

Mr Collins looked shocked at such an opinion as this, but Mr Abbot continued before he could interrupt, "Surely, Reverend, you can see that your wife had her reasons. Only think of the expense of travelling into London; then how much more inflated London prices are, not to mention how such an elegant fashionable milliner would price his wares. In addition, I daresay such a shop would not be as diverse as to stock bolts of material or many other haberdashery items, requiring Mrs Collins to patronise yet another shop. Indeed, I can think only that perhaps Mrs Collins was, in fact, thinking of the limits of her own purse, Reverend."

"Well, I... hmm," was all the reply he received.

"I daresay, Reverend, in this light, the punishment does not fit the crime, eh?"

Mr Abbot stood up and poured himself a cup of tea from the pot. He had no desire for more port.

Mr Collins sat staring into space, mulling over Mr Abbot's quite logical appraisal of the events. He fought within himself. On the one hand, Lady Catherine could not be disobeyed; but, on the other hand, what Charlotte had done was neither too terrible nor improper. In fact, the more he dwelt upon the matter, the more he realised the verity of Mr Abbot's words and the foolishness of such punishment. His obsequiousness to Lady Catherine would not so easily be quashed and fought back in his mind. He continued thus in such a position for the remainder of the evening, emptying and refilling his port glass until the decanter was empty.

The rest of the evening passed jovially, and Mr Abbot told the company a few wild stories of his travels to the Continent with Mrs Abbot. The card tables were cleared away, and a game of charades was suggested. Mr Abbot took the first go, and as the game progressed, Charlotte felt as though she had never laughed so much in all her life. She had pains in her sides and her face hurt from smiling. Mrs Brown then suggested word puzzles so that they might recover from the hilarity of the previous game.

Mr Collins walked out to the hallway on extremely unsteady legs and managed to wave farewell to his guests from the door. Charlotte was pleased with this turn of events, but perhaps was more pleased that he was not angry and, more specifically, not angry with her.

As he bid adieu to Mr Abbot, he said, "Thank you, Mr Abbot. I enjoyed our repartee."

"As did I, Reverend. We should do this again sometime." He paused to gauge Mr Collins' reaction, who was again lost in his thoughts. "Perhaps I might call on you in a day or two, Reverend, or maybe you would like to have luncheon with us after services tomorrow?"

Seeing no reaction still from Mr Collins, Mr Abbot turned his question to Charlotte, who had been standing close enough to her husband as to overhear every word. "Mrs Collins?"

"Indeed, Mr Abbot, I am sure my husband and I would be delighted."

"Excellent!"

Mrs Abbot then leant out of the carriage and joined in, "Then do come home with us straight after the service. We will bring the carriage, my dear."

Charlotte thanked them both on behalf of herself and her husband, who remained standing deep in thought and staring at nothing in particular.

She bid her guests adieu and noticed that Mr Simmons was the last to leave. "Mr Simmons, may I thank you heartily for coming this evening. It has been a pleasure."

"Mrs Collins, it is I who must thank you. It has indeed been a pleasure that I, for one, hope to repeat in the future and frequently."

"Indeed, I hope so." She smiled knowingly at him. Mr Simmons mounted his horse and rode off down the lane.

Charlotte made to return to the house when she noticed Mr Collins was still in the same position as before. "My dear, will you not come in from the cold?"

"Hmm?" His reverie interrupted, he stumbled back into the parsonage, embarrassed and awkward in her presence.

"My dear, you look exhausted. Why do you not take yourself off to bed? Mrs Higgs and I can clear up down here."

He merely replied, "Yes, yes," in agreement and mounted the stairs slowly, still obviously in thought.

Mrs Higgs joined Charlotte. "Well, ma'am, a good night's work, I think."

Charlotte smiled at her, "Yes, I believe so."

Mrs Higgs then chuckled as she and Charlotte began clearing up the sitting room. "Despite the monster of a headache he'll wake up with on the morrow!"

Chapter Fifteen

M r Collins' sermon the following morning was lacklustre and his voice muted owing to the pounding of cannon fire in his head. He fought as hard as possible to look at the sea of faces attending him, but found the sunlight was too hard on his eyes.

Thus, he paid little attention to his congregants and winced his way through the hymns, especially in the rousing choruses, wishing he had chosen more sedate ones that morning. He dared not look in Lady Catherine's direction and focussed on the papers in front of him instead. The sermon seemed interminably long, and he desired only to be free from the church and sleep more.

Were they not engaged to dine with the Abbots? He vaguely recalled from the previous night, giving up his hope for a nap. His mind and conscience were in turmoil of the events of the night before and he knew not what to do nor what to think of it. He was mightily relieved that Lady Catherine and her daughter departed first from the church and did not see Charlotte and himself climb into the Abbots' carriage. He did not wish to risk causing a scene or to be on the receiving end of Her Ladyship's wrath that morning.

Every jolt of the carriage on the road jarred his head, and he felt somehow deserving of the punishment. Whatever had induced him to drink so heavily? Moreover, how would he ever explain himself to Lady Catherine?

As they descended from the carriage at the Abbot home, Charlotte was keenly aware of the importance of being seen in public with her husband. She knew it would not be long before Hunsford's wagging tongues were silenced; but, on the other hand, she also wondered how long it would take for this event to reach the ears of the mistress of Rosings. That was something to which she did not look forward. *How are we to work on Lady Catherine?* she wondered. *And how can it be done with no harm to Mr Collins' living?* She was suddenly struck with remorse and regretted the card party; she all of a sudden saw the folly of going against their patroness and knew there could be dire consequences. She mentally shook herself and pushed such thoughts aside as Mrs Abbot greeted and welcomed them into her home.

During the meal, Mr Collins hardly ate a thing; his stomach did not know which way was up and which was down. Instead, he rearranged the food on his plate and his fellow diners smiled at him with barely hidden amusement. They did, however; accord him the courtesy of keeping their voices low so as not to worsen the crippling headache he was suffering.

Charlotte was enjoying the afternoon, despite her concerns of having gone too far against Her Ladyship. She knew this issue was not yet over and that as soon as Lady Catherine heard of Mr Collins' defection, she would again see red and goodness knows what would befall the *wayward wife* then. Charlotte took comfort in the presence of her new, dear friends and enjoyed their company more than ever.

Once they had returned to the sitting room, Mr Collins promptly fell asleep in an easy chair and remained so, snoring gently until it was time for them to leave.

Charlotte, on the other hand, enjoyed quiet conversation with the Abbots, and together they planned the return dinner invitation at the parsonage in three days' time. She just hoped to keep their intentions away from Lady Catherine's hearing as long as possible.

As Charlotte climbed into the carriage to be driven back home, she realised that three days were a long time and a lot could happen in that time. She bit her lip with worry and wondered if she should simply go and apologise after all.

* * *

Mr Collins was obliged every Monday morning to Rosings, and he passed Charlotte on her way home from her morning walk as he set off in that direction. He merely stopped and looked at her for a moment, a pained expression on his face, and continued on his way.

Charlotte had not, up until that moment, felt too much pity for Mr Collins' predicament. He had, after all, brought it entirely upon his own head. But the expression on his face brought a pang of pity to her heart, and again she wondered if she should accompany him to Rosings and end it all. Her husband was foolish, but he was now also going to pay, and could pay heavily, if Lady Catherine knew his hand had been forced and he had been unable to keep his side of their agreement.

Mr Collins, though, had no intention whatsoever of mentioning his duplicity to Her Ladyship. He knew her wrath would come down in full force upon his own weary head, and he had no desire to partake of such anger at present. He was like most people: keen on keeping his position in life and did not wish to endanger his living.

He had spent the remainder of Sunday in his book room, sleeping off the ill effects of the excesses of the night before, and this morning he still felt somewhat delicate. He had managed a little breakfast, but the thought of visiting Rosings had stolen his appetite. He now knew the meaning of the saying *to be between a rock and a hard place.* Keenly did he feel it. Although he still maintained that Charlotte was in the wrong for ignoring Lady Catherine's advice, he could also see the sagacity in what his wife had done and the pettiness with which Her Ladyship had reacted.

He stopped walking when that realisation hit him with full force. Her Ladyship had acted pettily. He shook his head, continued on his way to Rosings, and pushed the treacherous thought from his head entirely. This was not hard to do, for as soon as he arrived at the door of Rosings, his attention was drawn to the sound of hooves on the gravel. He glanced in the direction of the sound and saw that Colonel Fitzwilliam had just arrived and was heading to the stables.

Good, he thought, *a well-timed distraction.*

* * *

Mr Collins sat playing with the hem of his coat and making simpering noises throughout his visit. Lady Catherine did not ask her nephew about his trip to London or if the business was concluded. She did not enquire as to his health; neither did she ask him if he had a safe journey. She only launched into a lengthy speech on the infamous happenings in Hunsford of late. Mr Collins' attention went from Lady Catherine, then to Colonel Fitzwilliam, and back again to Her Ladyship. Her words made him cringe and sink lower in his chair. He felt ashamed.

The Colonel's brow was firmly knit, and his lips were tightly pressed into a hard, thin line. He certainly did not look happy. Mr Collins could not make out whether the Colonel was angry or frustrated, whether his facial expression was due to hearing of the situation so elaborately described by his aunt or to preoccupation with his business in and ride back from town.

When Lady Catherine had finally finished her discourse, she rose to indicate to Mr Collins that his visit was at an end, and Colonel Fitzwilliam rose also and declared his intention to visit the parsonage.

"Yes, Fitzwilliam, you feel the slight against my person as much as I do. I know you wish to talk to Mrs Collins, but I fear you will find her a most obstinate woman indeed."

Colonel Fitzwilliam made no reply. He simply bowed and departed Rosings at a speed that made Mr Collins have almost to run to keep pace with him.

Colonel Fitzwilliam did not let up on his pace, and upon their arrival, he did not wait for the maid to announce him but burst in on Charlotte, sitting quietly at her writing table in the sitting room.

"Mrs Collins, forgive me for interrupting you."

Charlotte, startled, jumped up from the desk, almost knocking over her inkwell in so doing, and stared at the Colonel. "Colonel Fitzwilliam!"

Mr Collins then arrived, huffing and puffing his way into the room. "Oh, my dear, here you are. You see Colonel Fitzwilliam wishes to visit with you."

"Mr Collins, I wish to visit with both you and your wife."

Mr Collins stood with his mouth open. Charlotte gained her wits first and invited the Colonel to be seated and called for tea. They quietly awaited the arrival of the tea things and talked about the weather, their health, and Mr Collins' garden.

Jenny fortunately brought the tea things just as the conversation had run dry and Charlotte was glad to busy herself with making the tea. She knew that the Colonel was by now acquainted with the situation and that he would have something to say on the subject. She felt chagrined, ashamed of her behaviour. When she thought of how he must view her now, she blushed with embarrassment. Colonel Fitzwilliam had become a friend, and she did not wish him to think ill of her, nor did she wish to lose his friendship so recently formed.

She handed the Colonel and her husband their tea and sat back down in her chair, nervously gripping her own saucer. She looked up at the Colonel apprehensively, and he took her gaze as his cue to say what was on his mind.

"Mrs Collins, I am sad to say that this is the second time I have had to apologise to you for my aunt's behaviour," the Colonel began as he stirred his tea. Mr Collins blinked in confusion. "I fear it is becoming a habit."

The sound of the Colonel replacing his spoon on the saucer brought Mr Collins to his senses. "I am afraid, Colonel, that I have failed to understand you."

"My aunt's behaviour to Mrs Collins," obliged the Colonel.

Mr Collins continued to look none the wiser, so Colonel Fitzwilliam continued, "Mr Collins, my aunt has no right whatsoever to dictate to another human being how they ought to or ought not to conduct themselves. Mrs Collins is not a servant and, therefore, has every right to do as she pleases. I am most ashamed of my aunt!"

This impassioned speech confused Mr Collins, making him more wide-eyed still.

He could not conceive of the idea that Colonel Fitzwilliam would take such a view and, indeed, thought he had misheard. "Forgive me, Colonel. You think your aunt was in the wrong?"

The Colonel finished taking a mouthful of tea and nodded, "Hmm, indeed I do, Mr Collins. Her behaviour is deplorable. My father told me that she was headstrong even as a child and was never corrected, but always indulged. She dominated her poor sister Anne, Mr Darcy's mother, and I also know she did the same with her poor husband, Sir Lewis, when he was alive."

He took more tea and continued. "You can see for yourself how she controls even the smallest part of my cousin Anne's life."

Charlotte nodded; Mr Collins was speechless.

111

"I deeply feel for Anne, and I wish I could do something to help her, but I fear even marriage will not free her from her mother's powerful grip. My aunt and Darcy have fallen out over his marriage, and as you know, Mrs Collins," he nodded towards Charlotte, "your friend is a most excellent and amiable woman. I think my cousin could not have asked for a better match. She is lively and extremely witty and brings out the best in my cousin. Yet so displeased was my aunt at their marriage and sent them such a scolding letter at Pemberley, that Darcy immediately wrote back and informed her that she was no longer permitted to set foot on Darcy land, for the insults to his person and his wife, until such time as she apologises to them. I fear they may be in for a long wait. As you see, you are not the only people whom she endeavours to control, not the only people she has hurt deeply, and I am confident that you will not be the last."

He looked at both of them sincerely. "So, Mr and Mrs Collins, please accept my heartfelt apologies. I can assure you that I will do all in my power to persuade her to retreat from her position, and if I cannot, I will write to my father to ask for his help. I sincerely pray all will return to normal as soon as possible."

Charlotte could not express her thanks and she sat focussed intently on the cup in her lap, a smile playing at her lips. She earnestly wanted to be able to express her gratitude for his words and understanding, but need not have worried as the Colonel read her expression perfectly.

They then sat in silence for a minute or two while drinking their tea. Mr Collins, never one to like a pause in conversation and with a partiality for his own voice, felt increasingly uncomfortable and so took the opportunity to apprise the Colonel of all the other parish news that he had missed. This included the death of Farmer Wilcox's prize bullock and Mrs Harris' having been recently delivered of twins. Colonel Fitzwilliam listened graciously and patiently whilst he was filled in on the goings-on of people with whom he was wholly unfamiliar.

When Mr Collins had finished his narration, Charlotte took the opportunity to invite Colonel Fitzwilliam to join their dinner party on the coming Wednesday night. She told him that it would be a small gathering with the Abbots only, and despite the fact that he had never met the Abbots, he felt inclined to think well of them since they wanted to keep Charlotte's company and brave Lady Catherine's displeasure in so doing. He eagerly accepted her invitation, thanked her, and took his leave, declaring his intention of speaking to his aunt as soon as an opportunity presented itself.

Mr Collins was most perplexed at this turn of events and sincerely could not account for it. He replayed what the Colonel had said over in his mind, and each time came to the same conclusion: the Colonel was in earnest and was genuinely discomfited by his aunt's behaviour. Mr Collins personally felt that Lady Catherine was one of the best and wisest people in the country, and the fact that her nephew had accompanied him back to the parsonage to deliver his own personal apology for the surely reasonable actions of such an esteemed woman bothered him exceedingly.

In this agitated spirit, he retired to his book room to think and left Charlotte alone to replay the events in her own head in peace and solitude.

Chapter Sixteen

Charlotte had three walks which she preferred, and she regularly alternated between them depending on her mood and the weather. There was one with wide-open countryside views, one within the woods, and the last with safer paths for when the weather was unsettled. She chose her favourite of the three and walked through the woods, revelling in the sounds of the wind whistling through the treetops. The weather had been more clement in the last few days, and she enjoyed looking and seeing the new leaves beginning to appear on the branches. She continued walking in this way with her face upturned and did not see Colonel Fitzwilliam's approach until he trod on a twig. The ensuing *snap* gave his presence away immediately. She turned towards him, startled.

"I am terribly sorry, Mrs Collins. I seem to be regularly startling you," he laughed.

"Yes, Colonel. But it does not follow that I am unhappy to see you," she replied with a smile.

"May I join you then?"

"Please do."

They walked together in silence a while, enjoying the tranquillity and each other's company.

"Colonel, forgive me, but may I enquire as to whether your business in London is concluded?"

He stopped walking, and his face looked haggard with grief. It made him look older than his years. She regretted asking upon seeing this change in him.

"It is, Mrs Collins. It is, and much quicker than I would have liked. The evidence was stacked against him. I am afraid," his voice choked, "there was nothing I could say to …" He could not continue.

"I am terribly sorry."

The Colonel did not reply but kept his attention on a stone which he had begun kicking around with the toe of his boot.

"May I ask if there has been a collection taken up for his mother?"

He looked up at her then. *Always so considerate, always so kind*, he thought. "No, there has not been. Why did I not think of that? How remiss of me!"

"Oh, Colonel, do not berate yourself. You had your own grief to contend with." She paused and looked up at his face and noticed the dark rings about his eyes from lack of sleep, "I have a little put by. Might I entrust it to you to deliver to his mother?"

"Mrs Collins, I do not know what to say! Your kindness astonishes me. You did not even know the boy."

"Ah, but I know you, and I know that you thought enough of him to grieve his loss deeply, I can see it plainly in your countenance. Therefore, I feel it is right to give a little something to a family who will have not only lost a son but, I am sure, a valuable source of income."

She slowly set off in the direction of the parsonage and stopped to look back at the Colonel when she realised he was not following her.

"If you would be so kind as to escort me home, Colonel, we can have tea, and I can give you the money for the poor boy's family." She smiled invitingly at him, and he did as he was bid, a fond look suffusing his face.

* * *

Charlotte took the liberty of calling upon the Misses Thomas once Colonel Fitzwilliam had taken his leave and returned to Rosings. He had stayed a while, unburdening his heavy heart with tales of the young boy so recently shot after a court-martial, and she let him talk uninterrupted until he was worn out. He left the parsonage feeling lighter and extremely grateful that he had Charlotte as a friend.

Charlotte stopped in the Thomas garden to admire how the tentative early spring sun had begun to entice the garden to life, surprised to discover herself engaged in such sentimentality.

116

She rang the bell, and as soon as she was shown into the sitting room, she was delighted to see that she was joined by Mrs Brown and, most happily of all, Mr Simmons. She learnt in the course of her visit that Mr Simmons had visited twice since renewing his acquaintance with Louisa at the card party, and Mrs Thomas cherished hopes that he would also renew his proposal to her sister-in-law very soon.

"He is indeed marking her out for especial attention. I am certain he will soon make his intentions known, Mrs Thomas," Charlotte commented.

"Without a doubt, Mrs Collins, he is just as besotted as ever with her."

They spoke as quietly as they could, so as not to disturb the couple who sat on the opposite side of the room, oblivious to their surroundings.

"They have eyes only for each other!" Quipped Mrs Brown.

"Aye, it is much as it was before. Well…"

Mrs Thomas left the rest of her statement unspoken, but they knew to what she alluded.

Charlotte's visit passed amiably, and before she left, she had received and accepted an invitation to an evening party with the Misses Thomas and, to her surprise, to dine with Mr Simmons at Oak Wood Farm. She had never been to his property, but had seen the magnificent Tudor brick house surrounded by the old oak wood, home of the old squires, from the road and was exceedingly gratified to be considered friend enough to be invited there.

* * *

When she arrived home, Mr Collins was concluding some business with one of the church deacons, and she happily conveyed the invitations to him, with confidence of his having to acquiesce in front of Dr Sawyer. She exchanged pleasantries with the deacon as he departed and asked Mr Collins to join her for tea. He declined, saying he would take the tea, but that he had much on his mind, as the church accounts needed going over. She nodded and left him to his work, her mind more agreeably engaged with hopes for Louisa.

117

When the Abbots arrived for dinner the following night, they were delighted to become acquainted with Colonel Fitzwilliam, a man of whom they had heard much but had never seen. He was equally delighted with this new acquaintance, as he found their conversation lively and jovial, and they were as respectable a couple as he had anticipated. He was heartily pleased to pass an evening with such company.

Mr Collins remained uncharacteristically quiet, owing to the memory of the last time he had entertained the Abbots and drank too heavily, and out of awe of the fact that the nephew of Lady Catherine de Bourgh was dining with him in his own home. Mr and Mrs Abbot merrily made conversation, and as they had travelled extensively, they told diverting stories of their journeys.

"Of course, that was all before 'Ole Boney' came along, eh? Now he has made a great confusion of Europe. Not a place to take your wife any longer, I fear!"

"You are absolutely right, Mr Abbot," agreed the Colonel.

"However," continued Mr Abbot, raising his glass to Colonel Fitzwilliam, "we are eternally grateful to brave men like yourself and the Duke. You have done sterling work in the Peninsula, so the papers say."

The Colonel humbly thanked Mr Abbot. "Although when in the thick of it, we cannot see the larger picture. I personally only discover how well we are doing when I arrive back in London and make enquiries."

"Then how do you get any information at all?" asked Mrs Abbot.

"Well, ma'am, the commanders and field generals get their dispatches through by special riders employed specifically for the task, but even they can be intercepted."

"How ghastly!"

"That's war, I'm afraid, Mrs Abbot," he said solemnly.

Mrs Abbot deftly changed the subject. "How long will you be with us, Colonel?"

"Well, His Majesty's officers are not always required to be in the fray, so to speak. Then again, I have been engaged recently in other Army business," he said with a forced smile. "And now I have some leave owing to me. Fortunate am I to be able to take it with such delightful people." He raised his glass in return to his companions.

Charlotte and Mrs Abbot repaired to the sitting room and left the menfolk to drink Mr Collins' port, something, this time, from which he personally refrained indulging.

When Charlotte and Mrs Abbot had settled themselves by the fire, they began to speak freely. Charlotte informed her friend of what had occurred when Colonel Fitzwilliam had returned from London and how he had personally apologised to her for his aunt's behaviour. Mrs Abbot was astonished and asked many questions in return, and soon was wholly acquainted with the situation. She had to admit that it relieved her to see that Charlotte now had a powerful ally, and one whose father could be called upon, if necessary. She relayed as much to Charlotte, who expressed her doubts to Mrs Abbot in return. Mrs Abbot tried to calm her young friend's nerves and assuage her fears, reassuring her that she was not the one at fault. Mrs Abbot was certain that, with a friend like Colonel Fitzwilliam, nothing untoward could happen and that Mr and Mrs Collins were safe from reprisal from Lady Catherine.

"It is, I am afraid, a matter of time. We just have to sit it out, until the old girl gives in!"

This amused Charlotte immensely. She had never heard Lady Catherine spoken of so irreverently. She wondered how Mr Collins would react if he had overheard, but decided that it was for the best that he had, indeed, not.

Charlotte rose and rang the bell for coffee. "I think it is time the gentlemen joined us."

The evening passed in such a relaxing way. Charlotte could not remember a time like it, except amongst her family. The familial feeling seemed to spread to all, including Mr Collins, who was smiling and laughing as though he had no cares in the world, and Charlotte was extremely pleased to perceive this change in her husband.

She learnt a lot from Mr Abbot about Europe that night. For most of her life, England had been at war in Europe. She had never travelled and did not think it likely that she would have the opportunity to travel, so his tales captivated her. They were punctuated by Mrs Abbot interjecting a correction here and there, which only heightened the atmosphere and produced more laughter at Mr Abbot's wanton exaggeration of the strange Europeans and their habits. She was also pleased to note that Colonel Fitzwilliam seemed relaxed and to be enjoying himself. She was so grateful to him and wished for an opportunity of enquiring as to whether he had spoken to his aunt yet.

That said opportunity presented itself when their guests were taking their leave.

Colonel Fitzwilliam drew Charlotte aside as he put on his greatcoat. "I am afraid that my dining here tonight will, indeed, force my hand and I will have to account for myself to my aunt on the morrow, I am sure, Mrs Collins. Nevertheless, pray, do not fret. All will be well. I promise you that." He reached out, took her hand, and kissed it while staring into her eyes meaningfully.

She stood speechless, her heart pounding, breathing with difficulty, and could only find the power to nod her understanding. He was gone before she came out of her reverie to realise Mr Collins was speaking to her.

"I said, that was a pleasant evening," he repeated.

"Yes, it was. They are all such lovely people. We are blessed, are we not, Mr Collins, to have such friends?"

She did not wait for a reply, but climbed the stairs to her room and bid Mr Collins good night from the landing.

Sleep would not come, however, and she paced the floor in thought. She was worried for Colonel Fitzwilliam and wondered how his aunt would react in the morning.

She decided to hunt down some hot chocolate, so she crept out of her room and down the stairs. As she reached the last stair, it creaked. She winced and hesitated, not wishing to wake anyone.

Mr Collins, however, was not asleep, and the sound drew him from his book room. He stood staring at his wife, her form visible through her nightgown and robe. The sight of her clearly stirred something in him, and he took a step towards her. She could see he was aroused and his breathing shallow as his eyes drank in the sight of her. He took another step towards her, his meaning clear.

"Charlotte." His voice was husky with desire, and as his eyes locked with hers, she began to feel a desire for him stirring inside her.

"William," her eyes and voice soft.

120

He raised his eyebrow meaningfully. She nodded, turned, and led the way back to her room.

Chapter Seventeen

The next morning brought new sensations to Charlotte. She had never had a fire ignite in her belly as she had experienced the night before while making love with Mr Collins, and it was the first time she had enjoyed being with her husband in such a way. She felt so agitated at the thought; she did not know whether to feel pleased or shocked. After examining her feelings while she lay still in bed, she decided to be pleased. Their marriage could be for a long duration, and it was better to remove as much of what was undesirable as was possible. He had behaved like a different man altogether. He had been aroused before but had never been in such a passion. He had devoured her with kisses and was quite the gentle lover, very different from the fumbling oaf that she was accustomed to. She smiled dreamily at the memory and wondered what could have possibly wrought such a change in him. She felt him stir beside her, and she froze in place, not wishing to wake him. She need not have worried; her husband was already awake.

Waking up next to Charlotte pleased him, the scent of her hair overwhelming his senses and awakening his passions, although just as overpowering was his conscience and the knowledge that he was going against his patroness's wishes. He lay still, not wishing to move and disturb his sleeping wife, thinking about their predicament; and, not for the first time, he questioned the wisdom of Her Ladyship's advice and the folly of following it.

* * *

The Collinses rose late, and when Charlotte descended the stair, she was greeted with a jubilant smile from Mrs Higgs as she announced their breakfast was waiting for them in the dining room. Charlotte merely blushed, went to the dining room, and helped herself to ham and eggs as it dawned on her how hungry she was. She poured tea for herself and Mr Collins and watched him eat with as much gusto as usual, cramming more food than was necessary into his mouth at a time. She looked down at her plate in dismay and began to eat, wondering whence the gentle man who had made love to her last night had disappeared. Here, breakfasting with her, was the same Mr Collins as before, the same one she been married. She was puzzled and a little irritated with herself. *Of course, he is the same man!* she thought, berating herself. *What on earth did you expect?*

She was suddenly angry with herself and did not wish to finish her breakfast. She had allowed the man who was responsible for their current predicament to make love to her, and she did not put any obstacles in his way; quite to the contrary, she welcomed his attentions. She had given in to a moment's passion instead of standing her ground. She viciously stabbed a piece of ham on her plate in frustration but could not bring herself to eat it.

She wanted to scream, but her attention was drawn back to Mr Collins, who, taking a gulp of his tea, rose from the table.

"My dear, I pray you will excuse my hasty departure this morning, but I fear I must attend to the business I was engaged in before I was so *joyously* interrupted last night." He raised his eyebrows suggestively as he left the room.

Charlotte threw her napkin down on the table, continuing to haul herself over the coals mentally. *What did you expect? For him to be an entirely different man in the morning? For him suddenly to turn into some dashing hero? To turn into someone like Colonel Fitzwilliam?*

The thought hit her with the force of a horse at full gallop, and she sat, shaken and numb, as realisation crept over her. She was attracted to Colonel Fitzwilliam, and it was the close contact with him the night before as he kissed her hand that had prevented her from sleeping and had aroused her passion.

She stood up abruptly, and the chair almost fell back behind her onto the rug. *Colonel Fitzwilliam!* She repeated over and over in her head. She could not breathe. She wanted air, and she rushed to collect her bonnet and pelisse, almost running out of the front door.

She had not gone more than three hundred yards from her front door when she ran into the precise person she wished to avoid the most: Colonel Fitzwilliam.

Her distress was clear, and he grew concerned as he walked up to her.

"Mrs Collins, are you well?" he enquired.

"Yes, thank you, Colonel. I am just out of sorts this morning; that is all, I assure you." She looked about her, eager for a means of escape.

"Oh, dear. Got out of the wrong side of the bed?" he smiled disarmingly.

"Yes, I suppose so." Her breathing was shallow, and she felt faint but forced herself to stand strong and face the man who, after all, had done no wrong.

"Come, Mrs Collins, you do seem ill. Allow me to escort you home."

She could not think of a reason to refuse him, so she reluctantly returned to the parsonage with Colonel Fitzwilliam by her side.

As they entered the hall, Mr Collins came to greet them. "Colonel Fitzwilliam, I confess myself surprised to see you this morning. However, you are here, and I will not discourage you."

Charlotte flushed at her husband's discourtesy and asked the Colonel if he would take tea. He replied that he would like that, and she led him to the sitting room.

Mr Collins lingered near the door, "I must beg your forgiveness, Colonel. I am afraid that I have urgent business to attend to, but I am sure you can content yourself with the company of my dear lady wife." He smirked at her and again she wondered to where the man from last night had vanished.

"Indeed, Mr Collins, I shall be most content to visit with your wife, and perhaps if you finish your business while I am still here, you will join us also?"

Mr Collins laughed nervously, promised he would join them if he finished soon, and left them alone with the door open, much to Charlotte's immediate relief.

She resisted the urge to pace the floor, rang for tea, and chose to sit as far away from the Colonel as she possibly could.

He looked at her with a puzzled expression on his face but decided not to press the matter. *Perhaps she and Mr Collins have quarrelled, and it would be best to leave well alone,* he thought.

125

Once the tea had been brought in, with a freshly baked fruitcake, the Colonel began to speak about why he had come to see her. "Mrs Collins, you remember what we spoke of last night?"

Remembering last night was not something Charlotte wished to do, and she paled at her own shameful thoughts and realisations. She managed to seat herself, after handing tea to the Colonel and not spilling her own.

The Colonel took her silence as a sign to continue. "As you may well imagine, my aunt did indeed accost me this morning." He laughed and expected her to also, but she simply looked at him paler than before. "Really, Mrs Collins, drink some tea and have some cake. You look most ill indeed." He stood to slice the cake.

She took the proffered slice and reluctantly ate some. Her throat was dry, and she had difficulty swallowing, but he did not witness her distress as he returned to his seat. She drank some tea to facilitate swallowing, and it brought tears to her eyes.

Colonel Fitzwilliam looked at her with pity. "Oh, Mrs Collins, how you must be suffering!"

Indeed, if only you knew, she thought avoiding his gaze.

He sat watching her for a moment as she attempted to compose herself.

"My predicament this morning was unenviable, to say the least."

Charlotte looked up at him in surprise, realising he meant he had spoken to Lady Catherine finally.

"Mrs Collins, I apologise most profusely. If the language my aunt used with me this morning was the same language that she used speaking to you and Mr Collins, then I am grieved indeed. I am mortified." He paused, a frown on his face. "I never thought my aunt could speak with such venom. I am no longer surprised at my cousin Darcy's reaction to her letter."

Charlotte suddenly remembered that Lady Catherine had written a letter to Mr Darcy disparaging his marriage to Lizzy, which had resulted in Her Ladyship being denied the right to set foot onto Darcy land.

Colonel Fitzwilliam rallied himself, straightened up in his chair, and looked her in the eye. "I will not insult you by relaying the particulars, Mrs Collins, and I confess I do not have the stomach to do so. It would cause me pain to grieve you."

She wished he would not look at her so intensely; her colour rose, and she looked down at the cup and saucer in her lap.

"You know, I am sure, that I said all in my power on your behalf." He stood, placed his cup and saucer on the table, and began to pace the room. "I believe at times I could not hold my temper, and I fully matched her venomous words. It is a scene I am glad no one witnessed. She is an obstinate woman, Mrs Collins. Obstinate!" He stopped, opening and closing his fist until his anger passed.

Charlotte stayed quietly watching him, allowing him to speak his piece without interruption.

"Finally, she conceded that she *might have* overreacted somewhat." Here, he let out a bitter laugh. He returned to Charlotte and sat near her. "It matters little whether she is repentant, Mrs Collins. What matters is that she has backed down a little, enough to leave you be for now. Regrettably, by "a little" I mean that she still wishes you to apologise to her."

Charlotte was angry that Lady Catherine still, despite the anger of her nephew and his persuasion, felt that she was deserving of an apology. "I shall do no such thing, Colonel."

He gazed at her sympathetically, saying, "And I would not expect you to, nor would I press the matter. I believe the best course would be to allow some time to pass. I will continue to visit with you and dine in your presence, if you permit?"

Charlotte coloured prettily and nodded her agreement. She was pleased to see him smile at her in return.

"And I would encourage Mr Collins to visit my aunt less frequently."

"I am not entirely sure that would be possible, Colonel."

He laughed outright at the thought. "Yes, indeed, he is extremely attentive to her, is he not? I will speak to him on this matter. He must see his priorities lie with you. Not that I would suggest that he neglect my aunt, but perhaps his visits should be no more than weekly."

"I do not envy you the task of persuading him of that, Colonel Fitzwilliam."

127

"I will do my best, Mrs Collins, for your sake." He reached out and patted her hand.

She could still feel his touch on her hand a few minutes later when she realised he had risen, refilled his tea cup, taken another slice of cake, and was now making himself comfortable in an easy chair.

"Oh, yes, Mrs Collins, I have just remembered!" he declared bringing her jarringly back to reality. "I received two surprising invitations this morning, both from people I have never met in the entire course of my life! I am assuming that I have you to thank for them."

"I assure you, Colonel, I cannot think what you mean," replied his puzzled hostess.

"Well, all the same, I am happy to have accepted an invitation from -" he paused to remove the invitations from his breast pocket. "- Mrs and Miss Thomas for a party tomorrow evening, and from Mr George Simmons to dine at Oak Wood Farm a week yesterday. There now, are you sure you have had no hand in these?" he asked teasingly.

"I confess, they are acquaintances of mine, but I assure you that I had no influence. I do believe that Mr and Mrs Abbot may well be responsible. They, too, are invited."

"Ah, there we have it! Mystery solved. Good, good!" He returned the invitations to his pocket. "I must confess that I am glad, after the spat I had with my aunt this morning, to be able to accept invitations to dine out." A look of understanding passed between them. "Is Oak Wood Farm the old Tudor brick house on the road to Westerham?"

"Yes, indeed, it is. I am told that it was the seat of the old squires before the de Bourghs came into the area."

"Oh, I see. And is Mr Simmons descended from the squires?"

"I believe not. I think I heard Miss Thomas say that Old Mr Simmons, the present Mr Simmons' father, had bought the place after the last squire had died leaving no heirs."

They continued to converse amiably for some time, and Charlotte relaxed once again in Colonel Fitzwilliam's presence, her earlier alarm subsiding and becoming a mere embarrassment that she could easily hide. She did not understand herself and such thoughts, nor did she wish to explore them, but it was very

128

agreeable to be able to continue to be in the Colonel's presence without discomfort.

Colonel Fitzwilliam, after stating that he was most pleased to see Charlotte looking much recovered, expressed his desire to speak with Mr Collins about his visits to Rosings and about his own conversation with Lady Catherine before he departed. Charlotte led her guest to Mr Collins' book room and left him there to speak with her husband. She returned to the sitting room to think and to pray for strength and composure.

Chapter Eighteen

M r Collins stood at the window of his book room and watched Colonel Fitzwilliam walk down the lane towards Rosings. The Colonel had been firm but kind in his advice. He had not become impassioned, nor did he address Mr Collins as he would a subordinate in the Army.

What astonished Mr Collins the most was that Colonel Fitzwilliam spoke to him as an equal. Lady Catherine was so insistent that Mr Collins know his place and station in life and that he keep within it, that having been spoken to by the son of an earl and the nephew of his lady patroness as though he were an equal, produced disquiet in the subservient parson. His mind was drawing comparisons between the Colonel and his aunt, and she came out severely lacking.

The Colonel's words about Charlotte reverberated in his head, and it set him thinking.

A little over a year ago, he had gone into Hertfordshire upon the bidding of Lady Catherine to find a wife. He had settled within himself that the best decision he could make concerning choosing a wife would be to choose one from amongst his cousins. He was well aware that he would be the means of injuring them and their mother upon the death of their father when he inherited the Longbourn Estate.

He had at first, been drawn to the eldest Bennet girl, Jane. Her beauty was unsurpassed, but Mrs Bennet had informed him that Jane was likely to be soon engaged to a man of large fortune. This turned out to be true. Jane was now happily married to Mr Bingley and residing at Netherfield Park, close to her parents and friends.

He then thought, with some bitterness and hurt, of his second choice, the Bennets' second daughter Elizabeth. Now that lady was settled fortuitously, married to one of the richest men in the land, and nephew of his lady patroness. He was pleased that she was well married; he had never wished her ill, despite her bruising his pride in refusing the offer of his hand. With hindsight, he knew her words were true: he would never have been able to make her happy, and she most probably would not have made him so either.

He sat back in his chair and remembered his quitting Longbourn in consternation and embarrassment and going to visit with the Lucases, where he began to see their eldest daughter Charlotte as the possible companion of his future life. Yet recent events had begun to show Charlotte in a different, more prudential light. He had married her because she was a sensible woman of respectable standing, not brought up too high, and with a ready wit. Mr Collins now realised that although his head had made an excellent choice in Charlotte, his heart had been uninvolved. He had never truly seen her real merits as a woman. He was now taken aback by the feeling of affection growing within him for his wife.

He stood up and began to pace, lost in thought.

The morning's events had led him to three startling realisations. One, that Lady Catherine was in error; two, that Charlotte had not been in error and was well-respected by those who knew her; and three, he was in danger of falling in love with his own wife.

Mr Collins had never thought much of love. There had been no love between his mother and father, although he knew it was love that had falsely persuaded his mother into matrimony and lack of love that had left her in misery.

He shook his head to rid himself of the thought of his poor sentimental mother and his cold father. Although he had professed an ardent passion for Charlotte when he had offered her his hand, he had, in truth, merely felt a high regard for her, he was now ashamed to admit. In his profession as a clergyman, he had witnessed many a man and woman do the most foolhardy things for love. He was not adverse to affection, but felt that love addled the brain, confused the senses, and made a mockery of a person. He had seen many a time how a sensible and intelligent person could be brought low by that sentiment, how love could induce one to break the law, act with impropriety, how love was disrespectful of rank. *No,* he thought gravely, *love is to be resisted; it was dangerous and to be avoided if possible.*

132

However, the longing in his heart to go to his wife, enfold her in his arms, and apologise for the past few weeks was overwhelming. He sat back in his chair. He forced himself to stay seated and to resist the urge to give in to sentimentality.

* * *

Charlotte knocked on Mr Collins' book room door and awaited a response. None came. She knew he was in there, but she did not wish to disturb him, especially if he was working on the church accounts still. Therefore, she informed Mrs Higgs that she was going out to visit Mrs Harris to welcome the twins and take the family a basket of fruit and vegetables.

* * *

Mr Collins had started at the sound of her knock on his book room door but had remained silent, staring at the door. He did not wish to see her at that moment; he was fighting with his feelings.

He heard her speaking to the housekeeper and preparing to leave. He overheard their conversation about the basket she was taking and Mrs Higgs asking Charlotte to pass on her own congratulations to the couple. He moved to the window as Charlotte left and watched her walk across their small drive and out of the gate towards the workers' cottages to the west of the village. His book room afforded the best view of the road of any room in the house, and he was able to keep her in sight for some minutes. He observed her make her way down the lane, stop to speak to a child, give him an apple from the basket, and continue on her way.

He was most certainly proud of Charlotte. She was indeed an uncommonly good wife, an ideal one for a clergyman. He realised with some embarrassment that it had taken him above a year to see his wife as clearly as everyone else immediately had. He was ashamed of himself. He knew she deserved better. He knew she deserved a husband who could love her, but he was not willing to give in to that particular emotion.

He returned to his chair by the fire and remembered some other words the Colonel had said to him, that he was overly zealous in his attentions to Lady Catherine.

"Could that also be true?" He wondered aloud. "Have I placed Lady Catherine's wishes above my wife's? Have I sacrificed domestic happiness for an overstated sense of obligation to Her Ladyship?"

He shook his head again and returned to his work. "Surely not. At least I hope not. If that were, in fact, true, that would make me an exceedingly foolish man indeed."

* * *

Over the following days, Charlotte and Mr Collins were busy with their parishioners. There had been three births in the last two weeks: the twins and two boys born to two sisters who had married two brothers. Charlotte attended to as many families as possible. She helped to prepare food for the younger children and helped the mothers to get back on their feet. She enjoyed helping to care for the newborn babes, even though she did not enjoy the jibes that were often aimed in her direction about her turn being next.

Mr Collins' task for that day was not as joyous as Charlotte's. He was called to wait on old Ted Norris, who, it was thought, was close to breathing his last on this earth. Ted had been the cobbler in the village since he was knee-high *to a grasshopper*, so he told it. His father had been the cobbler before him and his grandfather before that. He was proud that his son carried on the tradition, but was pained that his only grandson had wanted to join the Navy instead. He told Mr Collins that one of his great-grandsons, by his eldest granddaughter, had expressed a wish to be apprenticed to his son Eddie Norris, the current cobbler. Old Ted Norris was a tremendously loved character in Hunsford and the surrounding area, and every year, as the sun began to warm the earth, Ted fancied himself *a goner*, as he said.

Mr Collins sat with old Ted, listened to tales of his youth, of how the heart of Mrs Norris had been caught and won. Maisie Norris looked on fondly at the old man. They had been married most of their lives, and Mr Collins noticed they still were in love,

134

which was something he did not expect to see. Lasting love was a new idea to Mr Collins.

Mr Collins had been with Ted for most of the day, and was becoming tired. Maisie inclined her head to indicate he should follow her as old Ted fell asleep once again.

"You get on off home, Reverend. We will be all right. It ain't nought but old Ted getting one of his feelings on. He'll be as right as rain in a day or two, you'll see."

Relieved of his duty, Mr Collins bid farewell to Mrs Norris and made his way home.

Charlotte was awaiting him in the hall when he opened the door. "Good evening, Mr Collins. I trust you had a pleasant day?"

He handed his hat, coat, and walking-cane to Mrs Higgs and sighed wearily. "Testing, my dear, testing. I was visiting with old Ted Norris. He is having another of his early spring bouts, but I fear this time he seems weaker than he did last year."

"I am sorry to hear that, my dear. Would you like a cup of tea and tell me about it?"

He looked at her, once again realising that he did not honestly know her at all. He nodded, said he would like that, and together they went into the sitting room where he told her about Ted.

Dealing with the infirm or elderly was not something Mr Collins enjoyed, nor was it something for which he had any aptitude. He never knew the appropriate thing to say and. more often than not, ended by saying something inappropriate or insulting.

Charlotte, however, did not feel ill at ease in such situations and was often much help to those in need. All the same, she felt compassion for Mr Collins' predicament. It was never pleasant to act with ease in a situation that made one apprehensive.

They took tea together, and he talked over his day and his worries about Ted's health and concerns for the widow he would leave behind, and then remembered that she had also gone visiting that day.

"I do apologise, Charlotte. I have been chattering on, and I have entirely forgotten my manners. Oh, I am sorry. Do tell me how the infants and mothers are."

He managed to remain quiet for the whole of her discourse on the infants, the mothers, the poor conditions they lived in, and the

135

deficient diets they ate. He interrupted her only once and said that the church might do more for the families. Mr Collins seemed too tired to speak much that evening, and that allowed Charlotte to acquaint him with a few charitable ideas she had with regard to those families with more than their fair share of children.

She had been reading in the newspapers that the Sunday schools spreading across the nation were, indeed, doing a valuable job and wondered if that would be beneficial for the children of Hunsford.

"It is too far for the children to travel into Westerham and attend school at St. Mary's; therefore, I thought there might be a few volunteers to run one here. What do you think, my dear?"

He smiled at her sleepily. He agreed the idea had merit, that the children needed guidance and the parents some time away from their numerous offspring. He did not dismiss the idea, but to her surprise, assured her that he would give serious thought to the matter and, when the next meeting of deacons took place, present the idea to them.

Charlotte was beside herself with surprise and pleasure at his approbation. He had never entertained an idea of hers. His usual bent was to inform her that parochial business should be left to those more informed than herself. This time was different. This time he had listened to her and had actually said he would consider her idea.

She decided it was best not to say another word on the subject, but to order dinner to be served before Mr Collins fell asleep on the sofa.

Chapter Nineteen

T he next morning, the Collins household awoke early to the sound of someone hammering on the front door.

Mrs Higgs rushed from the kitchen, unbolted the door to find Joe Cousins, young Mr Norris's apprentice, on the doorstep and out of breath.

"Whatever is the meaning of all this young man?" she asked sharply, showing her disapproval that he had knocked on the front door instead of going around the back like all other tradesmen.

The boy was hardly able to breathe from running and was bent over double. "Begging ye pardon, Missus. Reverend Collins is wanted!"

"Wanted? Wanted where, boy?"

Charlotte who had risen early that morning with the intention of walking, then appeared by Mrs Higgs side. "I will deal with this, Mrs Higgs. Would you be so kind as to wake Mr Collins?"

"Very good, ma'am." She bobbed a curtsey at Charlotte, all the while keeping her eye on the boy at the door as she went to do her mistress's bidding.

"Oh, and, Mrs Higgs," called Charlotte after her, "when you are through there, be so good as to have the gig prepared. Mr Collins will want to leave immediately."

"Yes, ma'am."

Charlotte turned her attention to the panting boy in front of her. "You are Joe, are you not?"

"Yes, Mrs Reverend." He looked up at her with wide-eyed respect and touched his forelock.

She said soothingly, "Now, then, Joe, tell me what this is all about."

"It's great-grandpa, Missus. He's been taken real bad."

Charlotte looked at him in dismay. Mr Collins had believed that this would pass, not that Mr Norris himself would pass. "You mean, Mr Norris, old Ted the cobbler?"

"Yes, Missus. Great-granny is beside herself, she is. He ain't never been this bad afore, Missus."

Charlotte gazed at him with concern in her eyes, outweighed only by the sadness shown in his. "Have you eaten, Joe? Are you hungry?" He nodded that he was.

She led him inside to the kitchen, where Cook and Jenny were surprised to see his arrival. "This is young Joe. Do you have any breakfast for him?"

Cook curtseyed to Charlotte, saying that porridge was ready and that he was welcome to some of that.

"Do you like porridge, Joe?" Charlotte asked him.

"I don't know, Missus. I only have gruel in the morning usually."

Charlotte smiled, "Well, Joe this is like gruel, only thicker. I think you will like it, and it will fill you up more."

He eagerly sat down to the bowl of porridge and glass of milk Cook presented him with. They all watched him eat as he wolfed it all down, making him seem as though he had been starving.

As she led him back upstairs to wait for Mr Collins in the hall, Charlotte commented, "My, Joe, you have a voracious appetite."

"I don't know what that is, Missus, but I like me food."

She continued chatting to him while they waited, and he told her all about being an apprentice cobbler, about how his dreams of having more than one shop one day when he was the master. Charlotte told him that it was healthy to have dreams and encouraged him to do well in learning his trade. Joe had heard she was a nice lady, but he had only ever seen her sitting in the front pew at church. Now that he had spoken to her, he agreed that she was a nice lady.

Mr Collins arrived soon thereafter, and as Charlotte had taken the liberty of having the gig readied, and after hearing what the boy had to say, indeed wished to leave immediately.

Charlotte pressed him to take some bread and cheese and a cup of tea before leaving. "It is likely to be a long day, Mr Collins."

He saw the wisdom in her words, went into the dining room while putting on his coat, and took some bites of the bread and cheese and a few mouthfuls of tea.

While Mr Collins was thus occupied, Charlotte led Joe out to the gig. "Have you ever ridden in a gig before, Joe?"

"No, never, Missus. But Master Norris lets me ride on the back of his cart sometimes." He looked over the gig with awe.

"Well, then, today is your lucky day." She said lightly and heard his gasp. "Are you going back to the workshop or to your great-grandfather's home?"

"To great-grandpa's. There ain't going to be no work today, Missus," sadness suffusing his face.

"No, indeed not," she replied as she offered her hand to help him into the gig as Mr Collins appeared behind her. Joe did not need her assistance, as he was an agile boy, and had swung himself into the gig with ease as Mr Collins mounted sedately, as befit his rank.

Once seated, Mr Collins said, "My dear, I do not know when I will return."

"I understand, Mr Collins. Please take my kindest regards to the family."

Mr Collins flicked the reins, the horse began to walk, and they departed with little Joe waving back at her from the side. She walked out to the lane so she could wave at him in return until they had driven out of sight.

* * *

Charlotte took a leisurely breakfast and then walked into Hunsford to visit Louisa and Mrs Thomas. They were both extremely excited about their little evening party that night, and it was with regret that Charlotte had to inform the ladies of their having to cancel their acceptance. They regretted, indeed, that Charlotte and Mr Collins would not be able to attend. They listened attentively to Charlotte's tale of why Mr Collins was called away that morning and her sad expectation of an unfortunate ending to the day.

"Oh, my dear, how sad this is!" exclaimed Louisa.

"How hard it must be on, Mr Collins!" Mrs Thomas joined.

"Indeed, I believe this must be the hardest part of Mr Collins' profession," agreed Charlotte. "I must admit that I am relieved that I have not been asked to attend the bedside. Although, I would gladly do my duty in that respect, but it is not a task to be envied. Mr Collins will, of course, be needed to stay until... well..." Her friends nodded their understanding.

Louisa and Mrs Thomas did their best to lighten their friend's mood by involving her in the arrangements and preparations for the evening, and Charlotte passed as enjoyable as morning as she was able to in their home.

Charlotte visited with the Abbots also before returning to the parsonage. They expressed their grief at such news and offered any assistance that might be required. Charlotte stated that she did not know the particulars and that she had never attended a pauper's funeral; therefore, it would be best for Mr Abbot to appeal to Mr Collins to offer such assistance. He agreed to visit the parsonage in the morning to enquire of Mr Collins.

* * *

It was with a heavy heart that Charlotte walked back to the parsonage that day. In the time that she had been Mrs Collins, she had experienced a whole range of duties connected with the occupation of a clergyman and his wife: births, marriages, and now, it would seem, deaths. The full cycle of a person's life was under the care of a clergyman, and whilst most events were joyous, this particular part was not, yet it was the completion of the natural cycle. Charlotte knew that if she were to perform her part in it well, that she would need to steel herself and rein in her emotions that, of late, had become more unstable. *The last thing Mr Collins needs,* she thought, *is for me to break down and cry over every sorrowful event.*

* * *

When she arrived home, there had been no word from Mr Collins and she took a light lunch, her appetite gone.

The afternoon dragged on, with her watching the clock and the progression of the hands as they crept round the dial. She grew more and more agitated and felt useless simply waiting to hear any news. She thought of walking out to the Norris cottage, but it was fully two miles there, and Mr Collins would be in a fury with her for walking all that way alone. She saw the impropriety of such action, and so settled herself on the sofa to await her husband's return. As time marched on, she grew tired, lay down, her head upon the arm of the sofa, and was asleep before she knew it.

She was awoken at six o'clock by Mrs Higgs. The room was dark, and Mrs Higgs informed her that they had not wanted to disturb her. Jenny began to stoke up the fire, and Charlotte realised she had grown cold.

"Would you like me to prepare you a hot bath, Mrs Collins?" Mrs Higgs asked upon seeing her mistress shiver.

"No, no. I would like some tea, and I will fetch my shawl."

Mrs Higgs closed the curtains and lit the candles while Charlotte walked groggily upstairs for her shawl. Mr Collins still had not returned, and she knew he would be tired, cold, and terribly hungry when he arrived home.

Once she had found her crocheted shawl in the chest and placed it around her shoulders, she picked up her book, went back to the sitting room, and found Mrs Higgs awaiting her return with a steaming cup of tea in her hand.

"Oh, thank you, Mrs Higgs. How long was I asleep?"

"About two hours, ma'am," she replied, handing the cup to Charlotte. "I assume you will not be dining out this evening."

"Of course not, and Mr Collins will be very cold and hungry when he returns."

"Might I suggest a lamb stew, ma'am?"

Charlotte sighed appreciatively. "Yes, that would be perfect, Mrs Higgs. Is there any chocolate left?"

"Aye, ma'am, there is."

"Then perhaps a cup of hot chocolate will revive him upon his return."

"Will there be anything else?"

"No, not for the moment."

141

"Might I take the liberty of saying how it warms my heart that things are better between you and the master, ma'am?" She curtseyed and turned to leave.

"Thank you, Mrs Higgs. So am I."

* * *

Charlotte spent the next few hours reading her book, watching the clock, and listening for the sound of the gig on the gravel outside.

At last, the long-awaited sound of the wheels crunching on the gravel drive reached her ears, and she leapt from the sofa, almost running to the door, Mrs Higgs bustling closely behind her.

As he dismounted the gig and handed the reins to Dawkins, Mr Collins looked sadly at his wife and shook his head.

She silently led him into the house, where he quitted himself of his hat and coat and, with his shoulders bowed, went into the sitting room. Charlotte followed him and took hold of his hand as they sat down together, his countenance heavy with the sorrow of the day. Charlotte's look of entreaty prompted him to speak.

He shook his head and squeezed her hand. "He is in the Lord's hands now."

Chapter Twenty

The Collinses had taken their dinner of lamb stew and had retired to bed immediately afterwards. Mr Collins looked exhausted, and Charlotte knew that such duties weighed heavily upon him. The next morning, she slipped out of bed without a sound, wishing for Mr Collins to get all the sleep that he needed after such an exacting day as the previous one.

Charlotte sat alone in the sitting room and sewed by the window for a little above an hour before she heard Mr Collins ring the bell for hot water. She joined him in their bedroom and enquired if he had slept well. He replied that he had and thanked her for not waking him.

"I have many things which need my attention this morning with regards to the funeral and the earthly remains of Mr Norris; however, I do not wish to intrude on the family's grief by visiting too early in the day."

"You are truly wise, Mr Collins. One can assume that sleep did not come easily for any of the family last night." She added as she passed him a clean shirt, "One would also think that they would be unlikely be ready for visitors at any time today."

"Precisely, my dear. Your understanding is particularly good. It will also give me time to begin preparations for this Sunday's sermon, as I do not know if I will be permitted much time under such circumstances."

"Indeed, Mr Collins. Please do not forget that Mr Abbot is due to call upon you this morning. He expressed a desire to assist you, should you so wish."

Mr Collins pulled a face, indicating that he did not wish to accept such help.

Charlotte saw it and continued, "Perhaps it will be wise to accept his offer of help, William. After all, your tasks are many, and you merely have one pair of hands with which to do them all. I suggest you accept and allow him to shoulder some of the burden." She handed him his cravat. "I, for one, would not wish to see you overworking yourself, my dear."

Mr Collins turned to Charlotte and kissed her on her forehead. "Your concern does you credit. I believe you are right."

Twice in one week she had been right. *Things are looking up*! she thought cheekily.

* * *

Mr and Mrs Abbot joined them after they had breakfasted, and Mr Collins repaired to his book room with Mr Abbot to discuss the delegation of the required preparations ahead. Mr Collins felt that even the poor should be given a decent funeral. Charlotte and Mrs Abbot stayed in the sitting room, and the latter recounted the events of the previous evening's party at the Thomas home.

"Colonel Fitzwilliam was greatly grieved to find you were not present, Mrs Collins. You have yourself a great champion in that young man," Mrs Abbot stated as she sipped her tea.

"It is good to know that I was missed as much as I missed being present. And yes, I believe you are correct; Colonel Fitzwilliam has been a particularly useful friend, indeed. Mr Collins and I have heard nothing from Lady Catherine since he spoke with her. Mr Collins will visit her as usual on Monday mornings unless there presents any other calls upon his time." Mrs Collins and Mrs Abbot exchanged smiles, each pleased with the way the situation was developing.

"I would wish to thank you also, Mrs Abbot, for your hand in managing events. You have helped immeasurably, my dear friend."

"Nonsense, my dear! There is no need to thank me for doing what any friend would have done in my place."

"Oh, Mrs Abbot, you are too modest. I certainly do not accept that everyone would have acted as you did. For sure, the thought may have occurred to them, but let us be honest; there is a vast deal of difference between thinking about helping and actually acting upon that though." Mrs Abbot simply smiled back at Charlotte and nodded in acceptance of her proffered thanks.

"Do tell me, Mrs Abbot, how goes it with Miss Thomas and Mr Simmons?"

144

Mrs Abbot's face lit up at the question. "Oh, my dear! Mrs Thomas has high hopes for her sister-in-law. Mr Simmons continues in his addresses, and it is quite apparent for all to see that he esteems her much as he always did."

"I am extremely pleased to hear it. I was so aggrieved when Louisa related her history to me. I could not rest until I had done something to throw them into each other's path once again." Charlotte blushed at her own confession.

"Oh, no need to blush or be embarrassed, my dear. As you so rightly stated, many may have wished such a thing, but few would have acted to bring it about. I believe your idea to invite him that night to your card party was inspired and, I for one, applaud you. Miss Thomas, it is evident, is still in love with Mr Simmons and regrets what happened in the past and the interference of a certain person we know." She took a deep breath and exhaled heavily as if expelling the thought of Lady Catherine from her body. "Mr Simmons is now, shall we say, providently unshackled. No longer has either of them a tie to Rosings. I believe they are free at long last to follow their hearts, indeed I do. I believe that everyone should marry the person they love."

A shadow fell across Charlotte's countenance as she dropped her eyes, knowing that she and Mr Collins had not married for love but thought it was best not to say a word on that matter. There was no love in her marriage to Mr Collins, and she suspected that it was evident.

Mrs Abbot saw the look of sadness cross Charlotte's face but chose to ignore it by asking if she might have another cup of tea. As Charlotte obliged her, Mrs Abbot wished that Charlotte knew love in her marriage, but she reflected, *It is obvious that he did not marry her for love. The man can hardly see past the blinding light that is Lady Catherine, let alone see how wonderful a woman his wife is, long enough to fall in love with her and make her fall in love with him in return.*

* * *

Mr Collins and Mr Abbot were occupied considerably during the rest of the week preparing for old Ted Norris's funeral. It had been decided to hold a service in the church for friends and family rather than have it all at the graveside. Mr Collins was forced to agree with Mr Abbot that a pauper's funeral was distasteful. Old Ted had been an essential part of the community and deserved a much better send-off.

Charlotte had visited with Mrs Brown, who was usually in charge of flower arrangement at the church and was more than willing to do her part in beautifying the church for old Ted's funeral service. Once she had accomplished those tasks Mr Collins had set her, Charlotte was left without occupation. She was free to resume her long walks, which she had missed of late. It felt good to get out into the fresh air once again and to feel lightness of heart after the sorrow and misery of the last few weeks.

Like anyone who has had the hand of Death pass close by, Charlotte began to think about her life as she walked. She remembered her childhood, growing up in Meryton, fondly, the joy and excitement when her father was first made mayor, which was heightened further when he was knighted and became Sir Lucas.

She thought about what little schooling she had been given, but that it was no less than what the Bennet girls had received. She thought of those friends, so far away now, Jane and Lizzy, all the fun they had together: the balls, parties, the laughter they had shared. All three of them married, and how different their situations now were. She turned her thoughts to her own marriage, the first meeting with Mr Collins, his proposal.

Charlotte remembered when she had first arrived in Kent. She had been terribly lonely, but sanguine about her situation in life. Not long thereafter, she was visited by her father, her sister Maria, and Lizzy. It had given her immense satisfaction to be able to show them that she was happily settled, that her situation was tolerable, and that she did not regret a thing.

As she walked along her familiar path in the woods, she reflected that many things had changed since that time. Maria was being courted by the youngest son of an admiral whose acquaintance they had made at St. James last winter. Lizzy had married Mr Darcy, and had married for love. Charlotte knew that her friend had such high standards and that only the deepest love would have induced her into matrimony, and she was immensely pleased for her best friend. *Could I boast the same level of happiness I had professed when they had visited?* she asked herself.

She stopped walking and gave the question the consideration it deserved. "No, I cannot," she said aloud.

She continued walking and thought about what had changed. After deliberating on the subject for some time, she concluded that nothing had changed but that she had become more acquainted with life and herself. She had felt content about her situation in life because there was nothing wanting and nothing to reproach. Now she, reflected sadly, that was not true; there was much wanting and many things to reproach.

Mr Collins' behaviour towards her, while cordial, as he rarely raised his voice, was condescending, and he was often disrespectful of her even when in company. This grated on her emotions, and she turned her thoughts inward towards herself.

She discovered that she was not entirely without blame. She had believed herself not to be romantic, that she would be content to live without love and affection. How wrong she knew herself to be now! She had grown up part of a large family, and while they were not the kind of people to express their love in words or with embraces, it was felt by them all. She had also known the affection of intimate friends and their families, and now she lamented she had little of that.

She chided herself for such thoughts. *I have dear friends here, and their affection is true or they would never have braved Lady Catherine's displeasure by standing by me at all*! She kicked a stone in frustration. *No,* she now admitted, *what is lacking is love, affection, and respect in my home. Mr Collins may have softened towards me of late, but he does not love me and I most certainly do not love him. I am most unhappy.*

She stopped walking, tears welling in her eyes. "Oh, what is wrong with me? Why am I so unhappy? Why cannot I be contented once more?" she wept.

She sat down on a fallen tree trunk and waited until these sentiments had passed.

Only then did she slowly made her way home, with a new determination and resolve to find the best in her situation, to see that she was fortunate indeed, and to hope and pray that one day there might be affection between herself and her husband.

* * *

Once she had returned home, she asked for hot water, washed and changed. She was a little cross with herself for allowing herself to become discontented with her lot. Despite the friction with Lady Catherine, she mused, life was not all grim. She looked around her bedroom, and thought, *Indeed, things are not all bad in the least. I have a lovely home, and I must be sensible of that.*

She set about her housekeeping tasks and then her letter writing, and every few minutes she paused to think of a few things for which she was grateful. Her mother had taught them this game. When the children had been discouraged or dejected, they were to stop every half an hour and think of things for which they were grateful. Usually, within an hour or two the agitation was lessened, the hurt dulled, the melancholy lifted.

She reminded herself of her blessings: a good-tempered husband, the prospect of children, a charming house with its well-appointed rooms. She was thankful for being able to keep servants and their own horse and gig. She was exceedingly grateful for new friendships that were forming, people willing to stand by her through thick and thin.

"Yes, I have much to be thankful for."

* * *

The sombre atmosphere in the parsonage was contagious, and everyone seemed to be in a daze of melancholy that they all hoped would lift once the funeral had taken place. Mr Collins retreated into himself, spending more time in his book room than he had before. Charlotte began taking longer walks than she usually was wont to do, but they raised her spirits somewhat, so she deemed them productive, as nothing would be accomplished under this cloud of melancholy. Even the servants felt it, and Charlotte felt stifled indoors.

One of the greatest consolations to Charlotte at present was to see the continuation and progress of Louisa's romance with Mr Simmons. Because she did not wish to stifle them with her continuous presence during such a time, and no set of lovers wants a third person hanging about, she decided to limit her visits to every three or four days.

She was gratified to find that whenever she was visiting, Mrs Thomas was quite content to relinquish the role of chaperone over to her. One such visit coincided with such a beautiful day, that all four of them walked the lanes together. Mrs Thomas linked arms with Charlotte, and the two of them deftly began to slow their pace to allow the couple in front privacy for conversation. Once they knew that they could not overhear the lovers and that they would not be overheard, Mrs Thomas began to acquaint Charlotte with what had passed since her last visit.

"Mr Simmons is so attentive. He pays his respects to me constantly, as Louisa's sister-in-law, and his affection for Louisa seems to increase daily."

"You must be very pleased indeed, Mrs Thomas."

"Aye, I am, Mrs Collins. Indeed I am." They walked on in silence for a few minutes, both of them smiling at the couple walking before them.

"Mr Simmons formally asked me if he could ask for Louisa's hand last evening," Mrs Thomas said in an excited whisper. Charlotte gasped and stopped to look at her friend in surprise.

"Truly?"

"Yes, truly. Although I do not believe he has had an opportunity yet. Charlotte, I pray you will help me in allowing him as much opportunity as possible today."

They resumed walking, now with a joint purpose. Charlotte was astounded and overwhelmed with joy. She had intended to throw them into each other's paths once again, but that things were taking such a happy turn and so quickly, was beyond all her hopes and expectations.

Finally she managed to say, "I am so very happy for her." Mrs Thomas squeezed Charlotte's arm.

Soon they came to an elevated clearing, which overlooked the countryside thereabouts and was a popular place to picnic. There they stopped and rested. During his lifetime, Sir Lewis de Bourgh had been fond of picnicking there and had trees felled and the logs placed for sitting. They were still there, although some were rotten through, and the little party sat and enjoyed the view and the warmth of the sun. It had begun to be unseasonably warm, and they talked of the likelihood of an early spring and the weather lasting until Easter. The general consensus was that it would not last and it was best to enjoy it while it did.

"I believe it might be possible to buy hothouse flowers soon," remarked Louisa, "although their scent is nothing compared to wild or garden flowers."

"Indeed," agreed Charlotte. "Do you have a nice garden, Mr Simmons?"

He was surprised at the question, as he had eyes only for Louisa. He regained his composure sufficiently to reply, "Yes, Mrs Collins, I believe it is nice, but as they say, *beauty is in the eye of the beholder.* Therefore, I hope you will form your own opinion of it soon."

She smiled the obvious invitation. "It is then unfortunate that your dinner party will be at night, Mr Simmons," and discreetly left him to Louisa's company.

Charlotte and Mrs Thomas exchanged knowing glances as they endeavoured to look everywhere but at the pair of lovers before them and tried, to no avail, to not hear every word that passed between them. The conversation of lovers in general is never terribly stimulating, and soon Mrs Thomas and Charlotte conversed of everyday, menial things, as little else occurred to them.

It was with reluctance that Mrs Thomas declared it was time for them to begin the walk home.

She made a fuss of straightening and brushing off her skirts to enable Mr Simmons and Louisa to get a head start and then declared with a giggle, "There, that should give them sufficient privacy, do not you think?"

Charlotte smiled and linked arms with Mrs Thomas as they set off back down the lane to Hunsford.

Chapter Twenty-one

T he day of old Ted Norris's funeral came, and Charlotte walked solemnly and quietly by Mr Collins' side to the church. She greeted Mrs Brown, who was busily placing the last of the arrangements around the church.

"I regret I could not get many flowers, Mrs Collins. They're mostly greenery, but I did the best I could do with the money collected by Mr Abbot."

Charlotte looked around her and saw the flower arrangements. They were simply made, but Mrs Brown had done extremely well, sourcing flowers from hothouses and surrounding them with greenery.

"I think you have done remarkably well. I particularly like the white lily-of-the-valley surrounded by ivy."

"I know it is usually used for weddings, but I thought that, as this is its season, and therefore, economical."

Mrs Brown looked worried, but Charlotte reassured her, "My dear Mrs Brown, using what is in season is sensible, and the little posies are a delightful tribute to old Ted." She patted Mrs Brown on the arm and began to place songbooks on the pews as the villagers began to arrive to say their final farewells to the old man.

At eleven o'clock the horse and cart carrying the ordinary wooden box containing the earthly remains of Ted Norris stopped at the church door. Charlotte led Mrs Norris, who leant heavily on her son's arm, to the front pew. Mrs Norris looked startled.

"I can't sit there!"

Charlotte reached out and squeezed her hands, "Today you can, Mrs Norris."

The service was longer than expected. Many people came forward to say a few words about their dear friend, and Mr Collins' eulogy was sympathetically given. Charlotte was impressed with his delicacy, although he confessed to her on the way home that some of its contents had been copied out of a sermon book, as he often found himself at a loss for words at funerals.

They sang Psalm 23 the Lord is my shepherd; and as the sound of *Amazing Grace* filled the church, the coffin was carried out, the menfolk accompanying it to its final resting place in the churchyard.

After a minute or two, Charlotte walked Mrs Norris out to the graveside, where Mr Collins performed the interment.

Mr Norris Jr informed all that a small wake would be held at The Bell Inn in Hunsford, for any who wished to join them, as he led his weeping mother away from his father's grave. Mr Collins deemed it was best to leave the family and friends to their memories together and that he and Charlotte should return home.

* * *

Charlotte had no news from Hunsford or from Louisa until the night of the dinner party at Mr Simmons' Oak Wood Farm. It was a pleasure to attend a party, to shake off the sadness and melancholy that had invaded every part of their home of late. After dressing, she opened her jewellery box to choose something to wear, her eyes falling on the miniature Mr Collins had given her as a Christmas gift. She quickly pushed it to one side and chose the string of pearls she had inherited from her maternal grandmother instead.

Mr Collins wore his usual black clothing, which declared his profession before he could speak. Charlotte looked at him and wondered what he would look like in a blue or gold waistcoat. She had never seen him in anything else, other than his cassock or nightshirt, and contemplated the possibility of encouraging him in the future to dress as other men of their society when attending dinners, parties, or balls. She did not suppose that she would succeed in such an effort, but it amused her to think of him in red or blue or any colour other than black.

The gig was ordered, and as they prepared themselves in the hall for the cold night air, Charlotte noticed that Mr Collins appeared pensive. "Mr dear, is all well?"

"Perfectly, I assure you, Mrs Collins." After a moment, he continued, "You do recall that because of this business with old Ted, I was unable to visit with Lady Catherine?"

Charlotte's spirits sank at the mention of that name. "Yes, I recall."

"I was thinking that I have not spoken with her for a fortnight now, and this Monday our meeting will be necessary."

He actually looks sad at the prospect of seeing her! Charlotte thought, astounded at this change in her husband.

"You do not wish to attend, my dear?" she asked him.

"Shall we say instead that I am apprehensive?"

She squeezed his arm in encouragement just as the gig arrived, and they turned their minds to happier thoughts.

* * *

It was a long drive to Oak Wood Farm from the parsonage. They had to drive through Hunsford and out to the Westerham Road before the old house loomed in front of them.

As they approached the house, Charlotte shared her thoughts, "I think my dear, that we should not stay late. That was rather a long journey."

"I agree, and I do not wish to be overtired for services tomorrow."

Charlotte was excessively impressed with the house once they had arrived. A stone plaque on the front declared the house was built in 1558, during the final year of the reign of Queen Mary I. The main door opened into what would have been the great-hall. Charlotte stood looking around her in awe. The hall was galleried, and the walls were oak panelled. It was incredibly grand and belied the house's name as a mere farmhouse.

It was here that Mr Simmons greeted them, and they discovered that they were the last to arrive.

The Collinses were shown into the drawing room, and after they had given their salutations and greetings were exchanged, Mr Simmons cleared his throat loudly to attract everyone's attention. "Thank you all for gracing me with your presence, and welcome to my home. I am assured that dinner will not be long, so I would

153

like to take this opportunity to share an excellent piece of news, which I am sure will gladden your hearts as much as it has mine."

The guests exchanged looks, and Mr Simmons waved his hands to hush the tide of questions that began to be directed at him.

"Please, please!" he urged. The assembled party settled down and awaited his news.

"This morning I asked Miss Louisa Thomas for the honour of her hand in marriage, and she has accepted." The room exploded in a cacophony of cheers and voices calling out congratulations.

Mr Simmons slipped past his guests, to allow Louisa to accept the best wishes of her friends and neighbours, and drew near to Mr Collins. "Mr Collins, I wonder if I might call upon you during the coming week to set a date for the wedding? As you may imagine, we are desirous that it should take place as soon as is convenient."

Mr Collins replied that he would be delighted to receive Mr Simmons on Tuesday following and, with Charlotte's agreement, invited him and Louisa to lunch that day.

As the excitement abated, pre-dinner drinks were served, and Charlotte had the chance to talk with Colonel Fitzwilliam.

"I was sorry to have missed you at the Thomas's evening party and saddened about the circumstances of your absence, Mrs Collins."

"Thank you, Colonel. It was terribly sad. I was not well acquainted with old Ted Norris but knew him well enough to have liked him. He used to make me smile with his cheekiness."

"In contrast," he replied lightening the mood, "I am happy that you are here this evening and to have shared in such joyous news!"

"Oh, how correct you are, Colonel. It is indeed the best of news. I wonder if you are acquainted with their history at all."

She could not resist asking the question and wondered at the propriety of acquainting him with the history, but thought it was appropriate that he know if he intended to continue to be friends with them all, and perhaps they might need him if Her Ladyship flew into another of her rages.

"No, I did not realise there was a history. Would you be so kind as to enlighten me?"

"I would be glad to, Colonel, so as to help them perhaps, should they so need it before they are wed."

Colonel Fitzwilliam turned to face her. "Why do I get the impression that my aunt plays a part in this history, Mrs Collins?"

"Colonel, I suggest that you accompany Mr Collins home on Monday lunchtime after he meets with your aunt, and I will inform you of the part she has played."

Colonel Fitzwilliam straightened in his chair, a look of perturbation on his face. "Very well, and I pray my intervention is not needed."

"As do I, Colonel."

He stood, offered her his arm, and led her to the dining room as the dinner gong sounded. "It has been fortuitous having your friendship, Colonel. You have been a great help, to me in particular, and I thank you."

"Mrs Collins, there is no need to thank me. I abhor injustice and cruelty, and it saddens me to find both within my own family. Tell me, how are things at home now? I trust everything is to your satisfaction?"

"There is a closer semblance of normality, yes."

"I am glad to hear it. Tell me, do you still enjoy your walks? I have been occupied assisting my aunt with her estate business, and I should particularly like to resume walking with you again in the mornings, Mrs Collins."

Self-consciously, Charlotte confirmed that she had upheld her habit of walking and that he was welcome to join her whenever he wished to do so. He smiled at her and left her in no doubt of his intention to join her the following morning.

* * *

When dinner was concluded and the ladies made to return to the drawing room, Louisa pulled Charlotte aside in the hall. "Charlotte, I am so happy!"

"I am so pleased for you, Louisa. Congratulations!" She embraced her friend.

"Please do not think me ignorant of the part you played in bringing this about." Louisa looked earnestly at Charlotte, and held her hands. "I know you deliberately invited George to your card party."

"I assure you, Louisa, there was no design." Charlotte smiled tenderly at her friend. "I admit that once I was acquainted with your history, I was grieved by it and wished to help. The only design, if you wish to call it such, was that you were on my mind when Mrs Abbot pointed out that we would be only seven at the party and we needed eight to make up two card tables. Naturally, I immediately thought of your Mr Simmons."

"I am then more indebted to you! I thought this chance would not come again!"

"Oh, Louisa, all that was needed was the opportunity. You are both so in love. It was evident from the moment he walked into the parsonage and laid his eyes upon you."

Louisa's face glowed with happiness, and Charlotte was proud to have played her part. Together, they walked arm-in-arm to the drawing room.

* * *

On the journey home, Charlotte and Mr Collins chatted away in a manner they had rarely done before, and it was certainly a far cry from the last conversation they had going home in the gig. Charlotte was sure that the celebratory atmosphere and a generous helping of wine were responsible.

When they arrived home, they ordered hot chocolate, which they took to bed with them and which remained untouched and cold by the time they awoke in the morning.

Chapter Twenty-two

C harlotte knew that she would be accompanied by Colonel Fitzwilliam that morning while walking, and it came as no surprise to her that he joined her almost as soon as she had passed the gates to Rosings, giving the impression that he had been waiting for her. She shook her head at him, attempting to look disapproving.

He raised his hands in mock surrender. "What, Mrs Collins? You do not believe I came upon you by chance?" He fell in step beside her.

"Not at all, Colonel Fitzwilliam, in truth, I believe you contrived a meeting with me this morning." She threw him an accusing look belied by the smile at the corners of her mouth.

"All right, I admit it! What will be my punishment then?" he looked at her flirtatiously.

Charlotte blushed deeply and smiled shyly at him in return, wondering when they passed through friendship to the point where they were now flirting, but she could not reply.

They walked for some time discussing the previous evening and their joy over the coming nuptials of Mr Simmons and Miss Thomas. Charlotte was so engrossed in the topic and in thinking of how to explain to the Colonel his aunt's part in their history, that she did not realise her mistake in taking the path they were walking until it was too late. The path led through the densest part of the woods and finally opened into a small clearing that was so enclosed that the only way out was to return the same way they had come. She often went there and enjoyed the solitude to pray and sing aloud. However, this time she knew it was folly to be in such a secluded place with a man who was not her husband, and to whom she was so attracted.

She attempted to feign ignorance of the place. "Oh, it seems there is no way through. We had better turn back."

"Why? It seems a lovely place. The ground is dry. We can sit here and rest a while, and perhaps you can tell me what you

157

have been avoiding," she blanched, her thoughts on his proximity and her racing heartbeat, "my aunt's part in the story."

Of course, he is referring to our conversation! Calm down! She chided herself.

Despite his assurance that the ground was dry, Colonel Fitzwilliam removed his coat, laid it out all the same, and bid Charlotte to sit beside him. He leant back against a tree trunk and closed his eyes for a moment, enjoying the sun on his face.

Charlotte could not take her eyes off his face. He was so handsome with the sun playing across his features. She forced herself to look away into the woods but could not resist taking in his lithe, athletic form as she did so. Her face flushed as she recognised the effect he had on her and thought perhaps that she should sit on her hands, to prevent herself from reaching out and touching him. She jumped as he spoke again, and she wondered if he had been watching her as she looked at him.

"So are you going to tell me my aunt's infamous role?" he said with a playful grin playing across his face, his eyes apparently still closed.

Charlotte told Colonel Fitzwilliam the story Louisa related to her the day they had visited Westerham together. He listened quietly, watching her from under hooded eyes. As the story unfurled, he sat up, a look of concern on his face. When she had finished her tale, the Colonel was silent for some time. Charlotte took these moments as an opportunity to gaze upon his handsome features.

"I am heartily sorry to hear it. I give you my word that I shall not allow her to interfere in their lives again. They shall be married whether my aunt approves or not, and if she tries to impede his business, I shall intervene for his good. I too have contacts." He paused, looking grim. "Even if I have to live at Rosings for the remainder of my life to accomplish it." He reached out for Charlotte and clasped her hand. "I am most sorry for any hurt she has caused. Especially to you, Charlotte."

Charlotte's mind was in a whirl. The heat from the hand over hers was invading her entire being. And did he just speak her Christian name aloud? She raised peered at him through her lashes. She could not speak, did not wish to break the spell.

"Tell me, Charlotte, do you like it here in Kent?"

She found her voice enough to say, "Aye, but I prefer Hertfordshire."

The Colonel began to tell about Derbyshire where he had grown up whilst absent-mindedly circling the back of her hand with his thumb. Charlotte's reaction to this touch was instant and explosive. Her whole body was ablaze with the fire of her desire for him. She kept her head averted and looked into the trees to prevent him from seeing the passion she knew was so plainly to be seen in her eyes, yet she could not draw her hand from his; she did not wish to do so. She believed she heard but one word in twenty that he spoke. Her mind was sharply focussed on the skin on the back of her hand. Despite her glove between his skin and hers, she found that she could hardly breathe. She felt that her heart beat so fast and so loudly, it surely must be heard in the next county.

How could he not hear it too? she wondered.

Colonel Fitzwilliam knew what he was doing. He knew it was wrong. He could not stop himself. The more time he spent in Charlotte's presence, the more he wanted to be alone with her, get up close to her, to touch her, and here was an opportunity to hold her hand.

You are not just holding her hand, are you? he demanded of himself, trying to fight the urges that were threatening to overtake him. *If she were to look me in the eye right now, I would be a lost man.* He forced himself, despite his unwillingness, to stop his thumb's mesmerising exploration of the back of her hand.

They remained silent for some minutes, each fighting to bring for self-control. Slowly, reluctantly, their hands parted. Charlotte's breathing began to return to normal.

Colonel Fitzwilliam quietly expressed that he thought that it was time that they began to walk back and helped Charlotte to stand, his hand gripping hers, threatening to reignite the fire so recently subdued. She knew he felt the same way; his reactions, his lack of ease spoke volumes. They stood for a moment staring in opposite directions, both fighting the same thoughts and desire. In the distance, they heard a dog barking – and reality crashed back.

As they began their return to the parsonage, neither could find a topic of conversation, until the dog they had heard barking ran

159

across the path, chasing some imaginary prey, closely followed by Grieves, the Rosings gamekeeper.

"Gunner, Gunner! Get back here!" huffing and puffing as he ran after the escapee dog, pausing only long enough to touch his forelock to Charlotte and Colonel Fitzwilliam, and continued chasing the dog, bellowing its name as he went. They both watched after the gamekeeper until he was out of sight. They looked at each other and burst out laughing, the tension between them gone.

The Colonel left Charlotte at the parsonage gate, brushing his fingers across the back of her gloved hand as he turned to leave. For an instant, both of them relived the moment in the clearing.

* * *

Mr Collins had already departed for Rosings when Charlotte entered the parsonage. She retreated to her room and ordered hot water to bathe, with the single purpose of trying to bring herself back to her senses. She did her best not to think about what had passed between herself and the Colonel in the clearing. She tried not to allow herself to feel the guilt that kept trying to well up and engulf her. She stubbornly pushed it from her mind. She had done nothing for which she could be reproached. *A friend merely held my hand; that was all*, she kept telling herself. It was impossible that anything could pass between them. She was a married woman, and he would not be so foolish as to risk such a scandal so close to his family. *It was just a fleeting moment. It shall never be repeated,* she did her best to convince herself.

By the time she had bathed and changed her gown, Charlotte was sufficiently calm to go into the sitting room and await the return of Mr Collins. It was then that she recalled that she had invited Colonel Fitzwilliam to accompany her husband home that day. Would he attend? Again, she found herself discomposed at the thought of the Colonel and decided to err on the side of caution and to inform Mrs Higgs that they might have a guest for luncheon.

She could not decide whether she was more discomfited or happy when she observed Mr Collins and Colonel Fitzwilliam approach parsonage. She watched their arrival from the sitting room window. Mr Collins was giving the Colonel his full attention and conducting what Charlotte liked to call *the grand tour* of the garden. She smothered a smiled on seeing Colonel Fitzwilliam deign to be interested in Mr Collins' garden, when the Colonel turned to look directly at her standing by the window and winked. Charlotte gasped just as Mrs Higgs entered the room.

"Are you all right, ma'am?" she asked, concerned for her mistress.

"Yes, remarkably well, thank you. Mr Collins is giving our guest *the grand tour,*" she blurted out quickly, hoping to cover her discomfiture.

Mrs Higgs placed the tea things on the table, came to stand by her side, and watched the gentlemen walking around the garden.

She shook her head as she went back to the kitchen. "Poor Colonel Fitzwilliam."

* * *

However, it seemed that Colonel Fitzwilliam had enjoyed his tour of the garden, or so he said when the gentlemen finally came in to take tea before lunch was served. Charlotte fought down a smile as he talked about how lovely he thought Mr Collins garden was. Mr Collins then began to talk about the gardens at Rosings, the variety of plants therein, and how many gardeners were needed for its upkeep. Charlotte knew it would be some time before his discourse was over. She stole a glance at Colonel Fitzwilliam, who was the object of her husband's attention, saw he nodded and smiled in all the appropriate places, and knew he had learnt to do that at his aunt's home, apparently quite skilled at feigning interest. Charlotte drank more tea than she desired in order to disguise her amusement at the scene in front of her. It seemed that Mr Collins had found someone new to fawn over. She shook her head in disbelief. When would he stop such sycophancy?

Lunch was a light collation, and the Colonel informed Mr Collins of gardens he had seen on the Continent. Charlotte was surprised, that his mild mockery of her husband had turned into interest in the subject, and she wondered if they would notice if she slipped away. As if he had read her mind, the Colonel fixed her with a gaze that took her breath away as he continued to describe the gardens at Versailles.

They returned to the sitting room, and Mr Collins excused himself, claiming that he had to write some notes that Lady Catherine had insisted he include in his sermon the following Sunday while they were still fresh in his mind. Amidst promises that he would not be long, he departed and left Charlotte alone with Colonel Fitzwilliam.

Mrs Higgs came into the room to refresh the tea things and lay out some cake, and the Colonel struck up a conversation that was ambiguous enough not to raise the housekeeper's curiosity.

"Did you walk out this morning, Mrs Collins?"

"Yes, thank you, Colonel, I did."

"And did you have a pleasant walk?"

"It was most pleasant." She hesitated. "I enjoyed it very much."

"I am most pleased. Was that your usual walk, or did you try something different this morning?" he smirked at her from across the room.

She paused, hardly knowing what to say. "I admit that I had intended to walk my usual route, but I took another, more interesting path instead."

The Colonel raised his eyebrows. "More interesting? How exactly, Mrs Collins?" he asked, knowing that she was growing more uncomfortable with his questions which only they fully understood.

Charlotte glanced toward Mrs Higgs as she set the cake plates on the table. "It was more interesting, Colonel, as I chanced to see some fauna I had not had the pleasure of observing there before." *Two can play at this game,* she thought.

"Oh!" he exclaimed, enjoying the game immensely. "Some *fauna*?"

"Yes."

"From Rosings?"

"I believe so, yes."

"Which kind?"

"A stag." She smiled triumphantly as she saw his colour rising.

Mrs Higgs curtseyed at Charlotte and left them to their conversation.

"A stag?" he repeated. "And you do not often encounter a stag?"

Her blush deepened, her cheeks on fire. "Not in that part of the wood, no, Colonel."

"Were you fortunate enough to observe the stag for long, Mrs Collins?"

She stared at him, uncertain as to whether to reveal herself or not. Flirtation was generally acceptable in society, only not in hers. Nor was she sure that this was merely flirtation, but she felt a little adventurous after their encounter that morning so pressed on. "I believe I did for some time, although I admit, for my liking, it was not long enough."

To busy herself, Charlotte rose and poured two cups of tea, handing him one.

The Colonel fixed her eyes with his as he accepted the teacup. "Not long enough," he mimicked.

She returned to her seat, stirred her tea, and sipped it slowly, all the while her eyes locked on his. Returning the cup to its saucer, Charlotte replied, "It is my observation, Colonel, that such encounters are rarely of any duration."

The Colonel almost choked on his tea, "Do you find so?" he managed to ask.

"I do."

"Perhaps if the frequency of such encounters was increased, they might last longer and provide you with more pleasure."

It was Charlotte's turn almost to choke on her tea. It was obvious to both that this conversation was becoming dangerous, but neither wished to stop such intimacy.

"I do not know, Colonel. I have no experience in such matters," she pressed on brazenly, the meaning now thinly veiled.

"That is a pity. I would have it that you could spend as much time with the stag as you wished... *Charlotte.*"

She caught her breath to hear him speak her name so expressively.

"Did I say something amiss?" he enquired not having missed any of her reaction.

"Not at all." Her voice was husky, her throat dry.

"Then perhaps I might venture some advice?"

163

He waited for her reaction. Her breathing was shallow. She almost imperceptibly inclined her head. He accepted her encouragement. "Perhaps if you were to continue to return to the same place, the stag might become accustomed to your presence and might remain longer. He would become acquainted with you, and you may enjoy a sort of familiarity as you slowly tame him by your continued presence."

Charlotte paused with her cup halfway to her lips at his invitation to meet her again there in the clearing. She did not know how to react. Her mind screamed that she was a married woman and that her husband was a clergyman, but her body and heart were just as persuasive.

"Perhaps you are right, Colonel." She returned the cup to the saucer, regaining her composure.

"Maybe you are uncertain because you do not wish to frighten the creature away?"

Charlotte's brows arched. "I think, Colonel, that there is more chance of the stag scaring me away."

He looked meaningfully at her over his cup. "Really, Charlotte? Then we shall have to see what we can do to calm your fears."

"What do you suggest?" The room was airless suddenly, and Charlotte forced herself to resist the desire to rush to the window, throw open the sash, and breathe in deep gulps of air.

"Oh, I can think of one or two things," he said with a smirk, "but in such cases as these, it is best to proceed slowly, so as to permit time for yourself and the stag to get to know each other, so to speak."

"Yes, I see the wisdom in that."

At that moment, they were re-joined by Mr Collins, who came into the room expressing a desire for a cup of tea. He chatted away pleasantly to the room in general and was oblivious to the tension in the air between his wife and his guest.

The Colonel and Charlotte remained staring at each other for a few moments before Mr Collins' chatter drew their attention to him and they were obliged to join in his conversation.

Chapter Twenty-three

The following day Charlotte was prevented from walking due to the weather. The clouds had built up over night, and they poured down a steady stream of heavy rain all the day through. The following day was much the same, as was the day after. On the fourth day, the weather had relented somewhat and reduced the quantity of water falling from the sky to drizzle. On the fifth day, she almost leapt out of bed upon seeing the sun streaming through the curtains, but when she went to the window to see if the world around her had dried out, she was disappointed to see that the landscape resembled the Norfolk marshes.

She went about her daily routine despondently. This did not go unnoticed by Mr Collins, who did all he could to raise her spirits and entertain her. This resulted in provoking her. She did not wish to be read to from one of his sermon books, and when she stated as much, he thought that she was coming down with some illness and threatened to send for the apothecary.

Charlotte tried to lose herself in her novels, but in her mind, every heroine was she and every dashing hero, the Colonel. This would not do! She hunted to find some other occupation before she went out of her wits, although everything either bored her or reminded her of him.

At length, Mr Collins produced the backgammon board and enticed her to play, but she lost all but one game due to her mind being otherwise engaged.

* * *

The next day dawned bright, clear, and much drier; however, as it was Sunday, there was no prospect of seeing Colonel Fitzwilliam other than across the church. Charlotte did not dare to look at the Colonel directly during the service for fear of her face betraying her and, instead, kept her eyes straight ahead or on Mr Collins as he preached. She felt rather than saw Colonel Fitzwilliam's gaze upon her throughout the entire service and knew she was beginning to blush. She sincerely hoped that no one noticed.

Colonel Fitzwilliam followed his aunt out of the church as soon as the service was over without exchanging greetings. Charlotte knew that was due to Her Ladyship and that she was still unforgiven. However, Charlotte did not care one jot about Lady Catherine; she had other concerns to occupy her now.

* * *

Mr Simmons had been prevented from visiting with Mr Collins on Tuesday owing to the amount of rainfall and the ensuing state of the roads. He offered his sincere apologies to Mr Collins, who accepted them graciously.

"I suggest, if my dear wife is agreeable to my proposal," Mr Collins simpered at Charlotte, "that we all return to the parsonage now and see what can be done to set a date for your union, Mr Simmons, Miss Thomas, before the weather can conspire against you once again." He laughed at his own wit, while the others merely nodded in agreement.

Mr Simmons was desirous that the marriage take place as soon as possible, and over tea they consulted Mr Collins' diary and agreed upon a date three weeks hence. Charlotte and Louisa sat and discussed plans for the wedding, the flowers, the dress, and the latter's hope for the future, while Mr Collins and Mr Simmons became better acquainted.

"I find I am quite excited, Charlotte. And it is not too late, you know," confided Louisa.

"I am glad you are excited, but pray, what do you mean by it not being too late?"

Louisa lowered her voice so that the gentlemen could not overhear, "It is not too late for me to provide George with an heir." She coloured deeply at the implication.

"I am very glad to hear it, and I wish you every success."

"Although I admit I am nervous, but Anne has told me what to expect, and I am as ready as I can be, I believe."

Charlotte was not entirely sure she wished to discuss this with Louisa while the gentlemen were present, but she could not refuse without appearing rude. Fortunately, Louisa changed the subject.

"I am having a dress made. It is a gift from George. Mrs Owens did such a superb job on the dresses we had her make, that day we went to Westerham that George has insisted that we also ask her to make my wedding gown. I confess that I always wanted to be married in pink. That is what I planned the first time and what I have chosen for this gown."

Charlotte smiled at her friend's excitement and was pleased to allow her to chatter away happily. She could only imagine the relief and happiness that Louisa must have been feeling. To have all her hopes and dreams dashed by pure cruelty and then, years later, to find that the man she loved, loved her still in return must have been overwhelming. The very thought brought tears to Charlotte's eyes.

"Oh, my dear friend, why do you weep?"

"Louisa, I am so happy for you, to get your happy ending finally." She chuckled at the girlish sound of that statement.

Louisa leant forward and hugged her friend. "You are such a dear, caring friend, Charlotte. You are so correct in what you say. I never dreamt this day would come. I was unable to forget him; I did not wish to forget him. I loved him deeply then, and I love him even more deeply now. You can imagine, I am sure, the felicity I feel now, knowing that after all this time, I will indeed be Mrs Louisa Simmons as I always hoped I would be." She paused to dab the tears away that were welling up in her eyes. "After all," she giggled, "does not every girl deserve a happy ending?"

* * *

Mr Simmons and Louisa stayed until it was close to dinnertime, which was served in the middle of the day on Sundays. Charlotte had rarely seen anyone who could bear Mr Collins' company for so long, but Mr Simmons, it seemed, could and appeared to quite enjoy himself. Charlotte was pleased, as it meant that, upon her marriage, Louisa was not likely to give up her friendship.

Charlotte was loathe for them to leave, and so she drew Mr Collins aside and suggested that she invite them to stay for dinner. Mr Collins went even further than that. He invited them to take a collation with them then and suggested they all attend evensong together, hear the first reading of the banns, and return to the

167

parsonage afterwards for dinner. He was sure at evensong they would find a boy who, for ha'penny, would run into Hunsford and inform Mrs Thomas of their plan so that she would know that Louisa was in safe hands. Louisa was delighted with the plan; Mr Simmons could not have been happier.

Charlotte watched Mr Collins and Mr Simmons conversing while Louisa provided her friend with details of the gown that was being made for the wedding. Charlotte saw that Mr Simmons had a way of drawing out the sensible side of Mr Collins' character, and as this was the side she personally preferred, she thought it best to encourage Mr Simmons to visit as often as he pleased.

In the time that she had been acquainted with Mr Collins, Charlotte had never known him to have a friend, someone on whom to rely, with whom to share burdens, in whom to confide. She was the nearest thing her husband had to a friend, and she was certain that he kept many things from her. In recent weeks, she had discovered, to her surprise, that Mr Abbot and Mr Simmons seemed to be able to tolerate her husband reasonably well. She prayed that it boded well for the future.

She returned her attention to Louisa and discovered that she was continuing to describe lace and silk. In the last few days, it seemed that Louisa had become visibly younger, as though this new happiness, which the renewal of love had brought, had lifted all the years of hurt from her person. Her skin was more radiant, her eyes brighter, her demeanour lighter. Charlotte knew that her friend would be happily married.

Her thoughts then drifted to Colonel Fitzwilliam. What was she doing with him? What did she expect from such flirtation? She knew she ought to put an end to this dangerous business but was yet reluctant. She had never felt before the way she did when she was with the Colonel and did not wish to lose his friendship, but recognised that this behaviour could not continue. She decided to signal her decision by acting a little more distant each time they met.

"What do you think you will wear to the wedding, Charlotte?"

The sound of her own name snapped Charlotte out of her reverie and back to reality. "Louisa, I do beg your pardon."

Louisa giggled. "You were lost in thought, no doubt imaging the dress I was describing to you. I asked you what you thought you might wear."

"Oh, I do apologise. Yes, I was indeed imagining," she fibbed. "I have two new evening dresses that we had made in Westerham, and I thought one of those might suit. One is a striped blue silk, the other a silk of the palest green. They are nothing terribly grand, but thanks to the discount from Mr Abbot, I was at least able to purchase silk."

"Oh, yes, what a felicitous day that was! I thank God for that day Charlotte, for had we not visited Westerham and had I not told you of my disappointment, then you would not have known to have invited Mr Simmons to your card party!" She gratefully squeezed Charlotte's hands.

"Louisa, I have said before that it was no design of mine, although I was thinking on the subject, and I do admit that I intended to bring you two together somehow."

"There, you see? You have admitted it! You intended to do it, and Providence gave you a helping hand!"

They both giggled, and Charlotte shook her head fondly at her friend. Mr Simmons had not needed much encouragement. She remembered that he often sat at the back of the church when he attended once a month and would enter as the service began and would leave as it ended, thereby avoiding all contact with Louisa. She supposed he must have been just as injured as Louisa had been and could not face her in his pain.

Charlotte excused herself and went off to the kitchen to arrange luncheon. There was no leftover meat, as the only meat available was the lamb for dinner, so Mrs Higgs suggested that they have vegetable soup and apple pie for dessert. Charlotte agreed that that would be acceptable and knew that the dinner that evening would be a much grander affair now that the staff had more time to prepare.

She left the kitchen. having ordered tea, and returned to the sitting room, where she found Mr Collins telling their guests about Charlotte's parents, Lord and Lady Lucas, and their home, Lucas Lodge in Hertfordshire. Charlotte watched him as he spoke with awe and admiration of his father-in-law, the one-time Mayor of Meryton, about how gracious they were to him on every occasion that he had the pleasure of being in their home. She had to admit that she was excessively gratified to hear him speak of her relations in such a manner, and repaid the compliment by speaking of his relations, declaring them her oldest friends and dear to her heart.

Mr Collins observed his wife closely as she spoke in a manner that reflected his own moments before and recognised that she was paying him a kind compliment. He felt that new sensation, which was now becoming more and more familiar, tugging at his heart. His love for her was growing, but while he listened to her, he felt no inclination to quash the emotion or to harden himself against it. It was pleasant to hear her praise his relations and, in so doing, praise him.

Lunch was served, and Mr Collins was delighted to have the opportunity of having apple pie, made with his own apples, served to his guests. Even Charlotte was impressed and declared it was the best she had tasted since living there.

They attended evensong, and as predicted, they found a boy willing to inform Mrs Thomas of Louisa's whereabouts for a ha'penny. It was dark as they exited the church and turning chilly, the sky full of stars portending a lovely day on the morrow. The party walked the short way back to the parsonage, where Mrs Higgs greeted them at the door and informed them that she had prepared hot chocolate for them in the sitting room.

For the first time since she married Mr Collins, Charlotte felt at home and at ease. She had felt it for a little while when the Abbots had been to dinner, but now the feeling was stronger and enveloped her. The parsonage felt like home; their company felt familial; and even Mr Collins seemed more comfortable than ever.

Charlotte renewed her determination to back away from the foolish flirtation in which she and Colonel Fitzwilliam had been engaged. She sincerely hoped that he had not taken it too seriously and looked forward to tomorrow, planning in her head a route to walk that did not take them to the clearing, whilst she sipped her hot chocolate.

She sat down on the sofa next to Louisa, sipping the warming beverage, whilst Mr Collins talked about gardening and his vegetable plot and Mr Simmons offered his professional advice. She did not hear more than one in four words; she was deep in thought, fighting within herself. On the one hand, her attraction to Colonel Fitzwilliam was strong, and she craved more of the sensations, which made her desire to cast aside her usual prudence when he touched her. On the other hand, she knew she was a fool to risk everything she had here. The feeling of being *at home* pervaded every part of her mind and body. She relaxed against the cushion. *I certainly would be particularly foolish indeed to risk losing my place here,* she thought.

* * *

As she had expected, Mrs Higgs put on a bit of a display for dinner, as she whispered to Charlotte in explanation, "To make up for lunchtime."

They sat down to the roast lamb garnished with dried rosemary, again from Mr Collins' garden, he was proud to admit. The conversation stayed light and friendly, and Louisa and Mr Simmons proclaimed that they would prefer to wait until they were married to repay the invitation, so they may entertain the Collinses at Oak Wood Farm as man and wife.

"Mr Simmons, I would not expect anything else," Charlotte reassured him.

"Thank you Mrs Collins. I have to admit, I did not expect to find such a warm welcome at the parsonage. I had thought that a *certain person* held sway over this house with a firm hand. I am glad to find I am wrong."

Mr Collins flushed upon realising to whom Mr Simmons was referring, and to his relief Charlotte responded in a manner that left him curiously satisfied.

"Let us say that perhaps a *certain person* did at one time hold sway in this household, but that the inhabitants regained their hold. We are adults, Mr Simmons; we no longer need a nursemaid." She shrank inwardly at her boldness and hoped that her husband would not take exception to her words.

She glanced in his direction, and he merely beamed at her and patted her hand. Charlotte sipped some wine to cover her surprise, but deep inside, she was pleased. She had stated what, to her, and certainly to others, was obvious; however, Mr Collins had been slow in realising that Lady Catherine was overly controlling and far too officious over their lives.

"Louisa tells me that you join her in sewing and crocheting for the poor." Mr Simmons said, changing the subject.

171

"Yes, indeed. I was honoured that Mrs Brown invited me to join such an activity."

"Indeed, yes," chimed in Mr Collins, "I feel I am most fortunate in my choice of wife, Mr Simmons."

Charlotte raised her eyebrows. Was this the same Mr Collins who usually fawned over Lady Catherine, now dismissing the opportunity to praise Her Ladyship in favour of complimenting his wife?

"She is an amiable woman and a good friend to my Louisa," agreed Mr Simmons wholeheartedly.

"I have often thought that not every woman is cut out to be the wife of a clergyman, but I, as you will agree, have been blessed; indeed I have." He returned his attention to his plate, leaving Charlotte with an unaccustomed feeling of satisfaction.

Dessert was served, after which they returned to the sitting room, the long day beginning to tell on the little group, and it was not long before the first moves towards departure began. Charlotte promised to visit Louisa in the morning; Mr Collins invited the couple to tea the following Saturday. Good-bye and thanks were exchanged, and the guests set off for Hunsford in Mr Simmons' carriage.

Once the door was shut, Mr Collins turned to Charlotte and surprised her by saying, "Thank you, Charlotte my dear, for a wonderful day."

Overwhelmed by pleasure from the unaccustomed compliment, Charlotte had difficulty finding her voice. "You are quite welcome, William. It was very pleasant, was it not?"

Mr Collins smiled tentatively, touched her arm while nodding toward the stairs. She accepted his proffered hand and followed him up the stairs.

Chapter Twenty-four

W hen Charlotte awoke the next morning, she thought she was ill. She tried to sit up, and her head swam. Mr Collins did not notice as he was getting out of the other side of the bed. As she tried a second time to sit up, her head not only swam, but the room did also. Mr Collins heard her strangled cry and somehow managed to retrieve the chamber pot and hold his wife's shoulder to prevent her from falling off the bed at the same time. He gently held her hair and tenderly stroked her back until the vomiting stopped.

Once her bout of nausea was over and her stomach had no more to divulge, Mr Collins managed to persuade her to remain in bed and rest.

He rang the bell and called for Mrs Higgs, who repeated over and over again that the lamb had been thoroughly cooked and that her mistress must be ailing from another source. "It is dreadfully draughty in that church, sir. Perhaps she caught a chill."

Charlotte said she did not wish anyone to make a fuss over her, requested a cup of tea, and to be allowed to rest a while longer in bed. Unsatisfied, Mr Collins pressed the issue until she agreed that if she was not better in an hour or two, that she would permit him to call for the apothecary.

She dozed off to sleep, and upon awakening an hour later, she felt much better. She rang the bell, and Mr Collins arrived at the same time as did Jenny. Charlotte sent Jenny back to the kitchen for hot water and set about assuring Mr Collins that whatever had ailed her had, indeed, passed.

He was not so easily persuaded. "I would not be easy on my weekly visit to Rosings if I thought you were in any way unwell, my dear."

"That is very kind of you, but I assure you that I feel perfectly well again. I am certain that I ate something that did not agree with me last night."

Mr Collins looked unconvinced. "If you are not completely certain, my dear, I will, of course, remain at home."

There he was again, offering to forego visiting Lady Catherine in preference of Charlotte.

Charlotte smiled reassuringly at him. "I shall take some fresh air, walk to the end of the lane and back again. I shall not go far, I assure you, and shall be back within half an hour. I am certain that the fresh air will do me the world of good, William."

"Very well, my dear, but when you return, I wish you to rest. I shall explain the situation to Her Ladyship and return home as quickly as she releases me."

Charlotte smiled at that. He was certainly a changed man. "Very good. I shall rest in the sitting room and await your return. If the weather stays this beautiful, perhaps we may take tea together in the garden."

Mr Collins' eyes lit up at the suggestion, and she was pleased to see he approved the idea. He kissed his wife on the head, bid her adieu, and left the room to prepare himself for his visit to Rosings.

* * *

Charlotte's stomach certainly did not feel as settled as she professed, and she took only a cup of tea before setting out to walk down the lane. The fresh air calmed her mind, and she breathed deeply as she walked. Her mind was occupied with thoughts of Louisa's wedding when she spied a figure up ahead of her, leaning against a tree. It was Colonel Fitzwilliam. She paused and thought for a moment of turning back, but decided the situation needed to be addressed. Being unwell would serve as an excuse to keep her distance that morning.

He smiled at her as she drew near and tipped his hat in greeting.

"Good morning, Charlotte. I am glad we are finally able to meet today," he smiled charmingly. "How are you?"

She took the opening to explain that she was unwell, and would not walk for long that day. She could see plainly that he was disappointed; it had been a sennight since they had last had the opportunity to be alone together, and he clearly had been looking forward to seeing her again that morning.

"I am sorry to hear that. I do hope you will recover quickly," he said with concern.

"Thank you, Colonel. I believe it was due to something I ate and, therefore, should not be of long duration. You need not worry yourself on my account."

He looked seriously at her as they began to walk along the lane, "Oh, but I would worry about you. How could I, Charlotte?"

There, he spoke her name again, and she felt her heart flutter at the sound of it upon his lips, but this time it did not excite her as it had the Monday previous. This time the flutter in her heart fought with the churning in her stomach and made her feel queasy once again.

"Indeed, you are ill. Do you wish to return to the house?" he asked, his voice displaying the depth of his concern.

"Perhaps you are right," she said stopping to breathe deeper. "I so wished to take some fresh air."

"You can take fresh air from the comfort of your garden. Please allow me to escort you home."

"Very well, Colonel."

Colonel Fitzwilliam took hold of her hand and put it through his arm as though she needed his support to help her walk. She felt herself blush at the proximity of his body to hers, but he did not see it as her face was already flushed from whatever was ailing her. He closed his hand over hers and kept his eyes on her face as they walked back towards the parsonage. She was grateful for his assistance, but felt ashamed that she had not achieved her goal of preventing him from touching her once again.

They reached the parsonage, and the Colonel rang the bell once they entered the hallway. Mrs Higgs joined them immediately.

"Your mistress is unwell. Where is Mr Collins?" he addressed Mrs Higgs.

"He is at Rosings with your aunt," Charlotte informed him as she took off her bonnet.

"Then I will see you safely settled on the sofa, and I will fetch him at once." He turned to Mrs Higgs again, "Bring Mrs Collins something for her stomach, and make sure it is warm."

175

"Yes sir." She threw a look of concern at Charlotte and returned to the kitchen as she was bid.

Colonel Fitzwilliam helped Charlotte to the sofa. She thought to point out that although she felt unwell, she was not an invalid and could walk perfectly well, but recognised that it would show she was out of humour. It was clear that his solicitude was born of concern for her well-being. He bid her recline and asked Mrs Higgs for a blanket when she returned with a cup of hot chocolate.

"Now drink up your chocolate. It is good for you, ma'am," Mrs Higgs commanded as she placed the blanket over her mistress. She turned to the Colonel. "Is there anything I can get for you, sir?"

"No, thank you. I will just satisfy myself that Mrs Collins is comfortable and go to Rosings to fetch Mr Collins." He said keeping his eyes on Charlotte's face all the while.

Mrs Higgs left them to attend to her work, saying she would be back to check on Charlotte in a few minutes.

Colonel Fitzwilliam knelt in front of the sofa. "I do wish you well Charlotte. I will leave you now." He picked up her hand and lingeringly kissed the back of it, all the while his eyes boring into hers. He was reluctant to leave and kept his eyes on as he crossed the floor to the sitting room door, took a deep breathe to compose himself, and departed.

Charlotte breathed a deep sigh of relief at his departure. *Whatever am I to do about him?* she asked herself, knowing that it might be harder than she had anticipated to extricate herself from a situation that could so easily spiral out of control. When she had finished her cup of hot chocolate, she laid her head back on the cushion, and within a few minutes, she was fast asleep.

* * *

Mr Collins patiently sat through his patroness's criticisms of his sermon of yesterday, and now he was forced to listen to her *suggestions* for his sermon the following Sunday. He scribbled down what he could manage to, and silently resolved to add only the least offensive ones to his sermon,; one, to not aggravate his parishioners; and two, to not aggravate Her Ladyship by showing he had paid attention to her instructions. His writing skill was much slower than Her Ladyship's dictating skill, so he did not catch the half of what she said, but it mattered not to him. He had begun, in the last few weeks, to see her for who and what she was, and he was severely disappointed, in her and himself.

Colonel Fitzwilliam arrived, and Lady Catherine broke off her dictation to address him, "Ah, nephew, where have you been?"

"I have been walking, Aunt," he replied curtly, his eyes on Mr Collins. "I chanced to see Mrs Collins near the parsonage, Mr Collins."

Mr Collins looked up at hearing his wife's name, but Lady Catherine interrupted, "Yes, yes, never mind about Mrs Collins. You are needed, Richard. I need you to tell Mr Collins how poorly he delivered his sermon yesterday."

Colonel Fitzwilliam turned to address his aunt, "I am sorry, Aunt, but I must pass on a message to Mr Collins."

Lady Catherine was taken aback, but her nephew returned his attention to Mr Collins. "Mrs Collins is far from well, sir, and I would advise you to return to the parsonage as soon as you can."

Mr Collins stood immediately and made to leave. "Yes, thank you." He half bowed to Her Ladyship, nodded to the Colonel, and made for the door.

"And, Mr Collins," the Colonel called out after him, "your sermon yesterday was very good."

Mr Collins could not help but swell with pride at the compliment that Colonel Fitzwilliam had paid him. Oddly, the fact that it was delivered before Her Ladyship made it all the sweeter.

* * *

Mr Collins almost ran all the way back to the parsonage, and as he burst through the front door, he found Mrs Higgs sitting on the stair awaiting him. She gestured to him to be quiet with her finger to her lips. She then nodded towards the sitting room. Mr Collins opened the door quietly and saw Charlotte fast asleep on the sofa.

"Would you like some tea, sir?" Mrs Higgs whispered.

"Yes, please." Mr Collins removed his coat and hat and crept into the sitting room. He moved an easy chair so that he could sit

177

and face Charlotte while waiting for Mrs Higgs to bring his tea. He did not have to wait long, and he sat drinking the hot tea as he watched his wife sleep.

She looked so angelic and peaceful lying there. *I am so sorry I have treated you poorly; you deserve better, my dearest Charlotte,* he thought, replaying all that had passed over the previous few months. *Dear Lord, let her pass through this illness and recover soon,* he prayed. *It will all be different, my sweet Charlotte. I promise.*

How long Mr Collins remained thus, keeping his vigil over the sleeping form of his wife, he did not know. His stomach had begun to growl, indicating that it must have been around lunchtime. He had sat in quiet prayer and contemplation. He thought over the events of the previous few weeks, and he had to admit that he found himself severely lacking. He wished he could take back his actions. He wished he had not gone running to Lady Catherine to bemoan his wife. He nearly groaned aloud when he thought of his own behaviour.

When had he become sycophantic and ridiculous? He did not know, but realised he had been for some time now. He was sure Charlotte's illness was because of his own behaviour, at least in some part, and he was sorry she had been suffering for it. He had heard that the shock of a loved one becoming ill can change a person, make them reflect inwardly, and repent of earlier actions. He now felt it to be true.

Mr Collins knew he was not sensible, but he was not stupid. He knew now that he was often ridiculous and must have pained Charlotte on more than one occasion. He remembered with remorse the pompous things he was wont to say on occasion and was deeply mortified. *It shall be my earnest endeavour to demean myself with grateful respect towards Her Ladyship.* He hung his head in shame and prayed for forgiveness and for Charlotte's recovery. He resolved to endeavour to be a different man for her sake and prayed in earnest for Divine assistance.

Charlotte began to stir, and Mr Collins returned his attention to his wife. He prayed again for her recovery and at length she opened her eyes and stretched, smiling at him.

"William. How long have I been asleep?" she purred sleepily.

178

"I do not know, I can scarcely remember how long I have sat beside you. I do know that it has been some time. Are you feeling any better, my dear Charlotte?"

"I do feel better rested. I dare not move as yet for fear of further disturbing my stomach."

Mr Collins stood up and kissed his wife's forehead. "Let me fetch Mrs Higgs and see if we cannot take tea in the garden as you suggested. The day continues fine, and the fresh air will put some colour into your cheeks, I have no doubt."

He left the room, and Charlotte gingerly raised herself to sitting, fearing another bout of nausea. Mr Collins returned promptly and informed her that it would take Mrs Higgs and Jenny some time to set up the garden furniture for the first time that year and asked her if she would like to freshen up beforehand.

"I would like to splash a little water on my face, yes, and perhaps get a shawl and bonnet too."

Mr Collins helped her to rise, and Charlotte was appreciative of his help and the fact that the giddiness and nausea had not returned. They went up to the room that was now returned to its original use as theirs, and Mr Collins watched his wife prepare herself, a worried look diffusing his face.

"My dear William, you need not be so concerned for me. I believe I am better now. It seems to have passed."

"I am relieved to hear it," Mr Collins replied, helping her on with her shawl, "but I urge caution, my dear."

"Of course," she turned to face him and touched his arm, "and thank you, William, for attending me."

He wanted to say that it was nothing. He wanted to say that it was what was expected of him. He could not bring himself to say the words. The truth was that he was desperately worried about her. He had been praying for her and had been near tears on occasion. He recognised this was the power of his growing love for her and embraced it. He wanted to feel wretched owing to what he thought was the part he had played in her illness, and he feared she was not truly recovered and he might lose her now that he valued her more than he ever had. He blinked the tears away that began to sting his eyes and turned away from her so she would not see his distress.

179

* * *

They sat in the garden drinking tea and discussing plans for the vegetable plot that year. The day was warm, the air still, and it was pleasant to feel the sun's warmth on their skin and to hear the birdsong around them. Mr Collins' plans for the vegetable plot included its doubling in size to provide for the amount of guests they had entertained of late, and hoped to continue doing in the coming year. He outlined his ideas, and together they made a mental list of what they would like to grow.

"Oh, my word!" Charlotte exclaimed.

"What is it, my dear!" Mr Collins shot out of his chair. "Are you unwell again?"

"No, no, please be seated, my dear. It is only that I have just remembered I promised to call on Louisa this morning. I must write to her so she might not worry."

She rose and made her way back into the house, Mr Collins closely following on her heels. He went into the kitchen in order to fetch Jenny, and Charlotte went straight to her desk. She wrote a quick note to Louisa expressing her sorrow for not being able to visit with her that day and turned to ask Jenny, who had just arrived in the sitting room with Mr Collins, to see that it was delivered.

Mr Collins smiled and took Charlotte's hands once Jenny had left on her errand. "Is it safe to return to the garden, my dear? Have you anyone else to inform?"

She replied with a disarming giggle, "No, no one else, William. It is safe for us to return to the garden."

As they walked, back through the house, she asked him to continue to tell her about his plans for the garden and asked him if they might have a private, secluded sitting area where she might read. He thought it was a splendid idea and was glad to draw her into the conversation, to consult her and hear her thoughts.

Chapter Twenty-five

That evening they received a letter from Louisa saying how sad she was that Charlotte was unable to visit and wishing her a speedy recovery. The missive included an invitation to dine the following evening. Mrs Thomas was throwing a small dinner party to celebrate the coming wedding of her sister-in-law. Charlotte was eager to attend, but Mr Collins was apprehensive, owing to Charlotte's recent bout of illness. He did not wish her to have a recurrence.

"My dear, I am sure that, by tomorrow evening, I will be quite well; and if I am not, we shall do as you suggest and stay at home quietly."

"I merely wish to prevent you from overly exerting yourself, my dear."

"Of course you do, William," she said, patting his hand. "I cannot cloister myself away simply because I ate something that did not agree with me." She looked over the invitation once again. "Besides, we shall be a merry company. The Abbots are invited, as are Mr Simmons and Colonel Fitzwilliam."

The mention of the Colonel's name was a great encouragement to Mr Collins, who then happily accepted the invitation on their behalf and sent the letter off to Mrs Thomas immediately. The Colonel's name was somewhat of a nuisance to Charlotte, who began to feel nervous at the thought of seeing him again. Her stomach churned, much to her disappointment. She sat back down on the sofa where she closed her eyes for a moment and rested thus, until she felt that Mr Collins was watching her, and she opened her eyes again.

"You are not feeling recovered, are you, Charlotte?"

"It is passing, William, I assure you."

"Perhaps you should eat something. You have hardly eaten the whole day," he pressed.

"Only if you insist, but let it be bread and jam, nothing more, please."

He smiled down at her. It was obvious that she was still unwell, and he felt impotent in the face of it. He uttered a silent prayer as he went in search of Mrs Higgs to ask for something to be made up for them in the sitting room. He would join his wife for a light meal that evening.

They dined on bread and jam and laughed as they recalled their exploits as they had picked fruit the previous summer to be made into preserves. Mr Collins had almost fallen off the ladder picking apples. Charlotte's apron and dress had become covered in berry juice one day while picking, and Mr Collins teased her that there had been more juice around her mouth than on her clothing, a contention she vehemently denied.

It was rare to see Mr Collins laughing or joking, and Charlotte was loathe for the conversation to end, this side of him to be hidden once more. It seemed the more she smiled at him and laughed at what he said, the more he opened up to her. It mattered not to him that his wife was laughing at his tales of mishaps and silliness, of embarrassing situations from his time at Oxford, which, under any other circumstance, would have mortified him. What mattered to him most was that she was laughing and smiling at him, at what he said to her.

He never knew the pleasure of such things until that moment, and he began to exaggerate and make himself seem sillier in order to provoke her to laugh harder still. He found that he enjoyed the sound of it, the way she closed her eyes, threw back her head, and placed her hand on her breast. He admitted to himself that he liked exceedingly to hear her laugh. *No,* he corrected himself, *I love to hear her laugh.*

That night Charlotte did something she had never done before: she fell asleep with Mr Collins holding her in his arms, and she had to admit that it was a very comforting sleep indeed.

* * *

Charlotte woke slowly in the morning, dozing back to sleep repeatedly, and noticing the nausea was still present but lessened. She was confident that it would pass in a few days, snuggled down into her pillow more, and drifted off to sleep again.

182

She did not see that Mr Collins was seated in a chair by the bed watching her. He had risen early, worked in his book room for an hour or two, and then returned to their room to keep watch over his poorly wife.

He had contented himself for a while to watch her steady breathing, but had grown restless with nothing to do, so picked up a book which Charlotte had left on the windowpane. He read the cover and flipped it open to where Charlotte had placed a ribbon to mark where she had stopped, and began to read. The story did not engage him at first, but interest grew and became fascination as he turned page after page, devouring each one. His eyes grew wider and wider; his face flushed with colour at the scene described by the writer. He was shocked, appalled, intrigued, and hungry for more all at the same time. And he kept reading, glad that Charlotte remained sleeping. He had never in all his years read a novel before, and this one confirmed all his fears - that they excited the emotions and were full of loose morals - but he found it was inexplicably captivating. He squirmed as the feeling swept over him that he was reading someone's diary, and then shook himself to recall it was merely the epistolary form of the novel.

He took out his handkerchief and wiped his forehead, surprised to discover that he was perspiring. Was this what interested his wife? Did she crave such wild and passionate encounters? Was she, in fact, searching within a novel for the love and romance that was lacking in their marriage? The question brought him back to reality with a snap. He closed the book, replaced it where he had found it, and watched his wife sleep as he considered what he had read.

Charlotte began to stir again, and Mr Collins went to her side of the bed as she opened her eyes. "Good morning, my love. Did you sleep well?"

"Yes, I did, thank you, very well."

"I am exceedingly pleased to hear it. Would you like me to ring for the water?"

"No, not yet, William. I just want to rest here a while; it is so warm in the bed." Mr Collins shifted uncomfortably, connecting what she had just said to something that he had read a moment before in her novel, and turned away to face the window.

Charlotte sat upon the edge of the bed and beckoned Mr Collins to sit beside her. He did as he was bid, putting his arm around her shoulders and she rested her head against him.

"William, I wonder. Do you think Mrs Thomas be offended if we came home early this evening? I do not wish to stay late out of doors."

"Nonsense, my dear. Who could object when they are aware that you have been ill? We shall return home the very instant you inform me of your desire to do so."

"Thank you, William. I knew you would understand." She reached up and kissed his mouth.

He was a little surprised at first to receive a morning kiss, but soon he was hungrily responding to her, and they parted only to catch their breath.

"I do apologise, my dear Charlotte," he panted. "I... Forgive me." He rose and stood at the end of the bed. His was heart racing and thumping against his chest.

"I assure you, William, you have no need to apologise to me in such a way." She rose and joined him where he stood. "In fact, my dear, I rather enjoyed being kissed like that."

He studied her face, reading the same feelings that were flooding him. "I cannot. You are unwell." He looked away.

"Not so unwell."

That was all the encouragement he needed. He pulled her to him and claimed her mouth with his own, his teeth nipping at her bottom lip, his tongue probing her mouth, as he had just read in the novel. She responded hungrily to his ministrations, sighing with pleasure. He ran his hands around her waist, and on down to her hips, feeling her nakedness beneath her nightgown, and as he led her to the bed, he owned, *Perhaps there is some benefit from reading novels after all!*

* * *

The dinner party at the Thomas's home was not such an arduous event for Charlotte after all. Every attention was paid to her, every assurance of her comfort seen to. Mr Abbot made a fuss thinking she was too close to the fire, and Mr Collins countered Mr Abbot with a fuss of his own, thinking she was too far from the fire. This produced a fit of giggles in Charlotte, which resulted in hiccoughs.

The resulting tide of advice as to the cure of hiccoughs ended with all the women present joining her in having a fit of the giggles. All the men were smirking and making up even more ridiculous but ingenious ways of curing Charlotte of the hiccoughs, as to ensure that not only did they not go away, but that all the ladies were left crying with laughter.

The only uncomfortable part of the evening for Charlotte was that she felt that Colonel Fitzwilliam's eyes on her constantly. Every time she looked in his direction, he seemed to have his eyes fixed firmly on her. It began to make her feel self-conscious, and she wished for a way of escape.

Colonel Fitzwilliam stood next to the card table, feigning interest. His real object was to observe Charlotte, who was in conversation with Mrs Abbot and Miss Thomas. He wished for a moment alone with her. He had contrived ideas all evening as to how they could be alone for a minute or two, but it was to no avail. The closest he would get to her that evening was with his eyes alone. He willed her to look up at him.

Charlotte listened to Louisa's plans for the wedding with as much attention as she could muster, considering all her senses could feel the Colonel's eyes on her at every moment. Mrs Brown laughed at the card table. Charlotte involuntarily looked up in her direction, and Colonel Fitzwilliam caught her eye. He winked; she blushed; and it took all of her power to resist running from the room. She would not draw attention to herself and her foolishness in such a way.

The longer she avoided expressing her regret to the Colonel and begging to return simply to being friends, the more difficult the situation and the harder it was to maintain her countenance in his presence.

She shook her head to rid her mind of his image and inadvertently looked in the Colonel's direction again. He grinned at her, noticing her discomfort. She knew, there and then, that no matter what, she must seek him out tomorrow and stop this charade before more things beyond her pride were damaged. She silently wished Mr Collins would stop playing cards and come to her side so she might express a wish to return home.

Her wish, fortunately, was granted a half an hour later when Mrs Brown stifled a yawn behind her fan and declared it was high time she departed. Charlotte was took advantage of the opening and expressed her desire to do the same. She found Mr Collins was immediately by her side, attending to her every need, and leaving no opening whatsoever for Colonel Fitzwilliam to manoeuvre himself to her side. This did not last long, for as propriety demanded, she had to bid adieu to each of her friends. Colonel Fitzwilliam took her hand and kissed it, his eyes conveying too much passion for her comfort and his desire to see her in the morning.

Chapter Twenty-six

The next morning, feeling much recovered, Charlotte was up and out of bed before Mr Collins. She washed and dressed with as little noise as was possible and made her way down the stairs to don her pelisse, as there had been a hard frost the night before. She drew on her gloves as she walked to the door, remembering that they had been no impediment to the Colonel before. She determined to be strong with him; this had to stop today.

She walked out of the door and to the gate. It took all of her strength to behave as if she were merely enjoying a sunny morning and not heading off to a rendezvous. She deliberately stopped to look at some red berries in the hedgerow. It was something she normally would do; she loved how things looked when covered in a hoarfrost and was fearful that someone might be observing her. She wanted to be as natural-looking as possible.

Charlotte continued on her way, forcing herself to breathe deeply and to calm the butterflies that had already started their dance in her stomach at the thought of seeing the Colonel. She wondered why he had such an effect on her, why she could not be mistress of her own feelings.

She rounded the bend in the lane and walked straight past the gates to Rosings. She knew he would not be waiting there for her. Instinct told her that he was at the clearing and that he had been there for some time.

She was right. She walked along the path, much faster now as she could not be seen. She stopped upon seeing him in the clearing. He was pacing back and forth, obviously in desperation of seeing her. Despite fighting against the desire that was rising within her upon watching him there, the sight of him pleased her. There was a certain thrill in knowing that he was secretly sharing those feelings and that excitement was difficult to subdue. Charlotte stepped forward along the path and into the clearing.

187

Colonel Fitzwilliam had not seen her at first as he continued to pace, his mind in turmoil, but the sound of her rustling skirts soon caught his attention, and he swung round to face her.

Within seconds, he had crossed the space between them, taken hold of her hands and kissed them through her gloves. "Oh, my dear Charlotte, I am so glad you have come," he said, deep relief filling his voice.

"I felt I ought to." She slipped her hands from his. "We need to talk."

"There will be plenty of opportunities to talk. I cannot stay long. I am engaged to ride into town on an errand for my aunt this morning, but I had to see you." He took hold of her hands again, and this time she did not pull away. She did not wish to force a fight; she needed to deal with him gently. "You seem well again, Charlotte. Are you?" he asked.

"Yes, much recovered, thank you. Colonel, I..."

He hushed her by placing a finger on her lips. Despite his wearing gloves, she felt the heat from his finger on her lips; she could barely breathe. "Why can you not call me Richard when we are alone?"

Her breath caught in her throat. This was not the way she had planned this meeting. "I cannot. It would not be right."

"Right?" He let out an almost hysterical laugh. "Right? Charlotte you know this feels right, all of this. Despite its being wrong, it is perfectly right." He fought to control his breathing as he stepped even closer to her, their bodies mere inches apart. "I cannot rest. I cannot think. Everything I do contains you." She began to speak in protest. "No, do not say a thing. I know you feel the same way."

Charlotte forced herself to take a step backwards, widening the gap between their bodies, her hands still firmly grasped in his.

"I am married," was all she managed to say to him.

"Yes, and to a man who does not deserve you."

"Who are you to say whether he deserves me or not?" she demanded, outrage rising within her at this insult to her husband.

The irony hit her just as quickly. She was affronted at the Colonel's insult to her husband, yet here she was, intimately close to another man. Was not her own insult to her husband the greater of the two?

"Oh, come now," he placated, "let us not quarrel. Of course this is difficult for you. I assure you, my feelings are sincere and genuine. My heart is yours, Charlotte." He looked deeply into her eyes, and she felt her resolve slipping away, her body frozen in place.

"Colonel, I..."

"Do not deny it, Charlotte!" He stepped closer until their clothing was touching. "Can you deny feeling my heart beating? Can you deny your heart is pounding within your own breast? Can you deny wanting me to do this..." He bent his head down towards her and brushed her lips lightly with his.

Her breath caught in her throat; he heard it. "You see, cannot deny it. And this?" This time he kissed her gently.

She could not breathe. The world was spinning. All her being was centred on her lips and the bolts of lightning his produced within her.

"And this..." He kissed her more firmly, his tongue parting her lips, demanding entrance to her mouth.

To her surprise, she returned his kisses with equal desire and passion. She had begun to learn of late the passion that kisses could arouse, but the Colonel's kisses were something more. They contained a fire that she had never known, a fire that was threatening to burn its way completely through her body.

Their lips separated slightly so they could breathe deeply of the frosty air. Their breathing was hard and ragged; their pulses were racing. Charlotte wrapped her arms around the Colonel's body, and he pulled her tightly against him. She let out a strangled sob as an even more intense bolt of lightning ran through her at the feel of his hard, muscular body against hers.

He continued to kiss her, wanting to devour her entirely, but restricting himself, with considerable effort, to her mouth. He was emboldened by the little purring noises she made as he probed her mouth with his tongue. He broke his mouth away from hers and nibbled her ear, knocking her bonnet askew, and kissed down her neck, his teeth nipping gently at the skin.

Charlotte thought she would faint from the exquisite feelings with which he was tormenting her. She panted out his name, which resulted in his mouth crashing upon hers again, claiming it completely.

189

He finally found the strength to tear his lips from her and rested his forehead against hers. Their breathing loud and ragged still, as their pulses slowed and they struggled to calm themselves. He squeezed her against his body, and she felt the power of his arousal. She looked at him wide-eyed.

He smiled down at her and gently kissed her swollen lips. "Do not worry, Charlotte. This is neither the time nor place for that." He smirked suggestively. She started with the sudden realisation of what he had just suggested.

"I have to leave, my darling. I will be gone for a week." He kissed her forehead. "But do not worry. I shall return to you."

He kissed her one more time before turning to leave her. "Oh, I spoke with my aunt. She was furious to hear on Sunday the reading of the banns of Mr Simmons and Miss Thomas' wedding. Regardless of her fury, she has been *persuaded*, shall we say, not to interfere in the marriage plans of our friends." He smiled at her, and she was left standing in the clearing as he rushed off towards Rosings.

Charlotte heard what he said, but it did not register. Her mind was far more disagreeably engaged.

A wave of emotion flooded her. "Oh God forgive me! What have I done?" she cried, the tears flowing down her cheeks. "What a terrible woman I am!"

She gave in to the sobs and allowed her guilt to wash over and condemn her. *I had every intention of ending it this morning, and yet I gave in. I gave myself up to him completely. I must never see him again!*

* * *

Charlotte did not return home immediately, but remained in the clearing for some time mentally berating herself over her foolishness. *I should have never come in the first place,* she thought. *He would have realised sooner or later. He is not a stupid man; he would know what my absence meant. Now, oh, now what must he think? He must be congratulating himself on an easy conquest. He must think that I am his, that I will be his mistress now. Oh, what am I to do? I am a foolish, foolish girl!*

190

Charlotte walked about in the woods until her nerves were calmed and her stomach reminded her loudly that it must be time for breakfast. She reluctantly and slowly made her way back to the parsonage. Praying fervently that her eyes were not too puffy from crying and that Mr Collins would not suspect anything of what had passed that morning. She determined never to see the Colonel again, apart from when there was no chance of being alone with him. She knew she would have to find new places to walk in the mornings, but that was a small price to pay if only she could extricate herself from an increasingly complicated situation.

* * *

Upon her arrival home, she found Mr Collins pacing the hall in worry.

"Oh, my dear Charlotte, there you are," he said with great relief and helped her off with her pelisse.

"I was only walking."

"Yes, I thought perhaps you were, but I have had prepared a hearty breakfast to promote your health, and when you did not return at your usual time, well, I began to worry." He looked bashful and wrung his hands, his concern genuine.

She removed her gloves and squeezed his hands. "Well, I am here now. Shall we eat?"

Mr Collins led the way into the dining room, and Charlotte saw prepared on the table bacon, eggs, sausages, and all the things Mr Collins would call *hearty* and which, at that present time, turned her stomach. She smiled weakly at him, thanked him for his consideration, and began to load her plate with food. She knew she would have to eat more than she desired to satisfy him, but felt it a small price to pay to please the man she had so recently injured through her wanton behaviour with another man. She found it hard to swallow, the lump in her throat and the tears welling in her eyes preventing her. She drank copious amounts of coffee to wash it all down. Mr Collins seemed contented to see her eat well and began to eat with his usual keen enjoyment.

He asked her if she had any plans for the day, and when she replied that she had not, he suggested a drive out in the gig.

191

"Perhaps we might visit Westerham? You might show me Mr Abbot's shop."

She knew that he was apologising in his own way for the trouble over her visit to the said shop and for telling Lady Catherine too. It was then she remembered that she had bought him some new shoes and had hidden them away in the chest in the bedroom. Thankful for an excuse to stop eating the breakfast she did not want, she rushed out of the room to fetch the shoes.

To say that Mr Collins was pleased with the gift would be an understatement; he was overjoyed with the shoes. He declared his intention to wear them to perform the wedding ceremony and to keep them as his best dress shoes.

This brought another thing to Charlotte's mind: the idea of him dressing less like a clergyman when they went out to dinner. She delicately put it to him that he might like to have a suit tailor-made for such events. He was, needless to say, stunned at such a suggestion and asked her if she was ashamed of his attire or of his profession.

She assured him that was not the case. "But perhaps you are not overly comfortable in your cleric's clothes in all situations?"

"Whatever do you mean?" her husband asked, looking puzzled.

"Only that I wondered if you found your attire cumbersome?"

He thought a moment or two and then nodded. "Yes, on occasion I have thought that, but I do feel it important that people should know who I am."

"Mr Collins, I think there can be no doubt of that! And if a stranger should come into our midst, he would be informed in no time at all of your being the clergyman in these parts." She smiled at him and drank more coffee to rid her mouth of the taste of bacon.

"Yes, I see your point, I do indeed. I have on occasion, if I might confess," he said looking self-conscious, "fancied myself in a pair of trousers. They look particularly comfortable indeed, much more so than breeches."

"Yes, they do indeed," she concurred. "Perhaps you might try some when we are in Westerham." He seemed to contemplate the idea. "Just to see how they feel," she added.

"Yes, I see no harm in trying a pair of trousers, just to see how they feel." He nodded and turned his attention back to his breakfast.

Charlotte felt quite pleased with herself, and finished her cup of coffee before returning to their room to freshen up before their trip to town.

* * *

The air was still chilly, but as the sun rose in the sky, it warmed up and turned into a pleasant day. Charlotte always loved riding along in the gig when it was not wet or too cold. The view from its elevated position was unimpeded, excepting, of course the rear view of the horse. They passed through Hunsford. She waved at her acquaintance; Mr Collins sat up proudly as he drove his wife through town.

As the gig passed through the other side of town, they had an excellent view of Oak Wood Farm and Mr Simmons' land. Charlotte was happy to think that Louisa would soon be mistress of it all.

The road into Westerham was unremarkable, passing through farmland on either side. As they came to a crossroads, they found themselves waylaid by a flock of sheep being herded from one field to another. Charlotte laughed aloud to see themselves surrounded by a sea of sheep and even Mr Collins found the situation amusing. He was slowly learning to see the amusing things in life. Eventually, they were free to continue their journey onward to Westerham. Mr Collins chattered away to Charlotte about his parishioners and his ideas for the summer fête, and she was content to listen to him.

She realised she was content once again with Mr Collins; there had indeed been times when she was not. There had been times when he had upset her or insulted her, especially where Lady Catherine was concerned, but that all seemed to be in the past now. She had long forgiven him, and he seemed now to be trying to make amends. He was changing little by little it appeared. He seemed to be endeavouring to learn from his mistakes and to please her. All she had to do now was to remove herself from an extremely foolish situation and to begin to enjoy her life once again. She was determined not to allow thoughts of Colonel

Fitzwilliam to cloud her day out, and she pushed him aside in her mind and concentrated on what her husband was saying.

Charlotte thought Westerham a lovely place. She loved St. Mary's churchyard, and when she told Mr Collins about it, he expressed a desire to see it also. They walked slowly around the market square, and Charlotte pointed out to him the places she had visited with Louisa when she was there last. Mr Collins asked the whereabouts of Mr Abbot's shop, a place Charlotte was more than eager to show him. They walked slowly towards it, her arm through his, and he walked with his chin high, his hand upon hers.

Upon entering the shop, Mr Collins declared that he had never seen such a well-appointed place and that she had been quite correct in her praise of it. Mr Abbot Jr joined them, remembered Mrs Collins, who introduced him to her husband. They talked happily for some time about the shop, Mr Abbot Jr's parents, and of Hunsford, a subject close to Mr Collins' heart.

"I assume you have not come all the way to Westerham to tell me that my parents are in excellent health, so how can I help you today?" asked Mr Abbot Jr eagerly.

"Indeed we did not," chuckled Mr Collins, proceeding to inform the younger Mr Abbot what he wished to see.

Chapter Twenty-seven

M r Collins surprised Charlotte with a new turban to match the gown she intended to wear for Louisa's wedding. She was delighted; she had never had a hat like it. Mr Collins' chest puffed with pride as he insisted Mr Abbot Jr add feathers that curled backwards around the turban. It was elegant, and Charlotte knew it to be at the height of fashion. When presented with the total, Mr Collins was certain that Mr Abbot Jr either had miscalculated the price of the millinery or was giving him a discount. He was embarrassed to think it was the latter, so decided it was the former and was about to correct the man when he caught a glance at Charlotte out of the corner of his eye, who shook her head slightly. She informed him later that it had been a discount, that if he was displeased, he should take the matter up with Mr Abbot Sr.

Their next stop was the tailor's shop. Charlotte smiled with delight as Mr Collins tried on a pair of trousers which the tailor said ought to fit him. The pair was so long that Mr Collins had trouble walking, which amused Charlotte, but a little bit of folding and pinning by the tailor and Mr Collins was able to prance about in front of the mirror without mishap.

The transformation was astonishing. His legs no longer looked like spindles, the trousers giving them a better shape. Charlotte commented that she thought they also made him look taller. The tailor nodded in agreement and enquired as to whether they had a preference for a tailcoat. Charlotte beamed with excitement and suggested navy or maroon. Mr Collins was all in a whirl. He had never received such attention, and Charlotte's discerning eye as far as finances were concerned ensured that they did not overstretch their purse.

Next came waistcoats. Mr Collins felt uncomfortable with gold, so the tailor suggested brocade or stripes, both fashionable he said, and insisted on double-breasted. Mr Collins was finally kitted out with two of everything he would need, and Charlotte calmed his fears that he had spent too much on frivolities. She assured him that it would be pleasing to see him in a white shirt and cravat, and a tall hat. In his excitement, he declared his desire to wear one of the outfits for the rest of the day. They waited while the alterations were made there and then to one of the sets of clothing, while the other was to be ready later in the day. Charlotte was extremely pleased with this change in her husband and felt that it boded well for the future.

Mr Collins was self-conscious but well pleased with himself as he and his wife exited the tailor's establishment. Charlotte had to stifle a giggle to see the transformation. Mr Collins seemed to take on a new persona. Suddenly, Mr Collins the bumbling clergyman became Mr Collins the man-about-town, a man on whose arm she could be proud to be seen.

She smiled up at him, and he whispered, "How am I doing?"

"Very well indeed," she giggled to realise he was indeed playing the part, and doing it well. "I am quite proud of you, Mr Collins," she whispered back.

His eyes locked with hers, and Charlotte felt an unfamiliar sensation. Could she be falling in love with her husband? She was not frightened by the prospect. It made her feel happy. It made her strengthen her resolve, and she tightened her grip on his arm, an action which did not go unnoticed by Mr Collins.

They ate lunch in the same teashop Charlotte had visited with Louisa and then walked around St. Mary's and its churchyard, then around the market square. They peered in the shop windows as they slowly made their way back to the tailor's shop to collect the remainder of Mr Collins' purchase.

When it was time to return to Hunsford, Charlotte found that she was reluctant to leave.

"What is it, my dear?" Mr Collins asked as he helped the tailor's man to load up every available space in the gig.

"It is strange, but I feel that I do not wish to return home."

Mr Collins stopped what he was doing and came to her side. "That is strange indeed, my dear. Whatever can be the cause?"

"I do not know," she lied.

"I believe I can guess."

"Can you?" She looked at him, startled.

"Indeed I can. We have had such a pleasant day; you do not wish it to end." He took her hand and patted it. "But, my dear, we must return home. As a diversion, what if we were to return by another route? It would be a longer journey, I am afraid, but no one will know of our return, and we might spend the evening together in quiet and solitude."

She smiled at his consideration. "That sounds perfect, William."

He helped her into the gig, and they set off towards Hunsford, all the while Mr Collins hoping he remembered the way and that they would return to the parsonage before dark.

Fortunately for them, Mr Collins did indeed remember the way home, with the aid of the roadside markers, signposts, and help from Charlotte's excellent sense of direction. Once or twice, they did have to about-turn when they found they had stumbled upon the drive of a farm, and Charlotte laughed, while Mr Collins tried to control his anxiety.

It was twilight when they pulled into the little drive in front of the parsonage, and Charlotte was tired and grateful then to be home. Mrs Higgs, upon seeing Mr Collins in his new attire, was astonished, but smiled and paid him compliments enough to reassure him that he did, indeed, look well.

Mrs Higgs said there was a roast chicken keeping warm in the kitchen, and if they would like to wash and change, then she would set the table for their meal. Never had Charlotte felt so famished. She and Mr Collins quickly changed out of their now dusty clothes and went to the dining room. Mr Collins insisted that Mrs Higgs bring them a bottle of wine for their meal. Mrs Higgs did as she was bid, wondering what had caused such a change in Mr Collins; but as she returned later with their dessert, she saw the way in which he was gazing at Mrs Collins. "Why," realisation hitting her like a thunderbolt, "the master has fallen in love!"

* * *

The rest of the week was tranquil, and Charlotte was happy to see the new Mr Collins frequently. On Friday their peace and quiet was broken by the arrival of a large farm cart to the parsonage, accompanied by Mr Simmons on horseback.

Mr Simmons hallooed to them as they came out to greet him. "What a fine morning!" he declared, dismounting his horse. He shouted instructions to the men riding on the cart to unpack the whatever-it-was hidden under the canvas from the back of the cart and to take it inside.

He turned to Mr Collins. "Now, let me explain what I am about. Shall we go inside?"

They returned to the house, and Charlotte led Mr Simmons to the sitting room, where she and Mr Collins waiting with anticipation for an explanation.

"Mr and Mrs Collins, please do not think me impertinent, but I bring you a gift."

"A very large one, it seems." quipped Mr Collins.

"Yes, it is rather, but not too large for in here, I think. Now, let me explain."

"Please do," Charlotte encouraged, indicating that he should be seated.

"You may remember that this is not the first time that Louisa and I planned to be married." They nodded their remembrance, and he continued, "At our first engagement, I promised my dearest Louisa that I would buy her a new pianoforte as a wedding gift, and I intend to make good on that promise."

"That is very amiable, but pray, what has this to do with us?" asked Mr Collins, still none the wiser.

"When I married the first Mrs Simmons, God rest her soul, she brought to my home her old pianoforte. I observe that each time Louisa sees it, she looks distressed, so I mean to remove it and replace it with a new one." He sat back triumphantly, thinking his explanation more than adequate.

"Oh!" exclaimed Charlotte, realisation dawning on her. "You mean to give the late Mrs Simmons' pianoforte to me?"

Mr Collins sat with his mouth open in astonishment, and Charlotte stammered, "I... I do not know what to say, Mr Simmons. Such kindness! I thank you so very much indeed!"

Mr Simmons laughed at her at her delight, pleased to see the gift did not offend, and stood up again, waving off her thanks. "Well, Mrs Collins, the first thing you can do is to direct where you would like it placed."

198

Charlotte looked around her. The sitting room was the obvious choice for the pianoforte, and she realised, that being the case, there remained only one place to put the instrument - in place of the breakfast table. It was rarely used, and the table top folded down so as to be easily stowed away. She called Mrs Higgs and Jenny to help with the table's removal, just as the men brought the instrument in through the door. The pianoforte was not overly large, but large enough to take up one corner of the room and a part of a wall.

Mr Collins remained agog and astonished at Mr Simmons' generosity. Mr Simmons laughed heartily and clapped his friend on the back. Charlotte stepped up to her husband's side and squeezed his hand as they watched the pianoforte being carefully manoeuvred into place.

Once Mr Simmons' farmhands had left the parsonage to return the cart to Oak Wood Farm, Mr Collins found his voice, "Mr Simmons, really this is too much. Your generosity astounds me!"

Mr Simmons merely laughed his protestations off. "Sincerely, my friend, if your dear wife was not in need of the instrument I would have sent it to be scrapped. I know that Mrs Collins plays. and I have often heard Louisa lament the lack of a pianoforte here. Hence, I feel emboldened in presenting this to you."

"I confess it is the most generous gift I have ever received, and I am quite taken aback by it, Mr Simmons," joined Charlotte.

"I understand, truly I do, and I did hesitate in bringing it here. Then I realised you would both accept in the true spirit of Christian giving. I would not have liked to have seen it broken up for scrap, and I know you will make excellent use of it Mrs Collins."

"Indeed I will, will I not, Mr Collins?" She turned to her husband, eyes sparkling, "You have often wished we had a pianoforte here at the parsonage."

"Yes, you are quite right, Mrs Collins, I have certainly wished that on many occasions. I apologise for my initial incivility, Mr Simmons. I am quite beside myself!"

Mr Simmons clapped Mr Collins on the back once more and turned to the door. "Do not concern yourself. What are friends for?" He mounted his horse, tipped his hat and cried, "Adieu until tomorrow!" and trotted out of the gate.

Charlotte could barely contain her excitement. She touched Mr Collins' arm, smiled, and indicated they should go inside.

They stood beside the instrument for some time, admiring it. It certainly was an old pianoforte, but had been kept well, the wood in splendid condition.

"All that remains, my dear Charlotte, is for you to try it out," Mr Collins exclaimed with as much excitement as Charlotte herself felt.

She sat down on the stool, her back to the window, opened the lid, and stroked the keys in awe. She looked up at Mr Collins and saw that he was smiling down at her. He nodded encouragingly, and she placed her hands in the resting position and began to play. The instrument was still well tuned, and its timbre sounded delightful as its music filled the sitting room.

Mr Collins moved to sit in a chair facing Charlotte and closed his eyes, immersed in the sound of her playing. He had enjoyed listening to her play when they had first met, and from time to time, Lady Catherine asked her to play at Rosings, but he had always felt sad that he could not have provided her with her own instrument. She had told him that she did not mind in the least, but he sensed that, deep down, she longed for one. Now it seemed that Providence had rewarded them both, and Mr Simmons' gift was a blessing indeed. Mr Collins was not too proud to be above accepting such gifts. As a clergyman, he was often in receipt of a gift or two, although this was far beyond any gift he had heretofore received. He was content and immensely grateful to Mr Simmons' consideration. The sound of music would always now fill the air in the Collins' household, and Mr Collins could not have been more pleased.

When Charlotte finished playing the piece, she rose and went to stand next to her husband, her joy evident in her face.

"My dear, that was beautiful," Mr Collins praised her, his voice choked. "I own that I have missed hearing you play as you did for me in Hertfordshire before we were married. Now I hope to have the pleasure of hearing you play daily."

"Yes, William, it is a beautiful instrument. We are so blessed to have such a friend as Mr Simmons. I had hoped, that one day we would be in a position to purchase one for ourselves. That, I know, would have taken years to accomplish. I find myself moved to tears over such kindness." She wiped her eyes, and Mr

Collins stood up to comfort her. "I do apologize. I am being overly emotional."

"Not at all. I confess myself to be rather emotional about today's events also." Together they gazed at the pianoforte, which now graced their home, both reluctant to leave its presence.

"I really must finish my letter writing," Mr Collins declared, breaking the instrument's spell, and left to go to his book room, leaving the door ajar so he could hear in case Charlotte continued to play.

Charlotte herself had letters to write. That morning letters had arrived, one from her mother, which contained a missive from Maria, and one from Lizzy; and she still had to finish writing a letter to Jane at Netherfield. Nevertheless, her mind was not on letter writing; she was trying to remember where she had put all her sheet music when she had come to Kent upon her marriage. She suspected that they would be in the attic in one of her travelling chests and went in search of Mrs Higgs for the key to the attic door.

Together, mistress and housekeeper braved the cold attic in search of the sheet music, which they happily did find in one of the chests. Mrs Higgs had taken the liberty of placing all the things Charlotte could not find a home for into the oldest chest. It was one that she believed would not see much travelling again, but would serve as an excellent place in which to store things.

Having retrieved the sheet music, the two women hastily retreated downstairs to the warmth of the house, and Charlotte went directly to the pianoforte. She had not played much in months, merely a piece or two at Rosings and once or twice in Hertfordshire when they had visited, which resulted in her fingers being a little stiff and her playing a touch stilted. It did not take long before her hands seemed to remember their skill and their command of the instrument returned, Charlotte all the while lost in the pleasure of playing once again.

She reluctantly stopped playing when lunch was served, and joined Mr Collins in the dining room to eat their repast, both of them speaking in raptures about the new addition to their home.

* * *

Charlotte diligently settled down to her letter writing after lunch, but all she could write about was the pianoforte. She endeavoured to be interested in what she was doing and to respond correctly to her letters, but she feared she did not do them justice at all. One thing did please her and gave her pause to think of another subject: Lizzy and Mr Darcy had invited her and Mr Collins to visit in the summer. Apparently, Colonel Fitzwilliam had written to Mr Darcy explaining the goings-on at Rosings of late, and Mr Darcy felt that his inviting them to Pemberley would be seen as his seal of approval. Lizzy mentioned something about their being cousins-in-law now, but Charlotte was certain the invitation was more to do with repairing the injury done to her by Lady Catherine than familial ties. Regardless of the impetus, she was more than happy to accept such an invitation. She knew Mr Collins would agree wholeheartedly and decided to accept and inform him later at dinner.

Her mother's letter was full of Meryton gossip and Maria's full of Mr Lang, her intended. Jane's letter was the one with all the true information about Meryton and the people therein. Jane could always be counted on to keep her apprised of everything going on *back home*. Charlotte enjoyed most of the news, laughed aloud at some passages, and was intrigued to read that Mary Bennet was being courted by a young man in Meryton. Her hand flew to her mouth in astonishment as she read this. Mary had always been a severe young girl, and Charlotte was pleased to find that she was to have *her own happy ending,* as Louisa would call it.

* * *

Mr Collins called Charlotte to come into their bedroom an hour before their guests were to arrive. He was standing in his undergarments and staring at one of his newly acquired suits laid out on the bed.

"What is it, dear?" she asked upon seeing him thus.

"I am anxious, Charlotte, of wearing clothing with which I am not accustomed to wearing this evening," he confessed.

"You will be amongst friends, William. Surely, you do not fear being ridiculed?"

Mr Collins said nothing, but his face confirmed her query.

"You will have to take the plunge at some time, my dear, and Mr Simmons and Louisa are our friends. Surely, you would feel more comfortable debuting your new attire in their presence than in a large party?"

His alarm showed plainly on his face.

He is truly frightened, poor man, she thought. "Perhaps you might dress in the new clothing, and see how you feel upon seeing yourself in the looking glass? You felt confidence when we were in Westerham, and I am certain you shall feel the same again," she said reassuringly.

"You are undoubtedly right, Charlotte my dear." He paused and then admitted something that had been on his mind for a while. "I know I have been a ridiculous man all my life." She raised her eyebrows in surprise at his confession. "But I am no longer that man. I have changed, Charlotte, indeed I have." He looked earnestly at her.

She smiled, stepped forward, and embraced him.

He pulled away from her slightly so he could look her in the eye. "You believe me, Charlotte, when I say I want to be a better man than the one you married?"

Charlotte could not believe her ears. What miracle had taken place to bring about this change? She smiled and encouraged him to dress as she turned to leave the room.

As she closed the door behind her, he said, "I shall endeavour to deserve you, my dearest wife."

* * *

When Louisa and Mr Simmons arrived for dinner, Charlotte discovered that Mr Simmons had not informed Louisa that the pianoforte from his home was now happily settled at the parsonage. Louisa was overcome by surprise and joy. She declared she could not think of a better recipient of the instrument than Charlotte, and soon they were playing duets, the air at the parsonage filling with the unaccustomed sounds of song and laughter. The gentlemen sat on the sofa, watching their ladies and exchanging small talk, smiling as Charlotte and Louisa paraded through their repertoire of duets, laughing at each mistake.

Once more Mr Collins was struck by how lovely his wife was, how she warmed his heart with her smile and laughter, and he lamented his own foolishness and blindness. How had he never seen this before? His heart swelled with pride at her talent on the pianoforte, but he did not know how to show it. He decided he would simply tell her what he thought in private. He was also pleased that neither Mr Simmons nor Louisa seemed to have noticed his new apparel, and he relaxed in the knowledge that he did not, in fact, look ridiculous, relaxation contributed to by the comfort of the trousers. *Why had I resisted for so long?*

Charlotte's friendship with Louisa grew with each meeting, and they were fast becoming like sisters.

Upon finishing the last of their duets, Charlotte hugged her friend and said, "Just think, Louisa, in one and a-half weeks, you shall be married!"

"My goodness, yes! Oh, dear, now I am all nerves!" the bride-to-be tittered behind her hand.

"Has Mr Simmons indicated if you will have a wedding journey?"

"Yes, we will, but we shall not go until after the sowing at the farm has taken place."

"That is wise. It would be best for him to supervise the planting," agreed Charlotte.

"Oh, yes. And then we intend to travel to Prittlewell, where George's mother was from, for a fortnight."

"How lovely! I confess that I have never heard of Prittlewell. Is it lovely there?" Charlotte asked as Mrs Higgs arrived to announce that dinner was ready.

"I have no idea," replied Louisa, "but George says so. Of course, he would say that, it is his mother's home after all. He tells me that it is a coastal village approximately forty miles to the east of London."

"Only forty miles? That is not too large a distance to travel. You will break your journey in London?" Charlotte asked, rising to signal the gentlemen to escort the ladies to dinner.

"George says we shall try to make it to Ilford. I fear he is being optimistic," said Louisa indulgently, joining her hostess.

* * *

204

After dinner, the little party took a walk in the lanes beside Rosings. The evening was warmer than usual, as the day had been fair.

As Charlotte looked to the horizon, she saw the clouds moving in. "I think it will rain tomorrow."

"Oh, yes, so we shall all be wet and shivering in church tomorrow," Louisa said with a resigned laugh.

The couples walked as far as the crossroads, then turned back on themselves. When Mr Simmons told them all about Prittlewell and what it was like there, Charlotte became quite envious of their wedding journey. She had not had one, but travelled almost immediately into Kent upon her marriage to Mr Collins. She desired now to visit the sea. Mr Simmons continued by telling them stories of whelk hunting when he was a child, greatly amusing them with his childhood antics.

"I should so like to see the sea," Charlotte said wistfully.

"You have never seen it?" enquired Mr Simmons.

"No, I have not. I grew up in landlocked Hertfordshire," she replied. "I have seen many rivers, including the Thames, but never the sea."

Mr Collins squeezed her hand on his arm. "Then we must remedy that, my dear, if we have time this year." He turned his attention to Louisa. "Did my wife tell you, Miss Thomas, that we are bound for Derbyshire this summer?"

"Oh, no, she did not!"

"Aye, my cousin Elizabeth made a fortunate alliance with Lady Catherine de Bourgh's nephew Mr Darcy, who has a great estate in Derbyshire," he told her proudly. "We have been invited by Cousin Elizabeth, who, incidentally, is one of Charlotte's oldest friends, to stay with them for a while in the summer. I own I am quite looking forward to seeing his estate, the Peaks, and the county of Derbyshire."

Charlotte smiled up at her husband as they continued walking towards the parsonage, discussing the places they had all visited and would wish to visit in England. When they finally arrived at the house, it had begun to turn chilly. They were glad to get inside, where Jenny was lighting a fire in the sitting room.

Once their guests had departed that night, Charlotte asked Mr Collins if he had been in earnest about taking her to see the sea. He replied that he had, and together they talked about a route they could take home from Derbyshire at the end of the summer, one that would take them to the sea.

Chapter Twenty-eight

C harlotte was correct; it did rain the next day. It began to rain in the early hours of the morning and developed into a storm by dawn, which woke the Collinses early. Charlotte hated being awoken early, as it put her in an ill humour. Mr Collins insisted that they stay in bed and listen to the rain on the windowpane, and within half an hour, Charlotte had drifted back to sleep.

When she did wake again, Mr Collins was already up, dressed, and was standing next to her side of the bed proudly holding a tray with two cups of tea upon it.

She beamed at her husband and sat up to receive her cup, which was more welcome than usual as she felt her nausea return.

"You see, my dear? I am in earnest about being a better man."

She sipped some of her tea, which felt good in her unsettled stomach. "Oh that is a good cup of tea, William. Thank you."

He sat on the end of the bed facing her, and for the first time in their life together, she saw love reflected in his eyes. She, in truth, had never expected to see such a thing in Mr Collins' eyes, but there it was, as plain as day. She blushed under his scrutiny, and he smiled tenderly at her reaction.

* * *

Louisa's prediction that they would all shiver in church that morning was also accurate. Mr Collins did his best to speed along the service to allow everyone to get home and warm quickly. As soon as the final prayers were said and Mr Collins made his way to the door to shake hands with his congregants, the churchyard was flooded with a sea of umbrellas and everyone scattered in their various directions, rushing to get out of the cold and rain.

Charlotte and Mr Collins practically ran home and, when they arrived, they leant against each other in the hallway, laughing at their semi-drowned condition. Mrs Higgs ordered Jenny to get the hot water ready and insisted that Charlotte and Mr Collins take hot baths before they caught their deaths of cold.

Once bathed and wrapped up in warm clothing, Mr and Mrs Collins sat beside the fire in the living room drinking hot chocolate, and Mr Collins expressed his reluctance to perform evensong that night.

"Do you think anyone would notice if you were not there?" she asked boldly, a smirk playing at her lips.

"I would be surprised if anyone else were there to notice my absence."

She chuckled softly at the thought of that.

"You may laugh at that, Mrs Collins, for you may stay at home by the fire!" he retorted.

"Yes, *Mr Collins*," she mocked his seriousness. "How tiresome that will be for me. I do not know how I shall endure it."

Mr Collins was determined to join in the fun, solemnly pronouncing, "I do believe that the wife of a clergyman ought to accompany him to church whenever he performs his duty therein."

"Hmm..." she replied pretending to contemplate his words. "Even when there is a risk of drowning?"

He laughed aloud, "Especially when there is a risk of drowning, Mrs Collins. After all, who will read the last rites to her otherwise?"

Now it was her turn to laugh. "So your purpose in encouraging me to accompany you this evening is to lead me into peril, in the hope of seeing me off?" she affected to be affronted.

"That was surely not my intention," he replied, enjoying himself immensely.

"But now that the thought occurs to you?" she invited?

Mr Collins could not reply as he was laughing too hard at their banter. *When did it become so easy and fun to be with her?* he asked himself. The time it took him to control his laughter gave him ample time to think of a reply, and he stared into her eyes, reaching out his hand to her.

She took it; he kissed hers, finally replying earnestly, "If you were in peril, I would do everything in my power to save you, Charlotte."

He leant towards her and began to kiss her, she responded with equal feeling, and he nodded towards the door. She cast down her eyes, nodded, took his hand in hers, and led him upstairs to their room, where they spent the remainder of the afternoon.

* * *

Despite having rushed to church the previous evening under the protection of an umbrella and having driven the gig to Rosings on the following morning, Mr Collins returned that lunchtime full of cold and sneezing. He was immediately dispatched to bed and was cosseted by Charlotte and fussed about by Mrs Higgs, who were both fearful that the whole household might become infected from his violent sneezes, coughs, and splutters. The medicine chest was fetched, and Mr Collins was dosed up with as many remedies as were available.

On the Tuesday morning, they realised all their precautions had been for naught when Charlotte awoke with a thick head, sore throat, and beginning to sneeze.

It felt luxurious to stay in bed, but she disliked the feeling of being unwell. Her head was thumping, and she slept a lot. She was vaguely aware of Mrs Higgs's presence and her ministrations to the sick couple.

Wednesday morning, despite still sniffling and having a terribly runny nose, Mr Collins was able to get out of bed. Charlotte stayed warm in bed, indulging her cold, when a sudden thought occurred to her: Colonel Fitzwilliam would be back from his errands by now. It was almost worth having a cold in order to not have to meet him. She was not ignorant of the attraction between them and she freely admitted to herself that part of her wanted to be enfolded in his arms again and feel his hot mouth against hers kissing her, but the stark reality was that she was another man's wife. There could be no liaison between them without scandal. She would have to leave her home and all her family and friends to be with him.

Colonel Fitzwilliam also would suffer from such impropriety. She imagined that there would be none amongst his acquaintance who would associate with him if he were to elope with a married woman. She was convinced that he would not be so foolhardy. So what was his intention in kissing her? Did he wish to make her

209

his mistress? Did he think that she was so miserable in her life and marriage that she would sink so low as to accept being his mistress?

Moreover, what of Mr Collins? What was he expected to do? Would he be forced to stand by and raise any bastards that came along as his own offspring? No, Charlotte would never accept that. She was not a proud woman, but she would never betray her husband or her own good name for a fleeting moment of passion.

She reminded herself of her impotence when he touched her, when he kissed her. She would have to be strong in refusing the Colonel's advances or he would be able to take what he wanted with remarkably little resistance from her. The very thought made her groan and sink further under the covers, pulling them over her head. She prayed for a way out.

* * *

On Saturday, Charlotte was able to move about the house, but she still laboured under a lethargy that had her dosing off frequently and had a terribly sore, red nose from continually blowing it. Mr Collins was almost back to his normal self, which boded well that she would not be suffering the cold for much longer.

Mr Collins attended church alone on Sunday morning and returned with many messages from the parishioners wishing her a speedy recovery.

Mr Collins was glad to see she was up and in the sitting room when he returned from church.

"Are you feeling recovered, my dear?" he asked solicitously.

"Somewhat, yes. Thank you for asking. How was the church service this morning, William?"

"You would be astounded to discover how many well-wishers you have, Charlotte my dear. Indeed, had I not insisted that you need rest, I believe they would have all followed me home this morning," he chuckled, secretly proud of his wife's popularity.

She invited him to sit with her and tell her all about the service, which, of course, he was more than willing to do. As he talked, she moved closer to him on the sofa, and he put his arm around her. This was another new element to their relationship, one that was surprisingly easy to adopt. She rested her head

210

against his chest and remained silent as he spoke, listening to his heart beating. When he had finished, they remained as they were, silently enjoying this new intimacy.

Charlotte knew that they would be happy, that she could look forward to a successful marriage. She knew William was working hard at removing the ridiculousness from his character and at being a better man, that it was to please her. She had been fortunate in her husband. There was no grand passion, but there was a sort of love forming, a love which would grow and deepen over time, to become something strong and steadfast. She began to dose off to sleep in his arms, not for the first time wishing that her troubles would all disappear.

Mr Collins reluctantly left Charlotte to go to church that evening, but she reassured him that she was content to sit and read on the sofa and that she felt much better.

Upon his return, he was pleased to see that her appetite was returning, and she ate enough to satisfy him that she was truly on the mend. "I am glad you are recovered, my dear. I should not wish you to miss the wedding on Wednesday."

Throughout her illness, Charlotte had forgotten about the wedding. "Oh, yes! I utterly forgot. I shall endeavour to sit in the garden tomorrow, bask in the sun and take the air."

"Then I will join you, if you wish," offered Mr Collins.

"Of course, William," she replied fondly, and they continued to dine, talking over what they might do on the days before the wedding.

* * *

As Charlotte recovered, Mr Collins encouraged her to take advantage of the sun and to walk around the garden. Under any other circumstance, this would have bored her senseless, but she found herself weak after being in bed for almost a sennight and was relieved finally to be able to exercise her limbs. Together they walked up and down the vegetable garden and around the flowerbeds. The day of the wedding was looming, and Charlotte wanted to be strong enough to be able to stand for the service without becoming weak or faint, thereby drawing attention to herself.

Mr Collins had recovered quickly from the cold and, apart from having a chapped nose, showed no signs that he had been ill. Charlotte was fortunate in that she did not bear an unsightly chapped nose for long, but the weakness in her legs frustrated her. She was fond of walking and wished to resume her walks along the lanes and through Rosings Park, alone if that were possible. She leaned heavily on Mr Collins' arm and was grateful for his assistance.

After lunch, Charlotte slept while Mr Collins set to work in his book room, working on the sermon notes Lady Catherine had dictated to him that morning at Rosings. No matter how many times he read and reread his notes, there still remained a tone in them of which he did not approve. He had studied at Oxford, to become a clergyman; she had not. He had learnt under some of the best scholars in the land; she had not. Yet he was expected to take and agree with her interpretation of the Holy Scriptures. In this instance, he could not. In this instance, the meaning of the text was clear to him. He searched his reference books on the subject, cross-referenced, and prayed. He still came to the same conclusion. The text he wished to use, that he was inspired to use by Mr Simmons' generosity in giving them the pianoforte, stated the same thing in all his books that it was honourable and proper to give of oneself, of one's worldly goods, time, and skills as needed.

He straightened up in his chair. "No matter how arduous, how inconvenient, we ought to serve and help one another," he said to himself. "How on earth do I write this sermon about the right attitude to our fellow man without disregarding Lady Catherine? How do I stay true to the text, encourage my congregants to give freely of themselves, and not make Her Ladyship feel I am pointing a finger at her?"

He bowed his head to pray for wisdom and the strength to do what was right.

He had struggled more than once with this problem. Lady Catherine knew best and would not let the Bible tell her otherwise, especially when she was wrong. He knew that in order to maintain his integrity and to be a faithful minister, he would have to stand up for his beliefs and fight his corner. The fact remained that he was still a little in awe of Her Ladyship, but mostly he was afraid her. The inimitable Grande Dame of Rosings was terrifying when she was at her worst. He also knew that the only reason she could rescind on their contract was if he did not suit as a clergyman. Going against her opinions on the given text would unmistakably be classed as *not suiting*. He had to tread carefully and be exceptionally gentle if he wished to break out of his servitude. He knew it was the right thing to do, but he was reluctant all the same.

He thought about what Charlotte would advise him to do. She would say that, for Lady Catherine, his black-and-white view of the world would not do; it would insult her. He knew that she would suggest that he then grey the edges, be gentle in his approach, deliver the message in a way that Her Ladyship would neither be offended nor realise what he had done. He prayed that, in time, Lady Catherine might take heed of some of the lessons he wished to deliver from the pulpit.

* * *

The day of the wedding arrived. Charlotte felt recovered, and the sun was shining. All boded well for the happy couple. Mr Collins had been early to open up the church, to allow the flower arrangers to work, and had arrived home in time to have a bite to eat to prevent his stomach from rumbling during the service. Excitement filled the air at the parsonage, and Charlotte and Mr Collins were ready too early to go to church. They passed the time in the sitting room, gazing at each other and listening to Mrs Higgs compliment them on how they looked. Charlotte was extremely pleased with her turban, and Mr Collins was exceptionally happy in his new clothing, aware that being covered in his cassock during the ceremony would allow him time to accustom himself to the idea of appearing in public in such a fashionable suit.

Together the Collinses took a slow walk to the church and arrived to see that the arch over the gate to the churchyard was covered in flowers and there were ribbons adorning the doors. The church itself was transformed by flowers, greenery, and ribbons. Charlotte was certain that Louisa had been very specific about how she had wanted the church to look and was sure that she would not be disappointed. Mr Collins left Charlotte and went to the back, where he would change and prepare to perform the service. Charlotte assisted by placing songbooks on the pews,

213

then went outside to greet people as the family and friends began to arrive.

Mr Simmons appeared soon thereafter, just as Mr Collins came out of the church wearing his cassock and a special chasuble that he reserved for christenings, first communions, weddings, and funerals.

Mr Simmons greeted them both heartily, although he looked a little pale.

"You have a lovely day for it, Mr Simmons," Mr Collins reassured him.

"Aye, indeed," Mr Simmons replied, looking up at the sky as if noticing for the first time that day that the weather was, indeed, superb.

A gentleman at his side cleared his throat and drew attention to his presence.

"Oh, I am terribly sorry!" Mr Simmons laughed nervously. "Mr and Mrs Collins, please allow me to introduce you to my younger brother Edward."

Edward Simmons, although younger than his brother, was stouter and had the appearance of being older. He bowed to them both.

"I am pleased to make your acquaintance, Mr Simmons. This is my wife, Mrs Collins," Mr Collins proudly turned towards her, "who is a dear friend of your soon-to-be sister-in-law."

"I am exceedingly pleased to meet you both. My wife shall be along shortly with Miss Thomas, as she is to act as matron of honour, our two boys acting as pages."

Mr Collins led them to the front of the church, where they sat awaiting the arrival of the bride.

Soon the church began to fill. Charlotte took her place and smiled at Mr Simmons encouragingly. He had turned whiter than he had been on arrival.

Mr Collins was stationed at the entrance to the church and kept smiling at Charlotte each time she looked his way. She was very well pleased with how things were improving with him. She heard him declare the arrival of Colonel Fitzwilliam, and she immediately snapped her attention back to the front of the church. She closed her eyes, stayed very still, and silently prayed to be invisible.

It was to no avail. He sought her out and spoke to her from the end of the pew. "Good day to you, Mrs Collins. Would you mind if I joined you?"

She turned her face towards him. How could she not accept when he had been overheard asking politely? To refuse would draw attention. "Of course you may, Colonel," she replied, her voice remarkably steady.

He sat down a little closer to her than was necessary, and she moved to her left to allow him some room. He would not have been able to move again without being seen. They sat for some moments looking straight ahead.

When he could bear the silence no longer he spoke. "I was sorry to hear you have been unwell, Mrs Collins," he said frustrated that he had to adhere to such formalities.

"Thank you, Colonel"

"I trust you are much recovered?" he asked while he moved the toe of his left boot over to touch her slipper.

She stiffened involuntarily. "Indeed I am, Colonel. Thank you for asking."

"I expect you shall be glad to get back out into the fresh air after being cooped up indoors for so long." It was a statement designed to disconcert her, and he could not resist.

She took a deep breath, determined to resist him. "In fact, Colonel, I walked with Mr Collins in the garden while I regained my strength."

"Indeed?" He smiled impishly. "I am sure that satisfied you greatly." The sting in his voice was clear.

"Yes, it did," she replied coolly.

She plainly cut him. A fuss at the entrance precluded any response.

Mr Collins walked solemnly to his place at the front of the church, after speaking a few words of encouragement to the bride. The organist, taking his cue from Mr Collins, began to play, and Louisa began her walk up the aisle on the arm of Mrs Thomas' brother, Mr Frederick Fields, as the assembly stood.

Louisa was a beautiful bride. Her happiness radiated from her and was felt by all present. Charlotte eyes drank in the beautiful pink dress Louisa had dreamed of wearing, and as the bride drew level with her, they exchanged jubilant smiles. As Louisa made her way up the aisle, Charlotte examined Mr Simmons' face. He was beaming with pride. He was finally to marry his sweetheart, the love denied years ago finally expressed in the ceremony about to be performed.

Mr Collins smiled down at the bride before him and began to recite the words the couple had feared they would never hear together, "Dearly beloved, we are gathered here today, in the sight of God and in the presence of these witnesses, to join this man and this woman in holy matrimony…"

* * *

The wedding breakfast was to take place at The Bell Inn in Hunsford, and the guests made their way there after the ceremony.

The bride and groom greeted each guest as they arrived and accepted their congratulations. Then the feasting began. They all sat down to the usual wedding breakfast of bread, buttered toast, tongue, and eggs. Hot chocolate was served, and in the centre of a table set off to the side was the wedding cake.

Once the guests' hunger was sated, they moved into the larger hall, usually used for balls, where a quartet of musicians had begun to play. Some guests lingered to pick at the food and hoped for some cake, but the majority wished to dance.

Mr Collins still had not learnt how to dance well, but was now more aware of that fact. He stuck to a dance he was familiar with when dancing with Charlotte. They took their places in the set, and he managed to crush Charlotte's toes only three times, which, she declared with a grin, was a decided improvement. They sat out the next dance, and Charlotte teased Mr Collins that the feeling was returning to her toes.

When the call came that the couple was to cut the cake, there was such a crush to be near the front, Charlotte and Mr Collins were lost in the throng. Charlotte just managed to see the event by standing on tiptoes. She withdrew to the corridor while Mr Collins fetched her a slice of cake. Surveying the room, she noticed that Colonel Fitzwilliam had been cornered by three unmarried ladies of the town. *That should keep him occupied,* she thought with satisfaction. Mr Collins returned to her side with plates of fruitcake, which they enjoyed at the entrance to the dancing hall while listening to the lovely strains of the string quartet.

The day continued happily. Charlotte danced again with Mr Collins, who had improved, stepping on her toes only twice. She also had the pleasure of dancing with Mr Abbot. Mr Collins knew she would tease him again over stepping on her toes and laughed as he confessed as much to Mrs Abbot. Despite his apologising to Charlotte, he welcomed her teasing, recognising it as a sign of affection. The groom requested a dance of Mrs Collins; Mr Collins begged a dance with the bride. In a mock serious tone, belied by a playful countenance, Charlotte apologised to Mr Simmons for his new bride's soon-to-be bruised toes. She threw a warning look at Mr Collins, who took extra care with the new Mrs Simmons' feet during their dance.

To her vexation, Charlotte discovered that in the next dance, she was obliged to stand up with Colonel Fitzwilliam, whom she had been effectively eluding for most of the day.

"I think you have been avoiding me, Mrs Collins," he accused with a grin.

"Whatever gave you that impression, Colonel?" She tried to avoid his gaze and concentrate on the dance.

"Oh, simply the fact that you *have* been avoiding me, Mrs Collins," his grin slipping.

She laughed at him, making light of the conversation, "Honestly, Colonel, how funny you are!"

Colonel Fitzwilliam was not amused. As they passed each other in the line, the grin was gone, replaced with a grim look.

"Come, Colonel, what did you expect?" she whispered as they danced the do-si-do.

"You know what I expect," he whispered back with venom.

She shot him a sharp look, remembered herself, and smiled at the couple with whom they were dancing. "Whatever do you mean?" She smiled at him, her eyes hard with anger.

He did not have a chance to respond as the dance ended and he led her back to her husband. As they drew closer to Mr Collins, the Colonel hissed in her ear, "I suggest we meet tomorrow to discuss it, Charlotte."

She ignored his comment as he handed her back into her husband's care. She curtseyed and thanked him for the dance, deliberately turning her attention toward the musicians. Colonel Fitzwilliam bowed to Mr Collins and departed the Inn, his fury written across his face as he mounted his horse and galloped out of Hunsford.

Charlotte and Mr Collins stayed until the happy couple had been merrily sent on their way home to Oak Wood Farm. Charlotte then requested of Mr Collins if they also might return home.

Chapter Twenty-nine

Upon their return home, Charlotte went to their bedroom to her change, after asking Mrs Higgs for a bowl of warm water to be brought to the sitting room to soak her weary feet. Mr Collins declared the wedding a veritable success and spent the next three quarters of an hour detailing the entire event to Mrs Higgs, who eagerly drank in the details. She felt that Mr Collins, as a typical man, did not say enough about the dress. For that pertinent information, she turned to Charlotte as she helped her to place her feet in the hot water that Jenny had delivered.

Mr Collins left them alone in the sitting room to change, as he had been chattering away to Mrs Higgs since he had arrived and had not even considered changing until that moment. Mrs Higgs began to rub at Charlotte's ankles, who sighed with relief at the woman's expert touch.

"Ma'am, might I ask you a delicate question?" Mrs Higgs began, her fingers deftly massaging the soles of Charlotte's feet.

"Ooh," Charlotte sighed deliciously. "Yes, of course, Mrs Higgs. What is it?"

"I do not wish to offend you, ma'am, but… well, when was the last time you - you know?"

Charlotte looked blankly at her housekeeper. "I am afraid I do not understand you, Mrs Higgs. I what?"

"The last time you had your courses?" she whispered, not wishing to be overheard.

Charlotte's eyebrows shot up as she replied, "I have no idea. Why do you ask?"

"It is just that - well… you *are* showing signs, ma'am."

"Mrs Higgs, I am not following you. I am showing signs of what?"

Mrs Higgs lowered her voice even more, "Of being with child, ma'am."

Charlotte was too shocked to speak and gaped at Mrs Higgs, busily rubbing her mistress's feet.

Charlotte nodded down at her feet, "You think they are a sign?"

"Well, your ankles are swollen; you have been nauseated; you have been off your food; and most telling of all, I am sure it has been more than a month since your last course. Much more. Do you keep a note of the dates?"

"Yes, a mark in the corner of my journal," replied Charlotte, desperately trying to recall the last time she made such a mark.

"Might I suggest, ma'am, that we check once Mr Collins returns?" Mrs Higgs suggested.

When Mr Collins finally came returned to the sitting room and make himself comfortable on the sofa with a book, Charlotte made her excuses and took Mrs Higgs to the bedroom.

Charlotte retrieved her journal and searched back for the little mark in the corner. She turned went back page after page and still could not find the mark she sought. In all, she flipped through two months of pages. She shook her head, muttered that it was impossible, worked forward looking for the mark once again, merely confirming what she had initially refused to believe.

"Oh, ma'am!" exclaimed Mrs Higgs, clapping her hand over her mouth, eyes gleaming with happiness.

"Mrs Higgs…" Charlotte closed the journal carefully and looked at her housekeeper, a smile playing at the corners of her mouth, "I think we should send for the doctor."

Mrs Higgs sent immediately for the doctor, as Charlotte said she would not be able to sleep if she did not know and Mr Collins would wonder at her agitation. Charlotte remained in her room, pacing up and down, impatient for Dr Sawyer to arrive.

Dr Sawyer was a church deacon, and as such, felt that Mrs Collins was a priority patient so arrived at the parsonage within the hour.

Mr Collins was astonished to see the deacon in his front hall. "Dr Sawyer, it is a pleasure to see you. To what do I owe this honour?" He sincerely hoped the accounts were not in error once again.

"I am here to see Mrs Collins. Is she above stairs, sir?"

Mr Collins looked bewildered. He had seen his wife in the best of health just above an hour ago; yet here was the doctor, whom it seemed, had been summoned for the express purpose of attending Mrs Collins.

Mrs Higgs stepped in. "This way if you please, Doctor," she directed, leading the doctor to Charlotte and leaving Mr Collins unenlightened. Once she had seen that the doctor had all he required, the loyal housekeeper retreated to wait outside the room, barring Mr Collins' entry to the room.

Mr Collins glared at Mrs Higgs when she told him that he was forbidden to enter. He threatened; he cajoled; he feigned indifference – not very convincingly – to no avail. He proceeded to stomp, rather than to pace, up and down the landing. He grew visibly more and more worried as time passed and the doctor failed to emerge.

At last, he did emerge. He nodded to Mrs Higgs to attend to Mrs Collins.

"Reverend, I will bid you good day and ask that you not disturb Mrs Collins until she asks to see you." The doctor tipped his hat to Mr Collins and descended the stairs, departing the parsonage.

Mr Collins was beside himself with worry. First Charlotte had a bout of dizziness and nausea; then she caught a cold. They returned from the wedding with her complaining of aching feet and tired legs. He could not comprehend what could be ailing her, and his mind reeled thinking the worst. He leant helplessly against the wall, feeling its coolness against the back of his head. What would he do without her?

Mrs Higgs opened the door to their bedroom and stepped out just as his thoughts had reached their darkest point.

"You can go in now, sir," she announced, an odd smile on her face, and scurried off to the kitchen, a wash bowl in her hands.

Mr Collins tentatively stepped into the room and looked around for Charlotte. She was standing by the bed, straightening the counterpane. She held out her hands, and he went to her and took them in his.

"My dear Charlotte, tell me that you are not ill," his face creased with concern for his wife.

"No William, I am not ill."

"But… you had the doctor called," he stammered.

"Yes, that is true, but I am not ill. In fact, I am in fullness of health."

His confused look forced her to spell it out for him.

"I am in excellent health, William dear. Such excellent health, in fact, that you and I are going to be parents."

He blinked, her meaning still not registering. She continued with a note of triumphant pride, "William," she laughed, "I am going to have a baby!"

He stood staring at her while her words reverberated around in his head. "A baby?" he repeated foolishly.

"Yes, a baby!" She laughed again, her face radiant with joy.

He snatched her up and swung her round, then ceased abruptly, apologised for mistreating her in her condition. Charlotte laughed with delight. "Does this news please you, William?"

The tears welling in his eyes were all the answer she needed. Upon seeing him thus, she too began to cry.

He folded his wife in his arms, holding her tightly. "Oh, my precious Charlotte. My precious, precious Charlotte," he murmured into her hair.

"William, I am so happy," she wept, happy tears bathing her face.

* * *

The whole of that day Mr Collins treated Charlotte as though she were a delicate porcelain doll and liable to break. This amused and touched her, but all her protestations for him to stop and to treat her as usual were ignored, so she resigned herself to being coddled. She knew it would not last more than a day or two and decided to enjoy it while she could.

Mr Collins asked her if he could read to her, and Charlotte insisted that he read from one of her novels. This resulted in her laughing until her face hurt, as each time a character kissed another or there was some romantic encounter, Mr Collins blushed, stammered, and could not finish reading the words at all. To remedy this situation, they took it in turns to read the novel,

222

Charlotte reading the amorous parts, Mr Collins reading the remainder. All the same, when Charlotte read out the romantic parts of the novel to her husband, she noticed it produced on his countenance a comical look of discomfort, evoking yet more laughter on her part, making their progress decidedly slow.

They dined on trays on their laps in the sitting room that night, during which Charlotte expressed a desire to retire early. Mr Collins said he would join her, as he was understandably reluctant to be out of her presence at this precious time.

They retired to bed early. Charlotte laid her head upon her husband's chest, and they talked about the child they were to have and began picking names for the unborn babe. They began with names such as William for a boy and Charlotte for a girl, but Mr Collins made the mistake of telling Charlotte the names of his grandparents. The poor unfortunates were named Theophilus and Magdalene Collins. Charlotte then had another fit of the giggles, saying that they sounded like characters in a terrible Biblical romance novel. Mr Collins, rather than being affronted, saw the humour in that, and he too laughed; from then on they both suggested absurd names for their coming child until they fell asleep.

* * *

The next couple of days passed in a blur for Charlotte as she was cosseted and loved at every turn. Mr Collins was in a high state of emotion. *He is about to become a father*, thought Charlotte, *of course he was happy.* Charlotte spent time with Mrs Higgs learning what to expect, and Mrs Higgs dealt with the subject of childbirth delicately, not wishing to frighten Charlotte.

On Friday afternoon, they received an unexpected visitor. Mr Collins was in his book room putting the final changes to his sermon for the coming Sunday when Mrs Higgs led the guest into the sitting room where Charlotte was sewing.

She looked up from her work. "Colonel Fitzwilliam!" she exclaimed, almost dropping her needlework.

Colonel Fitzwilliam waited until Mrs Higgs had left the room before he spoke, "Charlotte, I had to see you."

223

When she did not reply, he continued to speak. "I have waited at the clearing two mornings now, and you did not come. When Dr Sawyer came to Rosings for his usual visit to my aunt and said he had been to see you at the parsonage, my heart was in my mouth." He sat beside her on the sofa. "You cannot imagine the agonies I have suffered worrying about you. Please tell me directly, Charlotte. Are you ill?"

"No, Colonel, I am not ill, not at all."

His relief was obvious, "You cannot imagine how I felt after we quarrelled at the wedding breakfast."

Charlotte was not aware they had quarrelled, but she allowed him the courtesy of continuing what he had to say.

"I have been in agony. You must know how I feel for you. You must know I love you Charlotte."

"Colonel, I…"

He interrupted her, "Please let me finish, and then you can say all you like."

She raised her eyebrows archly at his impertinence.

"I have loved you for some time now. I cannot get the memory of you out of my head." He stood up and began pacing in agitation. "I have been thinking it all through. We can elope to York or somewhere north. We can live there as man and wife."

Charlotte regarded him, stunned, gaping in disbelief.

"When sufficient time has passed, I can secure a lawyer to file for a divorce, claiming Mr Collins to be abandoned. Alternatively, if you prefer, we can fight for a divorce immediately. I have enough of an income to support us both and pay for a solicitor. It will be difficult, I have no doubt." He stopped pacing, ran his hand through his hair, and finally looked at her. "But I know with you by my side, dearest Charlotte, it will all be worthwhile."

Charlotte composed her face and fought hard to keep her temper and voice under control, "Colonel Fitzwilliam…"

"Please, my name is Richard. We have come too far for you to still call me Colonel Fitzwilliam."

"Colonel," she said pointedly, "if you would but allow me to finish."

He was bewildered at her angry reaction.

"I have no intention of getting a divorce now or ever. Let me make myself perfectly clear. I have no intention of ever leaving Mr Collins."

"But that day in the clearing. Are you going to deny that there is something between us, Charlotte?"

"What happened between us was foolhardy, and we should have known better. We are both adults, and we behaved like immoral degenerates." She stole a look at the door, praying that Mr Collins was not able to hear them.

"I cannot believe you, Charlotte." Colonel Fitzwilliam sat beside her in disbelief. "Tell me, please, Charlotte that you feel the same way I do. Do not leave me wretched. I love you."

She could not reply. She was angry with him for not accepting her words; she was angry with herself for allowing the situation to evolve.

* * *

Mr Collins quietly stepped out of his book room upon hearing raised voices coming from the sitting room. He knew that a guest had arrived but had wanted to put his final thoughts down on paper before joining his wife and their guest. Before he could complete his task, his train of thought had been interrupted by a raised masculine voice followed by his wife's somewhat hushed, angry-sounding voice. Concern and curiosity led him to creep quietly to the door of the sitting room and listen. The door was slightly ajar, and he was taken aback at what he saw therein.

* * *

"You cannot possibly love him, Charlotte! He is a bumbling idiot! The man is a fool!" the Colonel shouted.

"That man is my husband, and I love him dearly!" Charlotte shouted back, now no longer caring who heard her. "And I do not take kindly to you disparaging him in my presence!"

Colonel Fitzwilliam was beside himself. He stepped forward, knelt in front of Charlotte, took hold of her hand, and kissed the palm passionately, muttering his professions of love into it.

225

Mr Collins burst through the door. "What is the meaning of this? Unhand my wife this instant!"

The Colonel rounded on him, "Or what?" He stood up, drew himself up to his full height, and towered over the smaller Mr Collins, "Or shall you fawn all over me and simper me to death?"

Mr Collins had never been a fighting man, but he rushed headlong into the Colonel and pushed him backwards.

The Colonel laughed cruelly. "Get away from me, you pathetic little man!" He pushed the smaller man negligently; Mr Collins stumbled backwards and into the chair behind him.

Colonel Fitzwilliam turned his attention back to Charlotte, demanding, "Tell me that you do not prefer him to me! Tell me that you will come away with me now! I love you!"

Mr Collins saw red at the Colonel's words. His heart bursting with his newly discovered love for Charlotte, he picked up the fire poker, and raised it above his head intending to strike the Colonel with it. The Colonel caught the movement reflected in the mirror above the fireplace.

He turned round and grabbed by Mr Collins by the arm holding the poker. "You thought you could attack me, did you?" he snarled. This time he shoved Mr Collins with greater force than before.

The force sent Mr Collins off his feet and toward the fireplace. His head hit the corner of the mantle with a sickening thud, and he slid lifeless to the floor.

Everything seemed to move in slow motion as Charlotte watched the exchange between her husband and the Colonel. She watched in helpless horror as her husband's head hit the mantelpiece. She heard screaming and the thumping of her pulse in her ears.

She realised the screaming was hers and time snapped back to its regular speed. She rushed forward to the slumped body lying on the floor. She raised her husband's head, resting it against her lap. She felt the warm stickiness of his blood covering her hands and spreading across her skirts.

"Help! Please, somebody help me!" she screamed hysterically.

Mrs Higgs came running in closely followed by Jenny. Jenny screamed; Mrs Higgs let out an expletive. She shouted to Jenny to fetch the doctor immediately.

She then rounded on Colonel Fitzwilliam, who was frozen in place, staring in disbelief at Mr Collins on the floor. "You, get the master upstairs and put him on the bed."

Charlotte was unaware of what was going on around her. She kept screaming over and over again, "William! Please wake up, William!" The tears were rolling freely down her face.

Mrs Higgs pulled her mistress out of the way, and Colonel Fitzwilliam swept up Mr Collins in his arms and carried him upstairs. Once in the bedroom, with Mr Collins laid upon the bed, Mrs Higgs demanded of Colonel Fitzwilliam what had happened.

"He tripped," was all Colonel Fitzwilliam could say in response.

"Then you should make yourself scarce before someone questions your part in his tripping," she retorted, her eyes hard and accusing, not blind to what had likely occurred.

The Colonel looked imploringly at Charlotte.

Her gaze was cold and unmistakable. "Get out of my house."

He did not need to be told again; he turned and fled.

Charlotte knelt on the bed crying over Mr Collins and wiping his head with her skirts, attempting to staunch the flow of blood. Mrs Higgs joined her in cleaning up the blood, and together they attended to him until Dr Sawyer arrived.

Chapter Thirty

D r Sawyer took a long time examining the wound to Mr Collins' head, checking his eyes, his breathing, his pulse, and listening to his heart. Charlotte stood close by, wringing her hands; Mrs Higgs stood next to her, supporting her with an arm about her mistress's shoulders.

The doctor bound the wound with clean linen and turned to Charlotte. "Head wounds often appear worse than they actually are, Mrs Collins." He looked at her gravely. "What concerns me most is that he has not regained consciousness." When she looked at him blankly, he explained, "I shall not beat about the bush with you, Mrs Collins. Unless he wakes up, he will decline and not recover."

Charlotte began to cry again.

The doctor returned his instruments to his bag. "Keep talking to him. Do not leave him alone. We shall know more within forty-eight hours."

Before he made to leave, Dr Sawyer squeezed Charlotte's hand kindly. "And remember, Mrs Collins, you, too, need your rest." He looked at her meaningfully over his glasses, and she nodded her understanding.

Charlotte was not lax in her bedside vigil. She never once left the room, not even for meals, which she had brought up on a tray. She read to Mr Collins, spoke to him, prayed with him, all the while intently watched his face for signs of consciousness.

Mrs Higgs had asked her if she wanted the spare bedroom made up so she could sleep. Charlotte insisted that she would not, even for one moment, leave her husband's side. She thought her fatigue was overtaking her then, as she believed she saw Mr Collins eyelids flutter at her words.

Charlotte climbed into her side of the bed and laid her head on her pillow. She took hold of her husband's hand, and as her weariness overtook her and she drifted off to sleep, she whispered, "I love you, William."

* * *

During the night, Charlotte had become cold and had slipped under the covers, kissing Mr Collins' cheek before snuggling back into her pillow. She was relieved to find his skin still warm. Her mind eased, she was able to sleep once more.

The forty-eight hours that Dr Sawyer had said were critical were excruciatingly slow and heart breaking for Charlotte. She tenderly nursed her husband, regularly changing the linen bands and cleaning the wound, reassuring herself as she did so that the skin was knitting together and the bleeding was staunched.

When the doctor called again, Charlotte was pleased to be able to report that Mr Collins had moaned once or twice in the night. Dr Sawyer assured her that she was right to hope, that it was an encouraging sign.

Lady Catherine arrived that day to pay a call, and Charlotte insisted on receiving her in the bedroom as she still refused to leave Mr Collins' side, providing most of the nursing herself. Lady Catherine could barely look at Charlotte; she was obviously still not forgiven in Her Ladyship's eyes. Lady Catherine only stayed the polite quarter of an hour, and loudly lamented on what she deemed was Mr Collins' certain demise. Charlotte was relieved when Her Ladyship left.

The days passed in a blur. Mr Collins still gave hope by the occasional moan, his eyelids fluttering when Charlotte spoke words of comfort and encouragement to him as she pressed water to his lips. He became increasingly restless, which the doctor said was a clear sign that he would recover. Alas, he still did not awaken.

About four days after his fall, Mrs Higgs woke Charlotte early in the morning, "Mrs Collins," she shook her gently, "forgive me, ma'am, but an express just arrived for you."

Charlotte blinked groggily. Mrs Higgs repeated herself, pressing the letter on her mistress. Jenny arrived to change the water bowl and sponge at the bedside and began the daily changing of bed linens, Mrs Higgs assisting before leaving to make some tea and toast for her mistress.

Charlotte tore open the letter and her eyes flew immediately to the signature. Elizabeth Darcy. Charlotte's eyes returned to the top of the page. Lizzy stated that she and Mr Darcy had received an express from Colonel Fitzwilliam confessing all and begging their assistance for Charlotte and Mr Collins. The note was brief, ending, by informing her that Lizzy and Mr Darcy were on their way and would be with her as soon as they possibly could.

My goodness! The Colonel must be repentant, indeed, and goodness knows how much I want to have Lizzy here right now, but she certainly knows all and must blame me! This is all my fault. Oh, William! She thought clutching the note to her chest.

Charlotte sat on the edge of the bed, told her husband that they were to have visitors in Mr and Mrs Fitzwilliam Darcy. His eyelids fluttered, his head moved slightly. Charlotte felt hope rising, and smiled at Mrs Higgs as she returned with a cup of tea.

* * *

Mr and Mrs Darcy arrived two days later. Their horses were exhausted, and they, too, looked wearied from their hasty journey south. Dawkins saw to it that the horses were looked after, and Mrs Higgs had the guest room ready for the Darcys, but Lizzy would not even remove her bonnet until she had seen Charlotte.

Charlotte was in a chair beside Mr Collins when Lizzy entered the room. "Charlotte!" she exclaimed, opening her arms and embracing her friend, who rose to greet her guest. Lizzy kept her arms about Charlotte, turned her head towards the unconscious figure of Mr Collins, and enquired after his condition.

"I scarcely know," began Charlotte, her voice breaking with the pent-up emotion.

"I shall have your housekeeper make up some food and tea, and then you shall tell me all that I have not from heard Colonel Fitzwilliam."

Charlotte nodded but said she would not leave Mr Collins' side. Mrs Higgs and Jenny brought up the now redundant breakfast table and cleared an area in the bedroom where the friends might sit and talk.

Mr Darcy was all politeness. He bowed to Charlotte and enquired after her health. Charlotte was frightened that they

231

would judge her and treat her harshly for her part in what had happened to Mr Collins, but neither of them treated her with anything other than kindness and respect.

The tea things were brought in, Mrs Higgs laid out a small collation for Mr and Mrs Darcy, and they all sat down to refreshment. Charlotte positioned her chair in order to keep an eye on Mr Collins in the bed, her love and concern etched on her face. Rather than embarrass Charlotte by having her recount her version of events, Lizzy handed Charlotte Colonel Fitzwilliam's letter.

In his missive, the Colonel had laid all of the blame at his own door, none whatsoever on Charlotte. He stated that he had coerced Charlotte into an improper situation against her wishes, that he had foolishly fallen in love with a married woman, a woman never destined to be his. He wrote that he had gone to the parsonage that fateful day to persuade Charlotte to elope with him. He explained how he had not recognised that she was not as enamoured of him as he of her, and he mistakenly assumed that he could persuade her into taking desperate actions.

Charlotte could not believe what she was reading. She knew there were two sides to every story, but here the Colonel was protecting her reputation by laying all of the blame firmly with him. He stated that in his disappointment and anger at her rejection of him, he lashed out at Mr Collins, engaged in a tussle, and Mr Collins had met with his unfortunate accident.

Then she read something that she had not realised before that moment. Colonel Fitzwilliam was aware that, should Mr Collins die from his injuries, he himself would hang for murder. Charlotte pressed her hand against her chest. She did not know which thought frightened her more, Mr Collins' possible death, or Colonel Fitzwilliam being hanged as a murderer.

The Colonel then went on to beg his cousin's help in ensuring that all could be done for Mr Collins' recovery, and to help Charlotte in any way that she required. He closed by stating that he was returning to his regiment on the Peninsula, and would not return to England until he heard from Mr Darcy as to what his fate would be.

Charlotte felt weak and shaken by this knowledge, and knew not what to think or how to react.

Lizzy reached over and touched her friend's hand. "Charlotte, what is it?"

"I did not realise." She paused and lowered her voice to a whisper, as she was sure that Mr Collins could hear all that was said, "I did not realise he might hang."

Mr Darcy countenance was grave as he replied, "Yes, I am afraid so. My cousin has always been headstrong. If idea lodged in his head, he would run with it and damn the consequences. Please, Mrs Collins, allow me to extend my sincerest sympathies."

Charlotte gazed at him gratefully but could not respond, the tears falling freely from her eyes once again. Mr Darcy got up, took a plate of food, his cup of tea, and told the ladies he would leave them to talk and join them again within the hour.

Once he had left Lizzy asked, "Was it as the Colonel states in the letter?"

Charlotte nodded, but feeling the prick of her conscience, she confessed all to her friend. She cried, blamed herself, and cried more, but not once during the telling of the tale did Lizzy censure her or her actions.

"Oh, Lizzy! I have been more than foolish. I was childish, and my immaturity may have cost me the most important person in my life." Again, she looked at her husband, lying helpless and unresponsive on the bed. She stood up to retrieve a fresh handkerchief. When she regained her seat, she saw that Lizzy was regarding her with deep sympathy and compassion.

"I have learnt my lesson, Lizzy. I know now that there is no such thing as harmless flirtation. The more I considered it, the more I realised the foolishness and recklessness of it all. I was completely swept along on a tide of emotion." She looked down at her hands again. "I am heartily ashamed of myself, Lizzy."

"Oh, Charlotte. I do understand, truly I do." Charlotte looked at her friend, baffled. "George Wickham. Remember?"

"Yes, I do remember. Was there much flirtation, Lizzy?"

"Aye, there was. Flirtation, flattery, lies – and on my side, an enormous dose of stupidity." She reached out and squeezed Charlotte's hands again. "You are not the only person to behave in such a way, and I doubt very much that you will be the last. At least you had the wisdom and the presence of mind to realise your folly. Colonel Fitzwilliam, it seems, did not."

Lizzy stood up, moved to Mr Collins' bedside, and took hold of his hand. "Now, Charlotte, what other news is there to tell me?"

Charlotte smiled, the first smile she had indulged in for days.

She stood next to her friend and took Lizzy's free hand in her own. "It does not seem appropriate to tell you after all that has gone on, but Mr Collins and I are expecting our first child."

Lizzy was elated at the news, embraced her friend, kissing her cheek. "Oh, Charlotte, that is such wonderful news. I am so happy for you!" She turned back to Mr Collins and patted his hand as she leant closer so he could hear her words, "This is Cousin Elizabeth. I wish to offer you my congratulations, Mr Collins. Charlotte has just told me your happy news. Now I see you have plenty of reasons to get well and return to us. Your child will need his father, as will your wife need her husband."

Chapter Thirty-one

Mr and Mrs Darcy had settled in well in the parsonage and had taken over the usual running of the house while Charlotte continued to attend to her husband's needs. Mr Darcy had seen to it that one of the deacons took over responsibility of Mr Collins' parochial work and delegated what was necessary to ensure the required duties were performed.

Lizzy determinedly began to take charge of Charlotte, whose spirits were getting lower and lower with each day that passed without Mr Collins reviving. She felt that, in Charlotte's condition, this was a worrying sign.

Lizzy ordered a fire to be lit and a bath to be drawn in one of the empty bedrooms and insisted that Charlotte take a few minutes to herself to bathe. Charlotte resisted, laughing weakly as Lizzy threatened to bodily carry her into the room and bathe her herself if she did not go willingly.

"You shall not be of any use to Mr Collins if you do not take care of yourself, my dear," Lizzy gently pointed out as Charlotte continued to hesitate.

Seeing the wisdom in this, Charlotte agreed to take a few moments to herself. She kissed Mr Collins on the cheek and assured him that she would not be gone long. Lizzy was touched by the affection that Charlotte showed for Mr Collins and thought to herself that much must have changed between the couple since her last visit. Happily married herself, Lizzy wished the same for her dear friend. She shooed Charlotte out of the room, sat by Mr Collins' side, took up her own needlework, and began to tell him about her life at Pemberley.

* * *

Charlotte finally emerged from the empty bedroom, freshly bathed and in a clean dress, her hair still wet, and returned to her bedroom. She had not realised how weary she had been from the constant nursing and worry.

Lizzy informed Charlotte that there was a pile of calling cards building up on the hall table, from people who had stopped by to extend their wishes for Mr Collins' recovery. Charlotte, feeling that she had been away from her husband's side long enough, did not wish to go collect them. Lizzy fetched the cards and returned also with Mr Darcy who went to sit at Mr Collins' side. Together Lizzy and Charlotte began to go through the stack of cards; Charlotte describing whom they were from. Lizzy was interested in her friend's new life and her acquaintances in Hunsford, sharing, in turn, stories of the people she had met at Pemberley and Lambton. Naturally, the conversation turned to talking about Meryton and their shared friends and families.

Lizzy was trying to lighten Charlotte's mood, but a thought suddenly occurred to her. "Charlotte, have you informed your mother about Mr Collins?"

"No, I have not. You are doubtless shocked, but until this moment, the thought had not occurred to me."

"I understand. You have been so traumatised by his accident and have not taken a moment since, but I do think you ought to let her know."

"Yes, Lizzy, you are right. Oh, dear. What do I say to her? What can I say to prevent her from rushing here immediately?"

"I think that is where I might be of assistance," replied Mr Darcy from the bedside.

Mr Darcy had been reading to Mr Collins from one of the many books from the book room and had been desirous of doing something useful. "If I may, I shall acquaint Lord and Lady Lucas with the situation. I am certain that I can assure them that everything is in hand and their presence is not required."

Charlotte agreed that this would be wise, and Mr Darcy was about to leave the ladies to go to Mr Collins' book room to carry out his task, when Mrs Higgs came into the room.

"Begging your pardon, ma'am, but the butcher's bill has arrived."

"If permitted, Charlotte, I shall attend to this forthwith," Mr Darcy offered.

Charlotte knew that Mr Darcy was uncomfortable in the sick room, as many men are, and was happy to hand over those tasks into his competent hands. He departed with her thanks and left the ladies alone with Mr Collins.

* * *

"I wish he would open his eyes, if even for a moment," Charlotte said as she went to Mr Collins' side.

"That would be very encouraging. Have you noticed any significant change apart from his increased restlessness?" Lizzy queried.

"It will sound silly, Lizzy, but last night I could swear I woke up to him saying my name," Charlotte replied, caressing her husband's hand and gazing at him, worry puckering her brow.

"That would indeed be a favourable sign, Charlotte."

"I cannot be sure, Lizzy. I might have dreamt it."

Mr Collins let out a moan.

She looked startled. "Do you think he heard me?" she whispered.

"Dr Sawyer seems to think he can," Lizzy affirmed.

"William, dear William, it is Charlotte. Please wake up, my love." She kissed his cheek, her tears wetting his face.

Mr Collins eyes fluttered, but did not open. He moaned. His body tensed for a moment and then relaxed once more.

The ladies held their breath during this display, eyes fixed on the invalid.

"Charlotte, that is a sign indeed!" Lizzy exclaimed. "He is fighting whatever he is languishing under, and I think we might allow our hopes to rise. I shall ask Fitzwilliam what he thinks."

Lizzy left Charlotte standing smiling down at her husband, her tears of hope coursing down her face.

* * *

Lizzy tapped on the book room door, but it was already open and Mr Darcy saw her and smiled, bidding her entrance.

237

She entered the room, and her husband took her hands in his. "How is she, Elizabeth?"

"Charlotte is such a strong woman; she will be well. I did not think to find her in love with Mr Collins, but it appears she is. Such a pleasant turn of events! But that is not the reason I wish to speak to you."

Elizabeth recounted to her husband all that had just taken place in the bedroom above and asked what he thought it meant.

"I agree with your supposition. It appears that he is fighting his way back. Perhaps he needs more stimulus to which to react."

Mr Darcy stood and closed the door. "Elizabeth, I have something I want to show you."

He returned to the desk and picked up a pile of old letters. "I ran out of ink after having finished the letter to Lord and Lady Lucas, and I began to search in Mr Collins' desk for more. As I rummaged, these old letters fell out of the back of last year's household accounts ledger."

"Fitzwilliam, you have been prying!" Lizzy pretended to be shocked.

"No not exactly. Mrs Collins asked me to take care of his business, and that is what I am doing. I cannot help it if Mr Collins' desk is untidy and letters fall out of ledgers and I happen to read a line or two." Mr Darcy managed to look just a little ashamed.

Lizzy smiled at him teasingly. "But you have not read only a line or two, have you, Mr Darcy?

"No, I confess I have not," he admitted, an abashed smile playing at the corners of his mouth. "Once I read a few lines, I was compelled to read more. They are from Mr Collins Senior."

"Mr Collins' father?"

"Yes. He was not an amiable man, Elizabeth. The cruelty with which he treated his son, the harsh words are staggering. I believe they explain a lot about Mr Collins sycophantic behaviour."

"Whatever do you mean, Fitzwilliam?"

"It seems that Mr Collins had an elder brother who died. Mr Collins Senior never got over that death; indeed, he blamed our Mr Collins for being the one who survives." Lizzy gasped in dismay. "Our Mr Collins spent his entire youth trying to please a

238

parent who, by all accounts, disliked him intensely. It would appear that Mr Collins' mother was beaten severely, and Mr Collins too, I suspect, would have been a victim of his father's beatings. Our Mr Collins wanted only to be liked, loved, and respected, and still does."

"So that is why he fawns over and is so desperate to ingratiate himself with anyone of higher rank than his own," replied Lizzy thoughtfully.

"Indeed. I believe Mrs Collins should be informed of this."

"I do not know, Fitzwilliam. I agree that she ought to know, but I do not think it wise for her to know that we are acquainted with the contents of the letters. This is a delicate matter."

"Perhaps I shall ask Mrs Collins to check over my entries in the ledger; perhaps the letters are left where she might chance to see them."

"If her own curiosity rises as did yours, she shall learn of Mr Collins' history." Lizzy bit her bottom lip in thought. "I own that I am ashamed that I thought so poorly of him now. If only the character of his father had been known… but my father and Mr Collins Senior fell out many years ago, and my father never mentioned why."

"If you are in agreement, that is what we shall do. No one can be of as much help to a husband as can his wife," Mr Darcy said as he arranged the letters in the ledger where Charlotte would find them. "I find I pity him, Elizabeth, and regret having misjudged him so."

Lizzy took her husband's arm, squeezing it to signal her agreement, as together they left the room to return to Charlotte and Mr Collins.

* * *

That evening Charlotte left the sickroom for Mr Collins' book room to look over the accounts ledger Mr Darcy had checked, to sign it and count out the money for Mrs Higgs to pay the bills. She had just finishing these tasks when her eyes fell on a pile of letters, the very letters which Mr Darcy had deliberately left for her to discover. She picked them up, and saw that they were to Mr Collins from his father. Her interest piqued. Her husband had told her little about his family. She lit another candle, settled herself in Mr Collins' easy chair, and began to read.

* * *

It was some time before Charlotte re-joined Lizzy and Mr Darcy in her bedroom. Her tear-stained face spoke volumes, and Lizzy knew she would have either to admit to knowing or the letters or lie to her dearest friend.

She decided that Charlotte had been through enough and did not need her deception as well. "You have read them, then?" she asked gently, enfolding her friend in her arms.

Charlotte sobbed against Lizzy's shoulder in response.

There she remained for a while, allowing her tears to flow freely. Her emotions vented, Charlotte dried her eyes. "How did you know?" she asked.

"I am afraid that is down to me," Mr Darcy confessed. "I discovered them by accident and asked Elizabeth what we should do. She agreed that you ought to know, and I left them where you would find them. It was wrong of me to pry, and I do apologise, but perhaps it is for the best," he said, his hand on Charlotte's shoulder consolingly.

* * *

Dr Sawyer returned that evening and, after thoroughly examining Mr Collins and the wound to his head, indicated by inclining his head towards the door that they should all follow him out to the landing.

"Well, I do not understand it," he declared. "I have examined him thoroughly. His heart is strong, his lungs are clear, the wound is healing nicely. There is no reason I can find as to why Mr Collins remains unconscious."

"What can be done, Doctor?" Mr Darcy asked.

"I have on occasion seen cases like this, and I am afraid it is all down to will power now."

"What do you mean?" Charlotte asked.

"Will power, my dear, whether he wants to recover or not."

* * *

Charlotte was persuaded to walk around the garden with Lizzy while the dinner table was being laid and to eat with Mr and Mrs Darcy in the dining room that evening. She obediently did as she was bid, her heart and mind occupied on what she had learned that day. Charlotte did not eat much and was poor conversation for Lizzy and Mr Darcy, but felt the fresh air did her some good.

When Charlotte had retired that night, Lizzy told Mr Darcy all about the miraculous change that Mr Collins had undergone since the spat Charlotte had had with Lady Catherine. Mr Darcy was acquainted with that part of the story owing to the frequency with which his wife and Charlotte corresponded. The transformation of Mr Collins was news to him, and he listened eagerly and with amusement as he heard about what Lizzy termed *the new and improved Mr Collins.*

"I think I would like to meet this new Mr Collins, Elizabeth."

"As would I," Lizzy agreed.

* * *

Charlotte slipped into bed beside her still unconscious husband, wet his lips with the ever-handy sponge, then manoeuvred herself so that her mouth was close to his ear. "Mr Collins, it is your wife."

She took a deep breath and began to say what was on her mind. "My dear William, you cannot imagine how much pain it gives me to see you here in this bed day after day."

She reached down and took hold of his hand, holding it against her cheek. "Today I had to go into your book room to organise the payment of our receipts, my dear. I happened upon a pile of letters from your father. Now do not be cross with me William; but I read them. I am so sorry to discover what your life was like in your youth, how you must have suffered. Your father was a cruel man and your mother did not deserve his treatment, and neither did you."

She stopped to wipe the tears from her face, kissing his hand as she gently replaced it on the counterpane. "Do you recall when

241

I asked you about that scar on your back? You told me that it was from a fall as a boy. I did not believe you then, and after reading your father's letters, I know my suspicions were correct. That scar is from his beating you with a belt, is in the shape of a buckle, as I suspected."

She broke down and sobbed, not fearing his hearing her crying. She wanted him to know the verity of what she was conveying to him.

"My dear, precious husband, Dr Sawyer says that you have to want to recover and come back to me. So please listen to me, William. I want you to recover. I need you in my life."

She shifted her position to his face in the moonlight. "When we married, we were, neither of us, in love. That is not the case now, is it?"

His eyelids moved, and she pressed on, "These past few months with you have given me such joy. You are a changed man. You have acted differently towards me. I have seen a side of you I had not known. You have made me laugh. You have made me want to be with you more and more. You have shown me tenderness and affection of late, which I had never before known. I am proud, William Collins, to be bearing your child. I am proud to be your wife. I am proud to tell you, from the bottom of my heart, William, that I love you."

She laid her head on her pillow and closed her eyes, praying that he had heard her words.

On top of the counterpane, their hands remained entwined and, very slightly, his squeezed hers.

Chapter Thirty-two

M r Darcy sat beside Mr Collins' bed reading his correspondence out to him. He was reading a letter from Mr Bennet when Lady Catherine burst into the bedroom without being announced.

"Mrs Collins, you are well…" She stopped mid-sentence upon seeing Mr Darcy and Elizabeth in the room. "You! What are you doing here?" she demanded angrily.

Lizzy, always with a quick tongue, spoke first. "Good morning to you as well, Aunt," she dropped a curtsey. "I trust you are well."

"Hmm…" and a withering stare were all the response she received from Lady Catherine.

Mr Darcy rose and offered his aunt the chair he had been occupying, although he did not greet her, nor did he bow.

Lady Catherine seated herself beside Mr Collins, whom was now forgotten, and stared at her nephew. "Well, nephew, answer me. What are you doing here?"

"We are here to see Mr and Mrs Collins, of course, Aunt," came Mr Darcy's response.

"I can see that. Do not be insolent with me. What is Mr Collins to you, pray?"

Mr Darcy determinedly stepped toward the bed and laid his hand upon Mr Collins' feet, an action noted by both Charlotte and Lizzy. They looked at Mr Collins' face for any reaction he might have at Mr Darcy's coming words. "Mr Collins is my wife's cousin. Mr Collins is my cousin-in-law. Mrs Collins is Mr Collins' wife…"

"Do not be obtuse!" Lady Catherine cut in.

Mr Darcy continued, his voice became more forceful, "Mrs Collins is Mr Collins' wife, making her my wife's cousin-in-law. This, then, makes her my cousin-in-law. To make it plainer,

Aunt, William and Charlotte are family, and we are visiting them in their time of distress."

Lady Catherine's face became so red at his words that she looked as though she would burst a blood vessel. She rose from the chair and stormed from the room declaring, "It shall not be borne!"

Charlotte, Lizzy, and Mr Darcy heeded her not. They were fixed on Mr Collins, who was moaning and trying to open his eyes.

Lady Catherine's voice carried up the stairs to them from the hall, where she remained loudly complaining about her nephew and his wife's presence at the parsonage. Mr Darcy rolled his eyes and resignedly went downstairs to deal with her.

Charlotte was beside herself. Mr Collins was trying to wake up. Lizzy was smiling and crying at the same time.

* * *

When Mr Darcy returned to the room, he related all that his aunt had said to him and how she had threatened to repeal Mr Collins' contract with her if he and Lizzy did not quit the parsonage immediately.

"Insolent woman. How arrogant of her! Can she do that, Fitzwilliam?" Lizzy asked.

"She is rich enough. She probably can," replied Mr Darcy with distaste. "Charlotte, may I be impertinent and ask you how much is William's living here? A thought has just occurred to me."

"Of course, Mr Darcy…"

He interrupted her, "My name is Fitzwilliam, Charlotte. I think we have established a familial connection, do you not?" He smiled.

Charlotte smiled nervously at him. "It is but a trifling amount. William receives two hundred pounds from Lady Catherine, I believe."

"Indeed?" he said raising his eyebrows. "Then I think William…" Mr Darcy said directly to Mr Collins but stopped before he could finish. Charlotte and Lizzy turned to see Mr Collins' eyes opening slightly.

Charlotte rushed to him and kissed him repeatedly on his face. She did not care a jot that they were not alone, her happiness was so great.

Once all the shouts of joy and the tears had abated Mr Darcy continued what he had intended to say. "William, the living at Pemberley has just become vacant. Reverend Clements has retired, you see. My wife and I would be honoured if you would consider it yours."

Mr Darcy did not wait for a response, leading his wife to the door to leave Charlotte and Mr Collins alone. He turned as he closed the door, "Oh, and it is worth more than a trifle. Would eight hundred pounds suffice?" and was gratified by hearing Mr Collins utter through dry lips, "Thank you, *Cousin*."

Epilogue

A year later, Charlotte sat looking out of the sitting room window of the vicarage at Pemberley watching the snow melting off the trees outside. She recalled the incredible journey the past year had been.

The Collinses had quitted Hunsford and moved to Derbyshire. Lady Catherine had made it clear that she would not allow them to have anything to do with Mr and Mrs Darcy. Mr Collins had surprised and pleased Charlotte by standing up to Her Ladyship, declaring he would associate with whom he chose.

Mr Collins later told his wife how he had heard every word said in their bedroom while he was unconscious, how, when he heard Mr Darcy telling Lady Catherine that they were cousins, he felt the grip of the fog that was holding him down lift and his return to consciousness begin.

Charlotte and William had spoken at length on the subject of Colonel Fitzwilliam. Charlotte had confessed all to him, and he forgave her unreservedly. He had been deeply moved by what she had whispered to him that night in Hunsford while he had lain unconscious in bed. He wanted there and then to reach out to her, to declare his love for her, but he was unable to move. She described that when she had felt his hand squeeze hers, it had ignited hope in her that she had scarcely allowed before.

Mr Collins told Charlotte how the events at Hunsford, the visit to Westerham, the association with the Abbots had taught him to re-evaluate himself. He admitted how, little by little, he had realised how ridiculous a man he had been, how he had begun to see her for who she truly was, how he had fallen in love with her. He told her how all these things contributed to his finally seeing Lady Catherine for the overbearing tyrant she truly was, how he deeply regretted his previous high regard.

They had remained at Hunsford for two months more, then began the long journey into Derbyshire. Louisa and Mr Simmons joined the Collinses three weeks later, and Charlotte was glad

247

their friendship survived the distance and was grateful for Louisa's assistance in settling into her new home. Charlotte's dear friends Lizzy and Louisa developed an affable friendship. Mr and Mrs Simmons planned to visit the following summer, bringing the Abbots along; and Mr Darcy had invited Messrs Simmons, Abbots, and Collins to fish in his lake.

Their new patron was all that was to be expected of him. Mr Darcy was not overbearing and delegated a great deal to Mr Collins, especially in parochial matters, encouraging him to preach true Christian values from the pulpit on Sundays. He made a considerable effort to befriend Mr Collins, which pleased Charlotte and Lizzy both.

The vicarage at Pemberley was larger than the parsonage at Hunsford, as was the living. Charlotte appreciated the extra space. She had not realised how much room a baby would require.

William Lucas Collins was born in the autumn approximately nine months after his parents had fallen in love with each other. Mr Collins was a most attentive father and discovered a love of children he had never known before. He became a better man, a better husband, and a better minister than he had ever been before, and he was well liked throughout the Pemberley Estate and the village of Lambton.

* * *

Charlotte returned from her musings as she heard Mr Collins enter the sitting room, carrying baby William in his arms. He joined her on the sofa, passing the sleeping child to his mother.

Mr Collins put his arm around Charlotte's shoulders and kissed her head.

He then reached down, lifted her chin, and looked into her eyes, "I love you, Charlotte."

She kissed him lightly, "And I love you, William."

She smiled up at her husband, remembered something Louisa had once said to her, about every girl deserving a happy ending and thought;

Now I am living my own happy ending.

More from Karen Aminadra

PRIDE & PREJUDICE CONTINUES

BOOK TWO

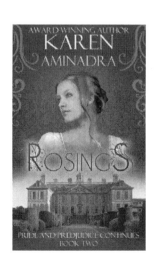

Trapped and cloistered in her own home.

Anne de Bourgh, wealthy heiress daughter of the inimitable Lady Catherine de Bourgh, yearns to be set free from her luxurious prison, Rosings Park.

Her life stretches out before her, ordered and planned, but it is a life she does not want. She wants more. She wants to be free. She wants to do everything that has been forbidden her, and she wants more than anything to fall in love with whom she chooses.

Lady Catherine de Bourgh has other plans for Anne.

Will Lady Catherine have her own way as always?

Will Anne succeed?

Can she break through the barriers of wealth, rank, and duty?

From the award-winning author of Charlotte ~ Pride & Prejudice Continues and Relative Deceit comes ROSINGS ~ Pride & Prejudice Continues Book Two!

The Uncanny Life of Polly

Book One of the "Polly" Series

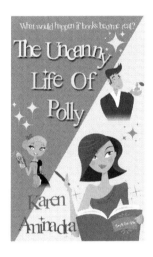

Polly writes chick lit and her debut novel is a worldwide bestseller. However, something strange starts to happen when she gets back from an international book tour. Polly finds that instead of art imitating life, her life starts to imitate art – or rather, her novel.

She arrives home to find her husband in the arms of the maid. Wasn't that in Chapter Three of her book, *Happily Ever After?*

Her best friend is having an affair with her husband, too, and is pregnant! Isn't that in Chapter Four?

Then she meets a bronzed Greek and embarks on a passionate love affair. Wasn't that in Chapter Seven?

Will anyone believe her life is mirroring her novel?

Can she prevent the ultimate tragedy or must the book play out, precisely as she wrote it, to the bitter end?

Her agent recommends that Polly go and live *Happily Ever After?* on the proceeds of her book, and keep away from drama!

You can find out more about Karen Aminadra at
http://kaminadra.blogspot.co.uk/

Follow her on Twitter @kaminadra

Join her on Facebook
http://www.facebook.com/karenaminadra

Printed in Germany
by Amazon Distribution
GmbH, Leipzig